The
Fire
Festival

Isioma Kasim

Isioma Kasim

The Fire Festival

Copyright © 2014 by Isioma Kasim

Published by Eos

ISBN 978-0-9862826-0-7

EOS

Fire from my heart.

In memory of my wife Juliet;

With you I lived out these fires.

You were (and still are) a blessing beyond measure.

Deep gratitude to Dustin and Jon,

The twin pillars of fire

From whom I have drawn much warmth.

Appreciation to Lisette Schuitemaker

For the burst of fire.

To my sister Rachael for not giving up on me, and to Sis. Ego

and my family in heart.

CONTENTS

CHAPTER 1:

FIRE BY FRICTION

B ecause I was pendant on the pendulum of desire; desire to hold her in love, full-bodied love; desire to be taken by her in love in fullest openness and surrender; desire to be one-in-love, just one-in-love in the bliss of non-dual botherlessness. And therein be still.

Because the whole of my petrol-soaked being was in the flames of that desire.

But she had no space for me in her heart, she of the mysterious heart. She had no space for me.

It was the fire festival, and three pots of fire were set up and placed at different sections of the altar. The first pot was placed just around the periphery of the altar where members of the congregation could easily offer their sacrifices. Thereafter, within the altar proper, was another and meant for the priests who would pick up the choice offerings of the congregation for the second pot. Then in the holy-of-holies, where she sat in poise, was the third pot – to receive the very best from the hands of the high priests. There she sat in radiance all her own, radiance I have never known.

But she has no space for me in her heart, my loved most faithful unlover.

Still the fire festival it was, and I was walking along the shore, musing and moaning over her faithful refusal. I was walking along the shore, listless but watching the ocean rise in layers and folds and then crash back into the deep of her mysterious heart.

Her heart is as deep and mysterious as the ocean.

The surfers were out there, they were out there speeding and twisting and turning, while the swimmers cut and stroked through the water. But I, bless my soul, I was only a grain of the mighty sand of faceless worshippers watching, watching that fit and fever for life. I was watching, hands empty, at the fire festival.

But she has no space for me in her heart, my desired and faithful unlover, and I have no space in mine for anyone but her. Yet she spares not the sharp arrows of her gaze nor the acid-force of her words, words so heartlessly and power-drunkenly fired at me – to shock and awe me to insignificance with her might.

Operation shock and awe!

She has no space in her heart for me, I a toilet-fly in the immense panorama of existence.

Still I was walking along the shore, the shore of the sea of lifelessness sucking me in and in. From the water, the ocean, emerged a man – or more appropriately a sculptured man – about seven feet tall. He was just a tight stretch of muscles of a sculptor's dreams, and all that he had in his stomach region seemed to have been drawn up to the chest. He had three 50-litre gallons, one balanced on his head and the other two on his shoulders. The gallons were full and overflowing – and he too seemed to be overflowing from all parts of his body.

The water of life more abundant.

As he passed, almost staggering, he momentarily fixed his gaze at me. It was benign, calm, and it stirred something in my heart, like his heart poured out to me. But he moved on, and I stood still, wondering whether or not to go after him – whether to aid with one of the gallons (wherever he was taking them to). Something, still in my heart, said yes yes yes, silently. But I was confused, and I knew not what to do.

Because I was pendant on the pendulum of desire.

And the whole of my petrol-soaked being was in flames, my tongue drooling for:

The healing hand of harmony

The just juice of joy

Of the fullness of life.

But she had no space for me in her heart.

"What truly did you expect of her? That she would cat-walk up to you in a Miss-World-white-teeth smile and declare: 'I yield up my treasures unto you!'" My cruel heart said softly, so softly that even Hiroshima and Nagasaki would shiver and swear never to make war with her. My heart knows how to do that, my heart.

"But why can't she love me a little, just a little?" I murmured back. But she had said, as always, what she wanted to say, and had no time for bickering – she never had.

My uncle it was who had, and he would hardly let me be as he stepped onto the podium of massed hatred at that fire festival.

"You are evil and you are evil. Even a bath with seven bars of salt in River Jordan will not redeem you. That's the absolute truth," he declared and smashed a grinding-stone on my head before gallantly striding away, his absolute truth continuously chiming:

You are evil

You are evil evil

You are evil evil evil

Still I walked along the shore, musing and circling around the blablabla of the huge heap of waste that was my life when the sound of my alarm clock jarred into that chaos and jolted me awake. I was rather too dazed to bother about stopping it. So I watched ivt as it rang to a stop. It was six o'clock.

Now from the sixth hour there was darkness over all the land.

"Will any light shine into the darkness of my being today?" I murmured as I looked from the ceiling to the walls of my room. It did not seem like I had any chance; for I saw that my room was smiling. Yes, my room was smiling, but not that kind of smile with which a loving mother enfolds and cradles her baby in her bosom. My room wore a smile, and on its face was boldly written.

Unceasing heart-wrenching accusation.

Much like the accusing silence (omni-present, omni-loud) of a guarding father after his daughter is found to have broken the family sex code.

For a thick stench of filth, oppressive and disconcerting, clouded the whole room, and every little space pointed its accusing fingers at me, sneering:

What a living corpse,

Living so so basely!

Then a hail of laughter followed, the rotten fruits of my life's failed efforts dangling before me.

"It's attacking my glass-cup of hope," I whispered.

This was torture condensed and most intense, and it seemed to attack in bouts, each trailing off with a soul-searing slash. Oh, only if you have known pain to that point just a little before beyond pain. Only if you have!

"It's attacking my glass-cup of hope," I whispered again – as it seemed that any effort beyond a whisper would precipitate an avalanche.

Only the avalanche of a hail of laughter crashed on me.

I closed my ears with my hands, but the laughter became the amplified scratching of a mad disc jockey in the hollow hall of my consciousness. Oh, the bare wretchedness of life, my life.

I sought solace, escape elsewhere.

I closed my eyes and tried to float in that darkness of nothingness. But it took only a few seconds for me to realise that somebody was smiling in that darkness, no, not smiling in but rather into that darkness. Truly, it was a smile, but it had that kind of fire which burns the heart of the guilty that one is unable to look an offended in the face. There was no hiding place here. So I opened my eyes, and it felt better to do so. But the walls and everything else were still there – grinning, all thirty-two out.

Did they know what joy was, did they?

The bare barrenness of this life! Must be from the line of the biblical job, I thought.

Then curse God and die.

"I will not. I will not. And tempt me no more, for thou shall not tempt the Lord thy God," I declared.

And, believe it, it did some magic. There was no laughter, no mockery seemed to be lurking. All was silent. And, was it the silence – it touched me somehow, something glowed in my heart, and I knew not why. Maybe within me was still that saving jewel of hope, I knew not. Perhaps because that spark of fire was still waiting and hoping to be stirred into flames and then burn up all obstacles and hindrances. Maybe there still was hope, some path still to my holy-of-holies, I cannot fully tell.

Or can you?

But it glowed in my heart, and from a glow it became a flicker, and then it was there no more. The glass-cup of hope melted, and I sank into that not-living which is not death, but just an interminable process of dying and dying and dying without termination.

I closed my eyes once again – oh fount of hope, can you still pour into the withered roots of my tree? – I closed my eyes and with determined effort I poked the nooks and crannies for an abiding place, if only for a momentary escape.

"Thou shall not tempt the Lord thy God," I murmured.

Perhaps I said it wrongly, for it set off a hail of raucous laughter from all around, and they laughed and laughed and laughed as only the mad could, and it reverberated and resounded down down the well of my being, saying and singing:

The sacrilege of
The sinful one
The evil one
Whose stain of life
Splashed on
The white-cloth of existence
Oh sacrilege! What sacrilege!

CHAPTER 1 | FIRE BY FRICTION

THE FIRE FESTIVAL

CHAPTER 2:

THE INCENDIARY BEGINNING

There are many accounts of the manner and circumstances of my birth. There was always something new each time my uncle's wife told the tale, always something new. And she always told it with a malicious glee whenever she felt that I had strayed towards some good conduct unbecoming of my true self.

I was an evil child, she would say, and it was no good thinking that I could be anything else. It was right from that moment when as a baby the ears open to human speech that I started hearing this lullaby; and I have heard little else. So from childhood I have always tried to make sacrifices to atone for my evil nature. And since I was always in the habit of attempting to be good, I had to be frequently told the story.

My father it was who broke the keg and thereby spread the wine of that revelation that I was an evil child; and everybody around took more than enough of that draught to remain eternally drunk. But my father did not live long thereafter for me to hear directly from his mouth the circumstances and manner of my birth and how he got his powers of clairvoyance and clairaudience to know that I was an evil child. He rather bequeathed that patriarchal duty to my uncle who did not always bother telling me the tale each time I strayed towards some good. He believed in more concrete ways of expressing my fate such as jamming my head against a brick wall or lashing my naked body under the sun with whip bathed with pepper. And whenever he bothered about telling the story – usually when he was drunk or whenever any of his children failed or disappointed him in anyway – he always had something new to add depending on the people present or on what point he wished to emphasise or – which was usually the case – on what filth was on his mind. And each account always differed from another, always differed, as it always differed from his wife's.

I have had to think over all the versions over time. I have had to think so hard over the matter that I dreamed up my own account of my birth. True it is that I am much given to dreams, and I will not bandy words with you if you find fault with me on this account. But you ought not blame me much, especially where and when dreams have remained the only thread holding the chaos of existence together. In any case, it is the tale of my life, not yours, and I ought to tell it as I see it, and not as you would want me to tell it for the satisfaction of your fancy. For how much do you think you can truly tell of another person's life from the prison-yard of your own tastes, values and ill-disguised sentiments called knowledge? Are you really able to stand beyond yourself to see and tell things as they are? And, more seriously, is there truly a way, just one way only, which can adequately present things as they are in their manifold manifestation? Is there truly a way of doing it without the tempering sourness of your stale saliva? Is there, indeed, such a way? Are you capable of it? How much in it is true to others as it is to you? How much?

But enough of all this now! Let me drop one or two lines of my evil-laden conscience while I still can, while there is still enough air allowed me. There you are now! There you are.

Oh, the irredeemable violence of that horror! That the ravishingly plum virginal youthfulness of my mother should be so crudely violated that grey evening, heartlessly plucking her unfolding rose as she ploughed the lonely furrow of her life.

Indeed, a lonely furrow she ploughed; for, as an only child gotten after fifteen years of marriage, and after losing both parents at the age of ten, she lived variously with different distant relations – indeed distant only in heart and not by blood – for about four years before she moved back to her parents' hut.

"I'll rather live with my dead parents than with these living demons," she declared. So that at the age of fourteen she was forced to learn to fend for herself, tilling the soil all by herself, planting the seeds and tubers and harvesting and selling them. This she did until she was sixteen, until that very grey evening when my grey fate was sealed. Undoubtedly over some bottles of beer.

He maketh his sun to rise on the just and the unjust, the evil and the good.

My father had only the word of a crooked finger pointed at my mother as she was going to the market, and seven men lay in wait to make his word flesh. As she was returning after the day's selling and buying, the seven men swooped on her, ferried her against her promethean will which she summoned and struggled and struggled and dug several teeth marks on the men, tearing off some flesh somewhere before they succeeded in forcing some stick between her jaws. Still they ferried her to an isolated hut in an island where my father had already bared his talons. There they stripped her of her clothes – and so exposed to the vile sight of those men, her horror was unnameable. Once again and in desperation she summoned the strength of her youth, but the strength of seven men was just too overpowering. So my father swooped and struck at her, forcefully striking off the lock of her innocence and penetrating into her holy chambers where no man had dared.

Who could have?

My mother, she was a lioness with a mane!

Oh, the fire next time.

Following the failure of her anguished prayers to restore to life her parents, she had believed that miracles and divine interventions only had the unreality of fairytales. Now her anguish, the fire raging through and eating her up, had an unreality of its own, and she screamed with all her might, calling on God to intervene and rescue her – how could He not hear such cries of anguish! But my father, burning with some other kind of fire, thrust and struck at her while the men nodded their heads and urged him on. She screamed and cursed and invoked hell and legions of demons, but the men tightened their hold and my father struck more forcefully until he was seized by a sudden fit of jerking, until his volcano erupted and poured. Oh, what a terrible downpour?

Every drop of that evil fluid went into her.

She froze and became still, like some arresting acid rapidly coursed through her. What amount of fire could ever after melt the thick wall of ice that gathered around her at that moment? Can you tell? What do you possibly know about it?

The deed was done and neither God nor Satan and his legions of demons had intervened. So the men licked their lips and, along with my father, walked out of the hut in triumphant strides. But they did not forget to secure the lock from outside, nor did they fail to keep two men to guard the hut while the rest went to celebrate. Nothing was impossible with this wild girl.

They poured acid into the jewel of her lotus.

She did not wail anymore. And she did not speak too, that is neither to anybody nor to herself. She was just there, just there. The sun shone all through the day, and the moon too leisurely strolled through the clear and serene sky. The sky was still clear and serene.

They poured acid into the jewel of her lotus.

On the third day they brought an older woman to stay with and pacify my mother who had not stirred from her position, much less eat or drink from their hands. The woman, on looking into my mother's eyes, much as a palmist does his patient's, let out a gasp before she gathered herself. But tears were in her eyes. She towel-dried my mother, oiled her skin and, laying my mother's head on her bosom, rocked her. The woman's tears were now streaming down.

She did not speak. My mother did not stir.

She reported to the men that my mother was responding well, and they were joyful and went ahead to celebrate the more.

And though the woman was supposed to go and return, she decided to stay, and so rocked and rocked and hummed lullaby for my mother day and night for seven days, taking some occasional break for snatches of sleep and for food. There they were, for seven days and seven nights, she rocking and lulling and humming, my lioness just there like an Egyptian mummy, the men coming and nodding approval and going away, the sun rising and setting and rising again, while the moon peeped with a half-open eye.

At the end of seven days the woman once again towel-dried my mother, oiled her skin and hair, and with song on her lips and love in her hands she, as a mermaid on her overflowing hair, gently combed the curly web of rich blackness that was my mother's hair. My lioness was a queen. Thereafter the woman passed some spoons of pepper soup into my mother's mouth, and my mother took the pepper soup. She took it.

They did not speak.

But the language of the heart, when translated, overflows into volumes. That language was in the rich repertoire of that woman.

She again reported that all was well, and my father was pleased. Then she left, after having promised to return in three days. Then my father discussed with my mother the need to forget the past and look ahead to the future that always held unbounded possibilities. My lioness only seemed to nod. And my father was pleased.

Three days later the woman returned, and after my father had left with his friends to drink, she fled with and ferried my mother across the muddy river to the woman's own hut where my mother was nursed back to activity in three weeks. Then she returned to her parents' hut.

My lioness with a mane!

She bought a brand new cutlass, sharpened it to taste, and walked about day and night with it. Nobody dared go near her except the woman who had rescued her, her only contact in the whole wild wicked world. Once her mother's sister came to explain that it was customary to so marry a woman as my father had done, and that she too, my mother's aunt, had been married that way. And when my mother asked her what she was expected to do, her aunt advised her to return to my father. Immediately the woman said that, my mother snatched the cutlass just by her. But the aunt fled, age and a matronly carriage disappearing in a flight for life. My lioness of luxuriant mane was in chase. The woman fled but my mother pursued with full fury. In no time she was close enough and lifted the cutlass high up in the air – so that the full force of the cutlass could descend with irredeemable violence. But as the cutlass began its descent, my mother's left foot kicked something on the ground – and the swift descent became hers.

A swift descent indeed it was, but I saw it all too clearly as a slow motion picture of a Holly-wood film. Desperately she struggled to maintain control of the cutlass, but as she hit her well formed and now enlarging breasts and mouth on the ground, she succeeded in slicing off the last toe. Still the aunt fled, now wailing and shouting for help. But my mother picked the little toe and returned home, not caring that blood was gushing from a deep cut on her upper lip.

The whole village concluded that she was possessed by the most malignant of evil spirits.

My lioness!

Weeks later she realised that she was not the same anymore; something had irretrievably gone out of her. More days of anxiety were to pass into weeks, and weeks into months before a hardening stomach made her realize that it was not the case that something had gone out of her, but rather into her; she was heavy with me. And she wailed, she really quaked and wailed like the ocean. She wailed inconsolably, her bitterness hardening and not pouring out – because the pressure of me inside her was hardening. Again it was the woman who rescued her from the claws of my father that came with a tender heart and words of comfort. So my mother somehow became calm, but could not completely stop wailing and bleeding inside. Which, in truth, was worse.

My lioness, she buried herself in work.

It was on the seventh month, during intensive labour in her farm, that the waters broke and poured forth as the flood of Noah. But she did not drown in it. Some women of the village still claim that they saw it still dripping as she hurried home that evening. Whatever happened thereafter nobody knows, and I have not been able to dream it up properly. All I can say is that my raucous cry attracted the attention of the villagers the following morning. They gathered and discussed but nobody was willing to enter the hut. And my mother's only friend, the woman that rescued her, had been laid low by illness. At last an old woman, who could barely walk, ventured. So she it was who saw the lifeless body of my mother, with me between her legs. I had come out legs first; an unthinkable abomination according to the lore of my people. And, added to that, I had taken the life of my mother in order to live.

When my father came he rained innumerable and unmentionable curses on me and my mother, even poking his fingers into my eye and kicking the lifeless body of my mother. (I often think I still see those fingers of his poking accusations at me). He then spoke out what seemed to have been in the minds of the villagers; that my mother and I were truly of the same stock – evil. Though the villagers did not cheer on my father, they exchanged glances and nodded approvingly.

Then my grandmother came, accompanied by the diviner. He it was who looked closely at my face and saw what nobody had noticed.

"Oh terror! Oh joy!" he chortled.

Then he drew my grandmother's attention to my face, asking her to look closely. And then my grandmother saw that one side of my face was wearing a grisly frown, but, paradoxically, a sparkling glint of light shone forth from the eye on that side, while the other seemed to be beaming a disarming smile as tears streamed down the eye on that side. In a breathless and trembling manner my grandmother stuttered before she found her voice:

"What, what can this mean?" she asked.

There was a funereal silence, and in this silence the diviner scoured the lines on my palms, and in a whisper declared:

"A bundle of contradictions so clearly conjoined into one. The joy in sorrow."

That night something happened to my father. While some say that he lost his speech, many still swear that he simply refused to speak. But it was the village minstrel's voice that was clearest and most articulate on the matter. According to him, it was the slow coach of death drawn by a smoky train that came knocking on my father's door that night. It took three months before the coach finally slouched away with him; and much to the relief of the villagers who had no more words to clothe their horror at watching a man gradually decompose while the breath of life had not left him. For this mysterious happening, accusing fingers pointed at my arrival, and the chorus was;

The sacrilege of
The sinful one
The evil one
Whose stain of life
 Splashed on
The white-cloth of existence
Oh sacrilege! What sacrilege!

THE FIRE FESTIVAL

CHAPTER 3:

FIRE ON THE MOUNTAIN

A nd the cloud of stench billowed rhythmically to that tune, making me shiver as it sounded down down the void of my being, turning my pant inside-out and thereby exposing the shit-stains on it.

Resolutely I sat upright on the bed. Then I jetted out a stream of saliva that had gathered in my mouth. But there was no relief in that, as the taste of a sour life could not so easily be expelled. But hope is the saving substance of all quests, the only anchor without which a final plunge into the abyss becomes the only possibility. So I hung on hope – no matter how indistinct – and tried again, only this time I blew my nose. And, bless my soul, there still was nothing in it to uplift. Nothing.

You are the salt of the earth

Looking round the room, I let out a low good morning to my most faithful companions – the void and its filth. But my words seemed to fly back at me, and I nodded my head and swallowed hard. It certainly did not appear like a good day to dare the devil and face the funny goings-on in that room. It did not seem like I had the needed strength to face those demons who were now threatening to rampage and empty all their slime into my mouth. Could this be my final untriumphant entry into Jerusalem, towards the place of skull?

I knew, though, I knew it deep within me, that this was no day to spend expecting any miracle. The miracle of the sky, if it chose to weep on us, or that of the Water Corporation, would be a welcome relief. But I was sure that, with my demons threatening to overwhelm me, I could not just hang around in expectation of any miracle. In spite of all the failures, in spite of the hard blows of life, I still had to strike if only a feeble blow into the air, if only a feeble blow. And the raging tempest of accusation would be met, somehow. After all, did I not try?

The cost of being human.

Because something there was somewhere in me which kept pushing. Because many many times vistas of infinite possibilities, wide expanse of conquerable territory, opened itself before my eyes, stirring towards the sun the nearly burnt-out roots of life in me. How could I be still ever after having partaken in this holy vision? How could I without first empting my memory of this vision? Tell me, how could I?

Woe am I that I see what I see, that I know what I know: which is that I see and see and see the glory but cannot touch; that I smell and smell the rich scents of life but cannot taste of it. Woe am I.

But I would continue to fret and struggle and fight, so long there was still life in me. I would. Because it seemed better that one should ceaselessly wage wars against hostile and life-threatening forces even though one knew that there was just a slim chance. Because in rare and high moments of tension some music deep in my soul was stirred, and in that silence I dived deep into the bosoms of life. One injunction there I always saw:

SHOW FORTH MY SIGNATURE
WHICH IS INSCRIBED IN YOU

But my demons would blare:

You are evil
You are evil evil
You are evil evil evil
You are the light of the world

I walked to the shelf, took a chewing stick and, sitting on the chair, started chewing, crushing and spitting away bits of the stick; bits of the stick of my life chopping off before my very eyes. And when this hollow stick of a failed life falls, is it going to be another beginning of itching without cure or an end, liberation to some place noble and free from the dividing pulls to the right and to the left? Or will it be some other bondage in the whirlpool of the sloughs of sorrow and suffering? Can I ever fly and soar free from these strictures of a debased and evil life, can I ever? From what I can see around me now, all roads lead to the Slough of Despond. For me, the evil one, the toilet-fly of existence. All the high hopes, all those hopes, where are you now? Tell me, where are you? Only crawling through existence, swimming only in the mud-water of life and getting myself messed up the more. The sun is not here now, does not reach me. Oh sun of my life, where are you?

Why keep jostling anymore anyway? What is it in here that keeps stirring, stirring little flames in my heart, so feeble now but anyhow still there? What more does it want from me? All I have known and held in concrete grasp is frustration and rot and death and destruction. That which seems good and lovely is only flighty and unenduring. And here I am still, still floating, with nowhere to call my own. All things that come to life ought to find a place, a spot within whose stillness to shelter and repose against the whirl-winds of life.

As a leaf separated from the branch and in the fury of those whirlwinds, that's what I am.

You are the salt of the earth

Some say one ought to try to the end. To the very bitter end. But, think of it, what more can there be, what more but those hard knocks that bring no saving meaning? Truly, where I am now I see neither goodness nor peace nor love, neither reason nor faith in all that surround me, all that tauntingly sing to raving madness:

Welcome to my world

Where all is in shards

Welcome to our mud

Welcome to my rot.

The clouds of stench and rot were squeezing, as a python its victim, the very life out of me that morning, and in spite of my woebegone defiance, I still sought some way of escape.

I stood up, resolutely, walked to the window, resolutely, unlatched it, commanded "let there be light in this void" and then threw the window open. Immediately a blinding effulgence of light hit my eyes, and a silent wind brushed past me. I remained still, not seeing, and breathed in, first through the nose and then through the mouth, in great gulps the fresh morning air. Then it was like the morning cloud, that morning life, descended on me, a flush of life and freshness and fullness flashing through me.

Could there be substance within that glass-cup?

So I breathed in again, this time rather greedily. But, expectedly and still more painfully, it was not there, it was not there anymore. Just as a momentary flash of inspiration which does not stay, leaving one burning the more in the flame of intensified desire.

"Casting pearls to a dog" I said and nodded my head in complete agreement as that feeling of vitality and life seemed to be lost forever.

The lot of a stunted sinful son of sorrow.

And who was I anyway to question anything anymore or to have that peace and tranquillity, that saving calm of balance which every heart craves? Oh, not to rule over the whole kingdoms of the world, but just that calm of a creature who finds its note in the orchestral symphony of life, who can stand with poise on that thread that stretches over and above the abyss of the raging ocean of dualism, over the deep gullies and precipices of the heart and shout:

"I have, I have found my note!"

All my life I have struggled to attain that, all my life. But it seems that even before my father pointed his crooked finger at my mother, I had already been cast out of the sphere of the cosmic heart, out of the wheel of life. How then am I ever going to catch a glimpse of that beauty, that harmony that is the bride of my heart? How am I? In spite of the fever! In spite of the fury! And that fire that ever warms and kindles all quests, it keeps stirring me. But there is no harmony here, just the raging chaos of desire for the fullness of life. There is no harmony. Life without music – perdition.

Still I breathed in, in great gulps, that fresh morning air. Because I still sought a space in her heart. But did she have, did she have any for me?

You are the light of the world.

The sun was not out yet – just as the sun of my life – and the sky was darkening with thick layers of cloud, layers folding and unfolding as if in preparation for a deluge, as if threatening to storm the land and wipe away the rot that had become so much a part of us. It was like the ocean had risen from the ground, ascended unto the sky and was now unfolding its layers in preparation for the cleansing ritual, the ritual to wipe away the sins of the world, the filth of Atlantis smelling to the high heavens.

She has no space for me in her heart. Would he have in the ark?

Still I breathed in that fresh morning air, hoping on its uplifting hand. I breathed in and it seemed to be there, somehow, for it stirred remembrances of things past and of everything good that would come. And in that moment, too, a tune, soft, sonorous and voiceless, echoed and thrilled through my heart. I remained still, almost breathless in expectant waiting as I hung on that indistinct and delicate hope. But it was all over, and with a definite finality it registered in my consciousness. And the darkness of despair instantly enveloped me; despair thick with the cream of death.

But, is this possible? I broke forth into a song. Maybe because he that is down need fear no fall; maybe because some hope always lurks by the corners of our hearts, I cannot tell. But I know that I broke forth into a song. I rhymed:

Today today
Today today
My saviour will answer me
Today today.

It was a church favourite with which our priest used to pour fuel into our frenzied emotions. But this time it stirred no fire in me. Still I declared:

"I will not give up," as I continued to hum silently.

From some distance not too far off came the sound of a train tearing through the city – as I would have wished to tear through my lethargy and inertia. But from my death-suffused enclave, the effort appeared superhuman.

A gentle wind blew, raising some dust into the air and causing polythene bags and dead leaves to stir – the dead leaves of the tree of my life. In a moment a black goat ran past my window, snorting and bleating while a hen fluttered its wings.

And life began to flutter its wings in my neighbourhood.

I stood there staring blankly at the sky and trying not to raise so much dust anymore, dust that might make me sneeze out my ugly past. For a new day it was. But though the wind that stirred little embers of life in the neighboured was cool and fresh and inviting, that which fanned the flame in my entrails had an acrid odour of death and rot and failure and waste, thereby throwing up those soiled sanitary towels of my life. And the much which I could do at that moment was to spit out a cupful of saliva which had gathered in my mouth. But not a measure, not even a small measure of relief was experienced.

There ought to be hope in a new day, expectancy from a darkening sky. So I breathed in, still, that fresh morning air, hoping on its uplifting splash. But, as before, it was not there anymore. Only the darkness of despair seemed to thicken around me.

As I turned to face the room, it was as if there was a swift movement in the room. It was all too swift for me to make out whether it was a figure or the stench. But whatever it was seemed to melt into the wall.

I shuddered at this possibility, though, and goose pimples stood out all over my body. And in some way I still felt some intangible presence in the room. I was used to the taunts and laughter of the room itself – always echoing down my consciousness – but I had not thought that it would get to this. So I rubbed my eyes with the back of my hand, and still I could see the clouds of stench and rot rising from every little object in the room – the bed, the dirty plates on the floor, the shelf blanketed with cobwebs, the dirty clothes and pants hanging from nails on the wall. And the void was just there, just there like an eternal presence, threatening to crush and grind into powder any life-enhancing endeavour. Was the void now condensing into a figure?

Somehow I had always lived with it. But it was different, glaringly and tauntingly unsettling this morning. And the light from outside mercilessly emphasised it, with a voice continuously echoing deep within me:

Nothing for you! I have seen it all, the bare wretchedness of your life.

This came with an increasing sting on my heart that as I stood there watching the clouds of stench, and the thought of the unidentified figure whirling, I realised that this was going to be a very trying day.

"Where is that sparkling fountain of my dreams?" I murmured. Because I had seen and seen and seen it many times too numerous to tell. Because even as the claws of inertia and rot gripped me on the throat that morning, I could still close my eyes and see that fountain. Because I knew, somehow, deep down my being and beyond any authoritative roar of any teacher, that death was only false and purposeless living, and that beyond this was the path of struggle and ascent to that living fountain of life abundant. I knew it in a way that is beyond the cosmetics and show of words, but I could never show it to anyone because I did not have it in my grasp. But what is knowledge if its fruits drop not into waiting hands, if its flowers stir no heart towards the sun and towards all that is noble and life-giving? Tell me, what is the value of that knowledge which can only yell and yawn in the face of acute need? How treat that dam which only swells with infinite satiety but cannot bestow a cooling drop on a parched tongue?

I was that knowledge and that dam fit only for the wastebasket and sewage of existence.

But there ought to be hope in a new day, in a darkening sky. This was no life, nor was it death which would have ended it all. I knew it. And I knew that I had to find a way either to live or to die that morning, or at least a way that would, at the end, make me exclaim a ha! of some relief, even if not victory. But I knew (or believed), somewhat vaguely, that within me was the power to overcome and shine forth in that resplendent glory of dreams.

Within me was that power and its glory. And I knew it. Something deep within me, deeper than the constant accusations of failure, told me that. And silently too.

"I must drink my share of the fountain of life," I murmured.

And as if words had powers of their own, I was suddenly seized by that impulse, as in a fit. And it stirred the deep void of my lethargy, of my inertia, and I could not be still. So I searched here and there, within and without, for a way unto a ha! At least something to attempt, to struggle towards, some sweat to justify my continuing debt to the breath of the air so freely given. If only that.

What to do?

It came, almost in a blinding flash of recognition. It came, voicelessly but with an unquestionable living presence. And I said:

"How can I live in such filth of a room?"

But water was more than an ordinary human necessity in my neighbourhood. It had become only dream-beautiful and precious as one of those unattainable cravings of humanity for ages, more of ambrosia enjoyed only in the privileged circle of Zeus and his deities, something distant and far removed from us as the manna of the Bible is to the modern man. Mud-water, from a pit near the incinerator, was all that we had. I had always wondered if, by using this water, we were not courting death. But much of the time I was past caring whether I lived or not – so silently I welcomed this possibility of an end-it-all. But some three weeks back when I last fetched and used the water, I stank and vomited for a whole week so much that my entrails nearly came out. Again in it was no death but just that indescribable, painful dying and dying without termination. Thereafter I vowed to die of filth than touch that water again.

"I must pluck my portion of the fruit of life," I declared, "or I will die of the effort."

I looked round the room once again, and in that moment it seemed hardly believable that this was not a madman's under-the-bridge abode.

"A door unto life must open for me today," I affirmed. I took the cup nearby, emptied the drops of water in it into my mouth and added! "Or this is my extreme unction."

CHAPTER 3 | FIRE ON THE MOUNTAIN

THE FIRE FESTIVAL

CHAPTER 4:

FIRE TWEETS

S trengthened by this resolve, I quickly dressed up and went out of the room. After inspecting the sky, I inadvertently closed my eyes for a moment as if I wanted to pray. This was instinctive but rather unusual because I could not even remember the last time I prayed. And in that moment of silence and unvoiced appeal, it seemed like a statement flashed into my consciousness. Not that I saw it like a picture, or that I heard it the way we normally hear another speak to us. I just became aware of it, and I knew and could bet my life that I knew it – without seeing, without hearing, and without tasting or smelling or touching it. The statement was: show forth the signature of divinity in you and thereby know joy enduring, gain the life abundant.

It was like a reminder of that skeletal blueprint of vision which had sunk in the deep sea of my society's din and the murky water of my fruitless existence. It flashed into my consciousness and thereby strengthened my resolve.

"I could join you and Ruth in an unholy wedlock." This was Dike my neighbour jolting me with his sarcasm.

I quickly opened my eyes and managed to say:

"Ah, Dike good morning."

"Was God speaking to you or you to Him?" he continued.

This question of his heightened my confusion, because, in truth, I was pondering precisely the same question. Was it possible, in any way, that Dike was reading my mind? This thought was rather disconcerting, and I quickly sought diversion. But he came to the rescue.

"How was your night?"

"Well, as you can see, I survived it. And how was yours?" I returned.

"It's another opportunity to wrest my kingdom by violence. There is no other way to break this stranglehold."

I agreed with him in my heart, but I also knew that this was no more than an ineffectual collection of words which had found no living expression either in his life or in mine. But we had become so used to this chest-thumping declaration that I often thought it served as his daily round of multivitamins which, however, had not given him the needed vitality to act. Nonetheless, it strengthened my resolve that some door must open for me – either way.

"You seem ready to do battle," he said.

Again he seemed to be hitting at matters as they were in my heart that morning, and this still caused me some unease.

"It would appear so," I returned. "Everything seems to have reached breaking point that either I break the stranglehold, as you call it, or it breaks me."

"That's the spirit, my brother, that's it. As I woke up this morning, I told myself that I must not allow this day to pass just like every other day, that I must destroy everything that stands on my way."

"But has one not always woken up with that feeling?" I asked, the sweat of all my years somehow trickling through my mind and irritating me. "How many times have I seen so clearly what must be done and at the same time seen so unmistakably why I must not make a move yet or that I have no such commensurate power to move?"

"We have the power and might to battle and dominate the forces of our own nature. Only that we are lazy and lack courage to fight hard enough."

Again this was somehow in line with my resolve for the day, but I could not be sure that Dike's 'we' meant human beings generally or was simply directed at me.

"So what's your plan for the day?" I asked in an attempt to change the subject.

"I'm still trying to work it out. You know, with all the mockery and treachery of the weather, it can hardly be believed that this over-hanging cloud means rain for us today. And then, there is nothing to suggest that the Water Corporation may wake up and remember us today. But I'll surely work out something."

Just like me, he was always working out something, something that never ever manifested in full-bodied livingness and presence. He was. We were just undulating flotsam and jetsam in the sea of life.

"We are undulating flotsam and jetsam on the tide of inscrutable forces," Dike said.

I had half-opened my mouth in shock to ask what game he was playing with my mind when I felt a strong impulse to say nothing. But I could not help wondering.

Because at the fire festival she was seated in grace within the innermost chamber of secrets, there she was taunting with her vast jewels and beckoning at me, and I jostled and languished around the periphery because I knew not how to reach her without burning in the separating central fire. I knew not how. Bless my soul.

Her heart is a mysterious chamber of secrets!

As once a spider and a fly were engaged in a battle of survival and of death on the net on my window. I was lying on the bed, wrapped in blanket, and watched unseen the battle and the fun. They were both perched on the net, the spider inside and the fly outside. The spider saw a sumptuous meal in the fly and crept towards it. It was a fat toilet-fly. And each time it got close the fly would move a little away. Then the spider rested a while, then crept again, and on getting close and about to leap for the catch, the fly still would move again and not far from the spider. The spider rested for sometime, tried again, but the same result. Then it refused to move anymore. The fly waited and waited but the spider refused to move.

Then the wheel seemed to turn.

For it was now the turn of the fly to move towards the spider, and each time it got close enough the spider would move a step away. This continued for some minutes until this time around, instead of creeping towards the spider, the fly simply took a leap which landed it almost directly face-to-face with the spider. And it appeared like a dream to the spider, for I could see its eyes widening in the thought of a feast. Suddenly it struck and grabbed the fly by the leg. The fly, horrified, fluttered and fluttered but the spider held on firmly. Again the fly fluttered and fluttered more desperately, even dashing its head against the net. But the net did no violence, and the spider held on. In no time the fly resigned itself to fate and struggled no more. It then became the turn of the spider to struggle. It pulled and pulled but the fly was too big to pass through the tiny spaces on the net. Then some knowledge dawned on the spider as I saw it nod its head reassuringly. It released its web, aiming to trap the fly in it, but the web could only trap the net and not the fly. The more the spider spun, the more impediments it seemed to create. Seeming to realise this, the spider ceased to spin; it just held on to the leg of the fly without stirring. And, finally, the spider became tired of just holding on, so it released the fly. And the fly flew away, while the spider moaned in hunger and anger and frustration.

The wheel of life rolls on.

After an interval of about ten minutes the battle resumed, only that this time it seemed to be re-enacted with some knowledge garnered from the experience of the earlier encounter. The spider was wise enough not to strike at every given opportunity – as it seemed to first contemplate its chance before acting – and the fly also appeared cautious not to let its legs pass through the net to the spider's side. And many a time the spider would come very close to the fly and, instead of attacking right away, would ponder and ponder. Only on very few occasions did it strike but to no avail, as the fly seemed intensely alert. Appearing to realise that it had no chances, the spider moved away in anger, tormented by renewed hunger. But the fly followed, enjoying the game. The spider would stop and the fly would also stop by it. The spider would then consider its chances, shakes its head and still crawl further away. Still the fly would follow. The spider once again stopped, swelling with fury as the fly moved directly opposite it and stopped too. Then the spider lost control over itself and struck with amazing vehemence. It really hit its head too hard against the net as it lost consciousness and fell on the windowsill where a portion of the net was torn. The fly too flew down, crept through the opening and laughed its heartiest laugh.

But the heartiest laugh could be the laugh of death.

And the fly did not just watch and laugh; it climbed on top of the spider to make a better mockery of it. And it did laugh and mock. But the spider was only down and not out, so that it grabbed the fly, spun its poison around it and sucked the juice out of it. The fly died while the spider sucked and fattened and even gloated at its success.

I flung away my blanket, took some machete from under the bed and moved towards the spider to slice it into pieces. And I was about lifting the machete when the shrill cry of a baby – from no identifiable direction or source – sent a trembling and chilling tremor through my whole being.

I feebly dropped the machete, walked back to the bed and sat down, shivering uncontrollably as the strings of my heart pulled and pulled and pulled.

I have never been more ashamed.

A door creaked and out came Hilary. He rubbed his eyes with the back of his hands before turning towards us, asking:

"How is it that the clouds still hang on Eno?"

I quickly picked the thread and responded: "I am too much in the sun, my Lord, and yet the sun of my life never shines."

"It's a fault to heaven," he returned, "and most retrograde to our desire for you to Wittenberg make."

By now he had joined us and, after shaking hands with us, asked me:

"So is it this water of a thing that's casting shadows over the sun of your life?"

"Is it only water? Just sick of everything – all beauty swallowed by stench," I replied, breathing out hard as the smell of a baby's faeces seemed to be stuck to my nostrils.

"Forget it, man, and cheer up. Hope we all slept well anyway?" Hilary still.

"Well, you can see I survived the night," I returned.

"Another day to wrest my kingdom," Dike put in, and after a brief silence, added; "So did the astral form of Shakespeare haunt you in your dream last night?"

"Oh no, brother, only his music tempered my sadness with joy," Hilary replied.

"What music? From Shakespeare?" Dike asked.

"Don't you know of that harmony beyond and behind his words, even beyond the melody of his words, that which keeps sounding and resounding long after its delivery? It transports to that high place where there is true joy, that joy which is much more than the most intense happiness. That height was my experience last night, and I will gladly share with you."

Then he dipped his hand into his pocket, brought out a short chewing stick, broke it into two and gave one-half to Dike, declaring;

"Take this and eat, it is the fruit of my joy."

Then he turned to me, cupped his hand against my lips and declared:

"This is the juice of my joy, shared to many for the remission of sorrow. Drink it and sorrow no more."

Thereafter he took a step backwards, made a sign of the cross and said:

"My joy I leave with you. Be of good cheer."

And for that moment I almost forgot about the stench and the shouting need for water. For as Hilary performed, the lightness of laughter pierced through the gloom that enveloped me, spread from my guts through the body but somehow got arrested in my lips as they refused to be stirred to open or widen for an outlet.

"When will you wake up to reality?" Dike asked Hilary.

"Come on, man, what's reality? Is it the key-hole parochialism of Ruth or the haunting banality and drudgery of your yet-to-be-wrested inauthentic kingdom, the old-woman's shrivelled breast of Eno's idealism or the commonplace concerns of the marketplace which have swallowed up all of you? Tell me, between –"

"How does this kind of discussion so early in the morning help anybody?" I asked, not quite sure whether it was because my name had been mentioned or because I truly cared for some suggestion on how to proceed for the day; after all I had resolved to make this day decisive – either for good or for ill.

"What more do you expect except the usual hunger and thirst and filth and failure and uncertainty? Diseases which have long been incubating will soon erupt, and after mindless suffering and pain a six feet pit alone welcomes you. Dust to dust. That's all. So what more do you want?"

This was from Hilary, and it deeply touched some chord in me that I remained silent, almost shivering within. Dike too must have been hard-hit by Hilary's bile, for he looked away and confusedly looked here and there as one searching for something. In his heart Hilary spat at the two of us. So uneasy was the silence.

But Ruth, seeker of a saviour and a saving grace, was our saviour from that awkward silence as she, that moment, came out of her room coughing and making a sign of the cross. But then she was the red cloth that always ignited the bull in Hilary – and worse, he was already charged. He attacked immediately:

"Here comes the rock of Christian faith who has surrendered it all to Jesus and prayer. Yet neither has cured her of her ageless cough or her husbandlessness. Oh faith so unrewarding."

Of course there was a time when I would have so flippantly uttered such harsh words. But not anymore. Things did not appear so straightforward as they had once seemed. So that as I looked at Hilary, saying in my mind that it was not fair of him to so mercilessly speak of a fellow human being's failings – if failings they were –, Dike seemed somewhat to nod in agreement. It was now Hilary's turn to look away, and after jetting out some saliva, turned towards us and almost whispered:

"Come on guys, I won't be too hard on her today. Promise."

"May the peace of Jesus, the Alpha and Omega, the Beginning and the End, the Saviour and Redeemer of the world, be with you all and good morning to each and everyone."

"Good morning," I replied quickly so as not to allow any sarcasm from Hilary.

"Good morning."

"Good morning, sis."

"I hope we all slept well?"

Again I was the first to respond, and deliberately too.

"Well, I survived the night."

"Another day to wrest my kingdom."

"I slept well, sis, really well."

"How's our baby?" Dike asked, meaning Ruth's four-year old daughter.

"Hmm, my brother, glory be to God the maker of all things. You know that child did not sleep a wink until about four o'clock this morning. She kept coughing and sneezing and crying. But thank God for everything. All is well."

"Won't she need to see a doctor, I mean, are you not taking her to some hospital?" Hilary asked, and, I supposed, sarcastically. Simple-hearted Ruth, she could be unimaginably deaf and blind to innuendoes. She replied.

"But I have already prayed for her. And my priest will be coming here later today. He, too, will pray for her. My God has told me that she will be alright after that."

"Come on, sister," Hilary pressed on, "take that child to some hospital. You are not going to let her die an avoidable death, because –"

That was how far she could take.

"The God I serve, the Omnipotent and Omniscient One, the Alpha and Omega, my God is a miracle-working God, and my child is not going to die. I destroy all spirits of negativity and doubt. Blood of Jesus! Blooooooood of Jesus I bind I rebuke I cast out I break all yoke I destroy I –" and then she went into a fit as she jerked and convulsed and muttered the unintelligible mishmash of noise called speaking in tongues.

Dike watched somewhat indifferently. An unmistakable glee mixed with scorn stood on Hilary's face. As I watched Ruth, a wave of immense pity swept through me. Because what I saw, as she conjured and invoked and shrieked and all else that's unwordable, was a terribly lonely human being, a heart soaked in the tears of the thirst and hunger for another heart to tell her that she too was a human being. That was how I saw her that moment, and it filled my heart with anguish because that too was all I asked of life. But she had no space for me in her heart. Nor did she seem to have for Ruth.

Still she convulsed in her lone world and we watched, indifference still on Dike's face, and Hilary still enjoying a free show. It all appeared too cruel, she in her yawning world of need, and no hand, no matter how feeble or false, reaching out to her. So I thought hard, I thought hard of how to reach her, to give her a sense of being. And, suddenly, the picture of my village priest laying his hand on the congregation flashed into my consciousness. It was so real and at the same time very much unreal; the film just rolled and rolled in my consciousness, but I also knew that there was nothing, if not filth, in those hands. But I took it all.

I took two steps forward, placed my hand on Ruth's forehead and muttered something I knew was nothing. And in descending degrees she calmed down until she seemed normal and went on her knees.

Without choice, and without even thinking about it at all but only sure that I could not abandon her just like that, more like leaving her between Heaven and Hell, I proclaimed.

"It is well with you, child."

She exhaled a loud amen and stood up, obviously relieved and strengthened and even looking happy.

"Bless me, father, for I have sinned." This was Hilary now kneeling before me and seemingly in a solemn mood as a nun approaching the Pope for the Eucharist.

Dike, too, joined and repeated:

"Bless me, Father, for I have sinned."

I almost burst out laughing, but some words formed in my mind.

"You are absolved of your irreverence. Go ye into the town and fetch us water."

This got us all laughing, even Ruth whom I thought might take offence.

"I would gladly go any length to get water. Only I obey my own command, and not that of a false priest," Dike said. "But this comic relief over, remember the day has just started and that you need more than comedy to cope with its problems and challenges."

With that statement, the full force of that earlier feeling of nausea and gut-rot descended on me. And the gloom too. I let out:

"But what on earth is wrong with the Water Corporation that they give no damn whether people are dying or not? And God, in His infinite wisdom, refuses to send down rain. Searching for water at this time of the year. I really wonder why things are the way they are."

"Things are the way they are because they are the way they are," Hilary responded.

"These are the signs of the end," end-time prophet Ruth added. "Sin has overtaken the world, and the Word is about to be fulfilled. The prophecy surely must come to pass."

I dared not add to or subtract from that. Nor did anybody else, Hilary seeming to exhaust his joy and jibes.

"There surely is a way out," was Dike's contribution, and this was somewhat slowly and gravely uttered.

Some uneasy silence fell on us thereafter, and I withdrew into myself, into my world. Still I stood there, flashes of lightning and thunder piercing the gloomy silence of the morning, the darkening sky seeming to add more to the burden on my mind. Either way I was going to say a definite yes. I told myself that repeatedly. I could go out and face it all in the streets where I just might run into some luck, and I could as well wander and loiter through the whole land and return with nothing. Some clean water, some clean water to clear that mess of a room. And the millennium surprise could just be a rainfall. For, truly, the sky was so overcast that in normal situations it would have taken only an incurable sceptic to doubt that rain would fall. But we had had many instances when the sky was so heavy with rain that people were ready to bet their lives that it would rain. And suddenly a strong wind would emerge from nowhere and drive away the promise. So that now it was convenient and better for people to remain in their scepticism than to suffer disappointment. And this attitude did not seem to be restricted to water alone – it had somehow crept into people's general disposition towards life. For many a time someone would, in the face of failure or disaster, sigh and declare: I had expected something worse. We had all become incurable sceptics through the acid strokes of circumstances.

"Brethren and sistren," Hilary now, "cheer up for I have been hoarding some good news. I heard it said yesterday that there would be water today."

"Who said so?" Dike asked.

"They said so last night," Hilary emphasised.

"I will walk any length – no matter how far – to get good water, but that's so long as there is hope that I will get. But, please, could you tell us who the 'they' are, and where did they say one could get water from?" This was from me, as some little ripple was already in motion.

"Come on, man, what do I care who the 'they' are, and how would that help seal up your mind that drains everything of life and leaving only filth? How will that help you? Anyway, it was in almost everyone's mouth last night, as I walked down the street, that there would be water today. Some said the public taps would run, others that the Local Government would go round with trucks to distribute water, and some more that a deep well with good water will open to the public. Some others even said that weather forecasters announced on television that there would be rain this morning. Surely, there should be some truth in one of these."

"I sincerely would like to hope there is," Dike said.

"I just pray so. Things are really getting out of hand. If not for God's mercies, I wonder where we would have been." Then she coughed her age-old cough.

It all added to my confusion on how to move on with the day and bend it to my purpose or break in the effort, all that talk about hope and prayer stirred my pot of confusion. Because whether there was strength and will-power in me or not, I was going to take a step definitive; because whether the fire of hope and prayer and age-old cough touches or not the incendiary roots of the tree of my life, I was going to take that step definitive; because one reaches that stage where one has to muster all available strength and take that decisive leap – leading either to life or to death. I must take that step definitive and leap decisive, but I knew not how. I threw the debate open:

"I wonder which is better: to wait for this rain or the Local Government bounty or to go out to the streets and face one's luck there."

Hilary affirmed his fence-sitting: "It's hard to choose one way or the other. But I'm sure there will be water."

Ruth's anchor never faltered: "I'll rather wait for the will of God to prevail. God's time is the best."

A kingdom wrester might have currents which ran more deeply than could be easily seen. Probe it, probe it.

"Dike doesn't think anything?" I asked.

"It sure is a jump into one of either intangibles, but –"

And the flash was frightening and almost blinding, snatching speech even from the very mouth of the power-seeker. Before I could move or even think, the thunderbolt was already on my feet, the whole world exploding and clapping deafness into me. Recovering from this after a while, I murmured to myself.

"Is this a promise of rain?"

They picked up in turns.

"God does not abandon His creation," making a sign of the cross.

"He ought not to."

"Yea, man, He ought not to."

And still in confusion, I led the choir again.

"Is this truly a promise of rain?"

"God does not abandon His creation," still making a sign of the cross.

"He ought not to."

"Indeed, man, he ought not to."

As we stood there, our hearts pounding, at least I was sure mine was, droplets of rain started falling. But it was not clear if this was not another level of mockery intensified. Ruth then suggested that we should each go into the privacy of our individual rooms and pray with all our strength and with all our might and with all our soul for rain.

From the silence that followed, I concluded that there was no support for this idea. Dike was not usually inclined to such, but his countenance suggested neither indifference nor hostility. Hilary evidently tightened his face, his teeth most likely clenched. I stood on the arid land of indecision, numbed by the desert possibility of either choice.

Quietly and without grace – the gracelessness of a woe-be-gone widow – Ruth walked away to her room and without a word. None from us, nor from her. In determined strides Dike too left, his intention being the big-bang lottery puzzle.

I remained there trying to recollect the last time that rain fell. It seemed like ages, far-removed like the time of Adam and Eve in that harmonious and pre-dualistic world of Eden, like the enchanting stories as told in folktales of that distant time when the good man always triumphed over the evil one and the orphan always received the help of supernatural beings to win against the wickedness of a step-mother. And how had one really managed to survive? Of course there was always the hope of an immi-nent relief, of better days ahead, that hope that was somehow being faintly stirred and awakened in me that morning by the rumblings in the sky. Without doubt this was a way of suffering and enduring today's pain in the hope of a better tomorrow. And that tomorrow seemed to be on my doorstep at that point in time.

I had not prayed for years, that is, what people generally call prayer in the manner of kneeling down or taking any other position to ask God to solve my problems for me and bless me with all the good things of life. But as I stood there that moment desperately in need of water, desperately in need of that which would either uplift or pulverise, I felt that if prayer was all that was needed for rain to fall, then I must pray. Because deep down my heart I did not dismiss the possibility of some Being or Beings greater than human beings and operating at a level of conscious-ness, a wavelength different from our own human reality and which thereby meant our inability to register such wavelength because we lacked the necessary equipment. Because the shore-less ocean of puzzles raging within my enquiring mind somehow always pointed to some intelligence. Because every little unit of life I tried to look at closely simply seemed to throw up all these puzzles. And because the general conception of God neither answered my questions nor gave any meaningful explanation for the purpose of existence.

Existence – that splash of mind-boggling symphonic infinitude.

I had started walking to my room when Hilary, of whom I was scarcely aware, cleared his throat. Then I turned.

"You, too, you mean you are going to pray?" he asked.

"In my present situation I am ready to bargain even with the devil himself."

"Man, you are a disappointment! You are a failure!" he roared.

"But I have never disputed that, have I?" I responded. "That is the chorus of the dirge that ceaselessly chimes in my consciousness. Only that I do not know why it has to be like this, I mean this low. That one has simple and honest human aspirations, that one seeks one's place in the bewildering grand scheme of things – tell me what could be wrong with that?"

Immediately I walked away, some fire beginning to rise within me. Getting to my door, I turned, "it doesn't cost you anything to pray – except, of course, the loss of your sense of pride in accepting your littleness. We could all try prayer, who knows", and entered my room.

CHAPTER 4 | FIRE TWEETS

THE FIRE FESTIVAL

CHAPTER 5:

FANNING THE FLAME

I was an evil child and everybody in my uncle's household watched with eagle eyes all my activities. My grandmother alone tried to love and care for me, but since she made little or nothing from her kola nut trade – and too old to do much else – she relied on my uncle her son for survival. So she dared not too strongly oppose my uncle's will regarding me. She learnt this lesson the hard way by being starved for two weeks by my uncle for her attempting to suggest that I be sent to school like every other child. Thereafter she had to publicly support my uncle's decisions, while privately she did the little she could to support me. And since she walked the length and breadth of our village and the neighbouring ones plying her trade, she was hardly home. So that there was no one to see how I was ground in the iron mill of my uncle and his family. Many a time I would repeat what somebody had just said or done in order to demonstrate to my Uncle and his wife that I was ready to conform. Immediately he or his wife would tear into pieces every step of my action or letter of my statement and show me how only my wicked and evil nature could have produced such an abomination.

Absurd, do you say? But much in life is, much is.

One day I came back from my uncle's farm alone – I was sent to the farm as punishment for daring to bath Peace, my Uncle's two year old child to whom I was not supposed to transfer my evil through too close a contact. I came back to see some money scattered at the entrance to the house. I picked and took the money to my uncle's wife who laughed at me and then took the money to my uncle who was grumbling and lamenting how difficult it was becoming to survive. I instinctively had a fair idea of what was going to follow, and I had not finished squeezing myself under a de-used table in a corner when my uncle came out laughing. I froze.

"You think you are going to escape it, eh? There is no point trying to be like my children. You are evil and you are evil. That's all."

Then he took one giant step and smashed his mighty hand through the table, landing it on my back. I fell flat on my stomach and waited for him to play football with me. But he did not. He violently pulled me up and ordered:

"Go to the sheep-house and lock yourself with that animal. I don't want to see you until tomorrow," and dropped me heavily on the pieces of the table. I was seven years old.

It was with heavy heart that my grandmother took me to the minstrel who lived in an isolated hut at the outskirts of the village. He was a gaunt old man buried in a forest of white hairs; the hair on his head remains the whitest I have ever seen, while his white beard brushed against the equally white forest of his chest. Tied round his waist was a wrapper which on that first day, as ever after, appeared to be an odd encumbrance to the man's inexplicable harmonious simplicity and poise. Much later when we had become close, he explained to me that:

"The wrapper is the yoke of our corruption which I must bear."

The discussion between him and my grandmother did not take time, as there was no financial requirement to haggle over. The training, the minstrel insisted, was free, and I was to spend the period of daytime activities with him.

It was also with heavy heart that I observed, the day after, the joyful chatter of children on their way to school while I walked in the opposite direction to the minstrel's. That picture has ever remained a metaphor for my whole life.

The minstrel was already up and seated beside the fire, his face somewhat toward the rising sun. I greeted him as soon as I entered the hut, but he did not respond. I greeted a second time and still there was no response. Ordinarily, this was enough to set fear into me, but somehow I was not afraid. There was a calm, a silence, a warmth, a light, a radiance, a something beyond these words which surrounded him and touched me and made me feel, it made me feel like I was not myself anymore, like I was not the evil-natured one. That magnetism of his touched the core of beingness inside me, a beingness I never considered a part of me, and within that core it spoke to me silently, wordlessly. It said: Sit and be quiet.

And I knew, in a way that left no grain of doubt, that this was the right thing to do. So quickly I sat down and remained quiet. It was only then it occurred to me that he was praying; praying without kneeling down and without the palms together before the face in order to help direct the prayer up to God our Father Who is in heaven so high above; praying so silently and solemnly without shouting out the prayer to our Father so far away and above. He was a strange man, my minstrel was.

There was something touching, soothing and overwhelming about the silence of that moment. And as the minstrel stretched out his hand (without opening his eyes), took the flute which also seemed to be having its own silent prayer, and started playing, that something increased in intensity, lifting me up and up until I realised that there were heights and spheres of intangible but beatific experience which could be reached through the wings of music. As the minstrel worked the magic of his flute, some vision beamed into my consciousness, not in form of pictures or sound or words. I just realised that I knew. And that knowledge, that vision (as little as I have been able to interpret its blinding flash), has indistinctly remained the goal of all my struggle as well as the bane and tragedy of my whole life.

Because, even though I did not immediately realise it, I just could not settle for things as they were anymore. Because in that very moment I set sail in life's stormy and tempestuous ocean for the full richness of the juice of life, but what that juice was I could not tell. Because in that very moment of high and rare intensity, a wide gate of infinite possibilities was thrown open before me, its road of shimmering light beckoning with the full tide of joy and fulfilment. Because what I heard, rather what I sensed, as I was transported on the wings of that music, was something I had never nor ever have fully sensed. Because what I saw, in that moment, was nothing like what I had been told and believed was the fixed compass of my possibilities. Because just as the minstrel drew forth the soul of his flute, that music, – its inexpressible harmony, its enchanting melody, the deep deep-life reaches of its magic – it stirred the dull and blunt roots of my life and pulled me up to a summit where all life flashed through my vision in eternal resplendence; and I knew, in that moment too, that there was so much inherited garbage to throw away, although what this garbage was I could not tell.

I knew not how long this lasted, for in that state everything was just intensely present and I had no idea of time. And as the minstrel finished with the flute and returned it to its former position, he placed his cool palm on my forehead. A ripple of life spread from my forehead through the spine and all over my body, and an immense peace settled on me.

"Silence amidst the noise of earth, calm in the midst of all storm, and peace, that peace in spite of the volcanoes of life."

A little silence followed this, and thereafter I realised the session was over. But the silence and calm and peace were not over within me, so I did not stir.

"Balance is the objective of the law of cycles. Always strive towards this", he said as he stood up, picked two tubers of yam and put them in the fire to roast. Then he added. "Start each day and each venture with in-breathing and re-charging session, and throughout there will be enough in you to beautify your activities. Otherwise, your sound will be hollow and noise to the soul."

When we finished eating the yams we went to the garden where, each day I spent with him, he tried to plant some seed on the soil of my uncultivated consciousness. That first day, he said:

"Seek not to weed your garden with the cutlass which never gets to the roots and will see you shortly returning to weed again. Rather, employ your God-given hands for the task of uprooting. This way, your crops stand free and mature before the weeds re-emerge."

And then he would walk round the garden, as I followed, tenderly touching the crops, affectionately speaking to them as a mother would speak to her child and then playing the flute to these crops – although the tune was never the same as the one he played for our morning prayer. He would also uproot the weeds with tenderness, and as he buried them in the beds, he would declare:

"Here lies your work of beautification, and I must aid you as much as I can."

I followed all his examples, touching and, in my mind, speaking affectionately to the crops – though it's difficult to say now how much of what I said truly came from me and not merely repetition of the minstrel's. But I did not speak to the weeds at all, rather I uprooted them quite without sympathy, if not viciously. My master the minstrel would only smile.

Afternoons were spent in lessons on the secrets of a beautiful life and the particular place of minstrelsy in the vast music of life – for he always told me that all of life, all of existence was a vast music. After the lesson followed some time of silence during which I was to contemplate his teaching. Much of the time I slipped into ever so profoundly peaceful sleep during this silence, a sleep much induced by the magic of my master on the flute.

Evenings were usually spent practising with the flute, and thereafter we would return to the garden to harvest – for he planned the garden in such a way that there was always something to harvest all through the year. Harvesting always was an experience as he usually sang a peculiar tune solemn and at the same time celebrative. Now and then he would punctuate his song with seed thoughts dropped on the still arable land of my mind:

"Just as these little lives have given of their best for our sustenance, and the heaven above freely pours out its heart in rain and sunshine on us, we too should learn to give to those who need us, for thus is all life connected into an endless ocean of music."

And he lived as he taught. What he called his "little garden" was more than twice the size of the farms of many of those who had nothing else but farming as profession. And since he sold nothing, he always kept what little stuff he needed for sustenance and gave out the rest. I never saw a day when someone in need came to him without going home with something.

Because of my master the minstrel, life became a beautiful piece of music, and since I spent virtually the whole of daytime activity with him, I had little or no contact with my uncle. And since I was fed by the minstrel, I also avoided my uncle's wife and children; for I would simply go straight to bed as soon as I returned, now and then speaking only with my grandmother when she was there.

At about the third month, I went as usual to my minstrel, and he was already in prayer when I got there. I had woken up with a terrible feeling of heaviness and dullness, so I left the house somewhat later than usual and almost missed our morning prayer. Quickly and quietly I joined him. When this was over, I put two tubers of yam in the fire and got set to go for water when he said.

"You may leave that for another day. We have enough water to take us through the day. Sit down and let's see what progress we are making."

My heart almost jumped out of my body as it dawned on me that he was going to put me to test. I sat down and tried to but could not remain calm. I could not afford to disappoint him; yet I knew that I was not ready for any kind of test. I wanted to ask if he could postpone the test to some other day when he said:

"We need no elaborate preparations to show what we truly know. And, my son, I know that you know more than you may think or realise now. Be calm."

So I tried to be calm, but the fact that he seemed to have read my mind worsened my anxiety. He continued:

"What have you learnt is the purpose of life?"

I almost answered before he finished asking, because there was hardly a day that passed without his hinting at this purpose. But I had to hold myself for him to finish, as I had learnt from him never to so jump into somebody's statement. He always said that such attitude shows eagerness, on the part of someone who does not know, to show that he knows. So I let him finish and waited a little, as if in reflection – again as he had taught me.

"The beautification of life through harmony," I said.

Some silence followed, and in that moment I could read no emotion on his face. After a while he said:

"What is that quality we need to cultivate to achieve this?"

Here many ideas and recollections of his teaching ran through my mind, and in that flash something settled, something that I was not sure I understood but which had a special appeal for me.

"We cultivate that stillness and silence and wordlessness which sounds," I said, recalling innumerable times he had said this in different ways.

He was evidently pleased as he smiled and said: "It really doesn't matter whether you fully understand or not the import of this statement. Your life demonstration will reveal to you its meaning." Some interval followed before he continued:

"How will you cultivate this silence?"

This was – or so it seemed – easy. "By listening to and obeying my master and living out his teaching."

"You have learnt well, my son, you've answered well," as he stroked my hair. "The teaching of any master is important and helpful, but there is a master whose silent voice is much more important and whom you must seek to obey. Tell me, my son, what voice is this?"

"The voice of the master within." I said.

"Strive with all that you have to reach the deep of this voice, and you will know all and your music will draw directly from the heart of life itself. You may throw away everything else I may have taught as the ranting of an old man, but hang on ever to this golden thread of truth. That's all you need."

During the afternoon lesson and silence, I fell into a deep sleep, and in that sleep I saw my minstrel in a blaze of very bright light. I was seated on a rock in the middle of a river of light, and he floated in the air towards me until the light that was his hand touched my head affectionately.

"My son," he said, "it is good to obey me or any other teacher. But you must always look within and only within yourself. Unless you discover that inexhaustible source of strength and knowledge, your sound will necessarily remain hollow – though enticing to minds of shallow depth. You also know that there is much inherited garbage you must throw off your shoulder. Discover what this is, and thereby become free to sound your note in the music of life. Blessings upon you always."

Then I opened my eyes to find him, my minstrel, staring fixedly at me. When he saw I was awake, he removed his gaze.

After the evening routine of harvesting, we sat by the fire discussing the harvest. Then in a solemn mood, my master the minstrel looked at the sky and then turned to me. For a moment he just stared without a word.

"Life will be hard and full of pain," he declared. "But it is only through pain that beauty and harmony are known and acquired. There is much to learn, and we learn only through pain. See to it that every problem before you is understood as an opportunity to grow; you must never think of it as the work of some evil force aimed at inflicting unnecessary suffering on you. Therefore cultivate pain and you will touch the sky wherein dwell the gods and the greatest of men. You are still young for much that I tell you, but they are ingrained in your consciousness, and, some day, at the right time, the meanings will unfold before you."

When I was about to leave for the day, my minstrel handed his flute over to me, saying: "This has become yours, and you will see to it that you sing through life. The way is rough and hard, but music is made only by harmonising discordant notes. You are well-fitted for all that you can do."

That the flute was finally mine, my minstrel's own very flute, I could pour my joy into the ocean and it would not be contained. And as I dashed out of the hut, I just managed to hear him:

"Don't come here early tomorrow because I will be travelling. You may come in the evening."

When I got home I went straight to the room and was glad to see that my grandmother had not returned – I wanted to play the flute and did not want it to disturb her. The joy in my heart was still overflowing. I took the flute and, lying on the bed, closed my eyes and observed some silent moment as my teacher always did. Thereafter I opened my eyes and started practising. But I could not strike up any harmonious tune. I had another quiet moment, and in that silence some pleasing tune came to mind. And without opening my eyes I started playing the tune. It was so uplifting and wonderful as I rose once again – almost as on that first day at my master's – on the wings of that music, the melody rising in intensity, and I too rising and rising. And when it seemed as if I was just about to step up further into the heart of it all, a mighty object smashed across my face, the laughter of my uncle's children – as I jumped from the bed and fell on the floor completely unable to see – their laughter brought recognition of my uncle's stone-weight wrath.

"Will I not have peace in my house because you are learning useless music?" he roared.

I was still on the floor, attempting by blinking repeatedly to clear my sight of the mass of stars twinkling before me. Something was dashed against the floor, and some splinters touched me. Then my uncle declared:

"Let me see you go to that lay-about of a minstrel, and that day we'll know who owns this house."

My flute was destroyed.

I was beginning to see a little when, as they strode away, my grandmother came in. She looked round, drew her conclusions, withdrew into herself and refused to speak to anybody or even respond to their greetings. That was the height of her anger. It was during the early hours of the morning that she asked me what had happened, and after I narrated, she lamented her fate and why God gave her such children as my dead father and my uncle. Then she declared:

"I have no money, but you must go to school like other children. Even at the cost of my life you must be sent to school."

She did not sleep for the remaining hours before daybreak.

Once it was daylight she asked me to call my uncle – a thing she never did as she would always go to him. When I told him, he looked at me curiously and asked:

"Is she dying?"

"I don't know?"

He had half-opened his mouth to say something when he changed his mind.

"Today is the market-day, and I am going there," my grandmother started.

"What is my business with that? Have you not always taken your wares there?" was my uncle's reply.

I was beginning to wonder what my grandmother was up to.

My uncle seemed to get some message that was beyond me, for his expression changed to that of intense anxiety as he inquiringly stared at my grandmother.

"I am going there with the begging bowl," she declared.

And it was like the universe became still. My uncle froze on hearing those words. My grandmother was still in desperate determination. I watched without stirring.

"I am going to the market with the begging bowl," she said again.

Still my uncle did not move. He did not even seem to blink as he stared and stared at my grandmother whose gaze went past me and my uncle and the room to that realm from where is inspired the solemn fixity of the suicide-bomber. Still I watched without stirring. And the song went on:

"I am going to the market with the begging bowl."

My uncle jumped out of his stupor and attacked:

"I will not be bothered, I am not bothered. If you like, go to the king or even to God, I don't care. I have provided a roof over your head, I feed you, I provide your needs. What more can any son do for the mother. Go wherever you like, I don't care."

Still the song went on:

"I am going to the market with the begging bowl."

And echoes of that song went round and round the walls of my uncle's pretended indifference until they fell. He knelt, shivering before my grandmother:

"Why do you want to ruin me this way, mother? You know you can't do this while I am alive, you can't. The Council will strip me of all titles and I will lose my place in the community. Is that what you want for your son? Tell me, is that a mother's prayer for her son?'

He waited, he waited for the result of this appeal to a mother's heart. It came, the result, not in words – for she did not speak this time, but in the statue-like rigidity of her gaze. But he might have seen only the signs of a softening heart. He offered:

"Mother, I promise that from today you will not need to hawk anymore. I will provide all your needs, and you will live out your remaining years in peace and ease, that's my promise."

"It's not me, it's the boy, my grandson. He has to go to school like other children," my grandmother declared.

"You!" my uncle roared as he turned toward me, "You," he still roared and then made for my throat.

Somehow, and for the first time in my life, I looked him in the face without any fear, a thing he seemed to realise as he struggled and struggled to choke me out of existence, out of his life. Still I did not stir. I only looked straight into his eyes, and what I saw in those eyes I immediately rejected – nor have I been able to accept them to date. Perhaps it was not so much what I saw in the eyes as the sensation and thought that flowed through me. When clothed with words, it is something like this: What if this man is a victim of forces he does not understand, a victim of his ignorance? Does he not deserve your sympathy and compassion?

My sympathy and compassion, for my Uncle!

I immediately rejected that which I saw between the lines of those eyes, and would have gone ahead, for the first time in my life, to strike a blow at him. My grandmother's song saved the situation:

"I am going to the market with the begging bowl."

He immediately released me and started pacing up and down the room, finally settling in front of my grandmother.

"Mother, I have heard you. Can we leave this matter till evening? I promise the issue of the boy's education will be sorted out, but let's leave it all till evening."

"Till evening", was the only thing my grandmother said, but it was good enough to make my uncle heave a sigh. He evidently deliberately avoided looking at me as he left the room.

My grandmother got set and then left to hawk for the day. As soon as my grandmother left, I locked the door and removed the key from the keyhole so that my uncle and family would not know that I was in. It was better to dream away the day in hunger till evening when I would go to my minstrel. And then, this question of my going to school, it no longer held the kind of attraction and enchanting light which it had before I met my minstrel. Still I wanted to be like other children, and still I wanted to remain with my minstrel. I wanted to go to school like other children, walking along that general direction as they did every school-day and chattering away in innocent abandon; at the same time, I wanted to walk along the opposite direction to my minstrel's, with whom I would sail on the wings of music and harmony and beauty. But

I was standing astride a gulf and knew not which side to step on firm-footedly.

But fate is a date we cannot but keep.

So in that gulf I floated and day-dreamed in snatches of sleep until my grandmother came back to announce that my minstrel, that man of immaculate heart, had passed on at night and had willed a portion of his garden to me. My uncle bewailed my fortune but rejoiced that he did not have to waste his money on my education. My grandmother took charge of the bequest, sold it and used part of the proceeds to put me in school. With her song of "I-am-going-to-the market-with-the-begging-bowl" more or less waiting on her lips, she warded off my uncle who laughed a let's-see-how-far-the-money-takes-him kind of laughter.

CHAPTER 5 | FANNING THE FLAME

THE FIRE FESTIVAL

CHAPTER 6:

THE FIRE OF SIN

S chool was not in any way like the minstrel's. Before
I stepped into the school, my uncle had gone ahead to
announce that everyone should steer clear of and watch
me closely because I was an evil child. So that as I walked into the
school I could feel eyes bulging out and steaming with hatred and
fear. Sometimes the glare was just too much that I could feel the
heat on the back of my head.

I had a seat in a corner at the back of the classroom, and it
was clearly separated so that my contagion would not easily get
to any of my classmates. The teacher too feared that he was not
immune to my contagion and, therefore, never bothered directing
any question at me, and he also always ignored me when I raised
my hand to answer any of his questions supposedly meant for any
interested member of the class. During playtime, every little cluster of children scattered the moment I came close, so that very
soon I started spending my break either at the graveyard where

there was ample peace or alone in the classroom when all the children would have gone out. Once I was sitting on my chair in the class when a classmate came to me and asked:

"Why do you look and smell so evil?"

I looked up at him but could not quite decide how to respond. He looked like one of those bread-and-butter children – soft and glass-smooth cheeks and skin. He was fresh and oily as a grilled chicken from mummy's oven of values. I admired him much and wished I had his privilege, and because of this I was confused as to what to say. I just kept looking at him, softly pulling in my imagination those cheeks of his, and … But he came up to me and struck me hard on the cheek. I was not confused anymore as I was instantly filled with venom and did not delay in striking back at him on the cheek. He fell, but then got up and walked away crying. It did not pain much again after I struck him.

Moments later the Headmistress came, flushed and in a flurry, with eight male teachers. When they got to me, they surrounded and surveyed me like a group about to attack a very dangerous snake. And when the time appeared right to them, they pounced on me and carried me away. At the Headmistress' office, I was placed on a desk, two men holding my legs, one my right hand and another my left, and one more holding my head. Two men, one on my right side and another on my left and both facing each other, whipped me with all their strength, while the Headmistress and another man standing by as reserve oversaw the whole thing. At the end of it all, I was taken to the field, given a cutlass and asked to cut grass for the rest of the day.

Our immediate community, of course, was aware of my evil nature and nobody pretended about it. Only one old widow who lived not very far from us took an unusual interest in my welfare and treated me with kindness. Her house was the only place I could enter and eat and drink and be free as a bird. But I had to watch with care the times I went to her because of my uncle who always looked out for anyone who would meddle into my matter.

But fate is a date we cannot but keep.

And my life rolled on and on like that on its tracks, always stirred by glimpses of the vision I saw at the minstrel's, but knocked here and there by hard cold stones along the path until one Sunday when my grandmother took me to a church for thanksgiving. She was not a Christian, but she had taken me there after she had rescued me from between the legs of my dead mother and discovered later that I had little life in me and responded no longer to any stimulus. She had pledged that if God preserved my life, she would give thanks on my fifteenth birthday. And that Sunday happened to be the day.

I went with her to the church with no clearly marked inclination. It was a small church, but the congregation filled up virtually every little space. When we entered the church, we were well received and there were no curious eyes staring at me – I mean, I did not see any. Yet, they all knew me. I truly felt free among them.

That day's service was elaborate and full of life, with drums and other musical instruments pouring fuel into the frenzied state of the congregation. Many amongst that congregation, especially women and children, danced and jumped and clapped and spoke in strange languages that nobody seemed to understand. A girl of about sixteen jumped and clapped and spoke to God above everyone else. When the priest raised his staff indicating time for prayer, everybody stopped singing and knelt down. But the girl did not stop. She continued singing and clapping and jumping and speaking in her strange language.

The prayer was a brief blessing on the congregation by the priest, but at the end of that prayer the girl was still jumping and clapping and speaking. What words, if those were words, that came out of her mouth sounded so strange and funny that everybody, except the priest and a few elderly women of holy carriage, started laughing. Then the priest went to the girl, placed his hand on her forehead and muttered some words. And in diminishing degrees she jumped and spoke and clapped until she finally returned to us from the world of spirits.

This must be a very powerful and holy church.

The priest then asked my grandmother and me to present our offering. We did bring it forward – a large basin of rice with stew, some bunches of banana, oranges and some tubers of yam (only God knows how my grandmother managed to provide it all). The priest then asked us to kneel down so that he might pray for and bless us. This we did, and he started praying. And then something suddenly seized or seemed to seize him, for he started shaking all over, he too started speaking his own strange language that I could not make anything out of except the intermittent mention of 'Jesus' and 'yes-Lord'. And as the priest was thus seized, the congregation too became possessed as they all joined the priest, everyone struggling to be heard above the other, some speaking in tongues, others shouting 'yes-Lord', and many more walking around my grandmother and me and shouting 'Jesus'.

The priest stopped and swiftly raised his staff. Everybody suddenly froze. Then he coughed, somewhat methodically, and everybody coughed. This time he laughed, and the whole congregation laughed. Again he said "thank you Lord," and the whole congregation said "thank you Lord," and he said "because you are good," and they all said "because you are good." Finally he shouted a long hallelujah and the congregation did the same, then he clapped and laughed for the Lord and the congregation did likewise.

In all, it was like the train of the Lord had left my grandmother and me behind; for though we (my grandmother in particular) tried to tag along, this aspect of that communion was unexpected and could not easily be followed.

Still the priest clapped and laughed for the Lord, and the congregation clapped and laughed for the Lord. Then he became calm, and the congregation too became calm. For the Lord.

"Shall we sit for the Lord," he said.

They sat, for the Lord, and my grandmother and I got up and sat too, though I could not tell whether it was for the Lord or not.

Then the priest declared that while praying for us, he saw, before God and man, some poison in the rice we had presented as offering. An old woman, he said, who lived alone and not far from us was responsible for the poison. He said that the woman had put the poison so that anybody who ate the rice would become a witch or a wizard. She was a witch, the priest declared, and even the leader of the witches in our village. Her mission was to draw the children of God into evil and witchcraft. But the rice would be eaten, he announced, and it would not harm anybody since the Lord had stepped over it.

This revelation was more than a shock to me, and it threw me into a wild internal turmoil. For as I knew, there was only one such woman who lived near us. How could it be that the only woman who singled out herself and treated me with love and kindness in our village, how could it be that she was a witch? But the priest did not give me much chance.

"You," he said, pointing his staff at me.

Everybody turned towards me, and the women around me ordered that I should kneel down. I did.

"Your days are numbered," the priest continued "Your life is in danger, great danger!"

He paused, fixed his gaze at me for some seconds and then shook his head. The congregation too shook their heads. Then he started humming a song, and still they joined him. After sometime he stopped, and they too stopped. Then he shouted a halleluiah, and the congregation did same. Again he shouted another halleluiah, and the congregation still did same. Then he laughed.

And the congregation laughed. And he said "thank you Lord", and the congregation chorused the same.

"Before God and man," he declared, "as I was praying, I saw you tied to a tree, with a group of women preparing fire to roast you. Their leader is that same woman who poisoned the rice," he paused and sighed. "They want you for a feast. But the God of Abraham, the God of Isaac, the God of Israel whom I serve has prepared you for great things in this life. The God who answereth by fire has prepared you in His fire for great things. The witch knows of the great task ahead of you, and she will do everything to stop the work of God, particularly when that work is of considerable importance. But you need now only rejoice that you have come to the house of the Lord, the God of Isaac and Jacob, the God of Daniel, of Shedrach, Meshach and Abednego, our great God who does not turn His back on the child who comes to Him in humility and repentance. Under His pinion and wings He shall cover you now and all the days of your life, and no harm from the wicked and evil ones shall befall you."

Here he took a break once again, paced up and down muttering to himself, or to his God. Then he laughed, and the whole churched followed once again. He finally returned to me.

"Be careful where you eat and drink. Otherwise, you will fall into the hands of the destroyers, and the plan of the devil, instead of the plan of God, will manifest in your life. But having come to the house of God, you need not fear anything or anybody. Only that you shall come for a seven-day retreat here, and you shall fast and sleep in the church for those seven days so that the Lord can cleanse you of the filth of the hand of the evil ones. Our prayer-warriors will be with you throughout, and, surely, goodness and mercy shall follow you all the days of your life and you shall dwell in the house of the Lord for ever and ever, amen."

And the congregation amplified and chorused 'amen.'

When I went to bed that night I kept wondering what on earth I might have done to this woman, this woman who appeared loving and kind, she who seemed to see beyond the narrow boundaries of my humanity foisted on me by my father and his brother my uncle. What could I have done to make her want to kill me? And why should such a woman, who appeared harmless and radiated goodwill, why would she be a witch and even want to kill me? If there was any witch in our neighbourhood, it must be my uncle's wife, and if anybody wanted me dead it was my uncle along with his family. So I searched all night for the reason why this woman wanted me dead, but I did not find anything satisfactory. And when I seemed to begin to doubt, I realised that it was the priest who had spoken and could not be doubted – for he simply was an instrument in God's hands, and so God spoke through him. Who was I to doubt the words of God? Rather – as I realised that this was the unquestionable voice of God speaking – I discovered how evil men could be, and how they could lure one to destruction and death with all sorts of good things and seemingly impenetrable logic. For why else would she show me so much kindness only to, at the same time, plot my death? Why if not for the sake of death? Because death has the habit of wearing the colours and garments of life. Because sweet and tasty things are the corrosives that wash away the firm and virile roots of life. Because the wide gate of easeful life is the gateway to death, the death to which she lured with her pretended love.

But my grandmother did not seem to worry about any of these things. That night she bought the candles and early the following day, before she left to hawk, she took me to the church for the seven-day prayer.

While on that spiritual retreat, I fasted from six in the morning to six in the evening, after which I was served very little food by the attendants. Intensive praying and bible lessons by the prayer-warriors dominated the whole day, while the priest, after the evening service, read selected chapters of the Psalms for me, cursing and invoking hell fire on my enemies and the enemies of the church and the Lord. Throughout the period of that retreat, I was robed in white and was not allowed to have my bath until the seventh day.

On that last day, a special deliverance service was held for me during which the priest drenched me with water and oil. And he prayed and prayed and prayed for so long that the twenty-one sticks of red candle with which I was surrounded almost burnt out and my knees became numb. When the prayer ended, the priest made a mark of the cross on my forehead, saying:

"I anoint you with the Olive oil of God and you are henceforth free from the bondage of the evil and wicked ones. Go ye now into the world and be a bearer of the light and word of God. Forget not that you have been chosen as a channel for the light and word of God. You are now a special instrument and tool in the hands of God. Therefore abandon not the task which is ahead, and let no persecution deter you from the work of God. It is, and always will be, well with you all the days of your life, so long you don't turn your back on God."

As I walked back home that night, I was filled with a certain lightness which pervaded my whole being. And a sense of worth seemed to be hanging somewhere at the periphery of my consciousness, dangling and blown hither and thither by the wind of my pasts. Still, that sense hung there. For what could be more reassuring than the revelation of God through the priest that I had been chosen for great things ahead? My life, after all, was going to have some direction and meaning. And having gone through that purificatory retreat, I felt somewhat relieved of the evil and wickedness of my life. If this proved enduring, then it would mean I would have a chance to start a fresh and clean life; and I truly was in a hurry to start that new life. As I rejoiced in what seemed a new life, I remembered the old woman, that witch. And I became worried. What should my attitude towards her now be like, knowing that she was not the good woman I had thought her to be, and also bearing in mind that I was now a special instrument in the hands of God, a tool for a great task. Could I hold this knowledge (of my position as a worker in God's garden and of her damned and wretched life as a witch) and then continue to relate to her as I used to? Or would I suddenly turn a hostile back on her, the only woman who, apart from my grandmother, endeavoured to treat me as a human being, the only one in that community of ours. And suppose I succeeded in doing this, how would I explain to her, if she came asking? But she was a witch, an instrument of the devil, and now I knew I was chosen, an instrument of God. There could not be any compromise on this marked difference, indeed no common ground on which to stand and forge ahead. The ways of God must not in any way mingle with those of Satan. That should never happen.

Give not that which is holy unto the dogs, neither cast ye your pearls before swine

My grandmother had not returned when I got home. After a short prayer, I went to bath with the holy water which the priest had sanctified and directed that I should so use. I was just about pouring water on my body when my uncle entered, the door having no lock.

"Even a bath in the ocean with a thousand bars of salt won't change you one bit," he said and lifted the bucket high and smashed it on my head. "You have multiplied your suffering," he added and walked away.

And he, in truth, tightened his grip on me, making every attempt to stop me from continuing with the church. But he was not so bold and loud about this as he had been on matters about me, and this mainly because my grandmother, though now frail and ailing from age, had become rather desperate about protecting me. For one day, as I stepped out of the house for the church, my uncle stopped me and asked where I was going. But before I could say anything, my grandmother answered:

"I took that child to that church, and anybody who tries to stop him must go down the grave with me. That's my word."

My uncle did not dare utter a word in response.

When I returned, I was more or less waylaid by my uncle just as I was entering the house,

"I will destroy you in seven days," he threatened and then jammed my head against the wall.

The word 'persecution' instantly flashed into my consciousness and took away the pain that was still there, and I nodded my head and walked into the room.

Indeed he descended on me those seven days, my grandmother ever out on her profitless trade. He descended on me in full fury, and always either that my foot steps were too noisy and therefore disturbed his peace or I was too sluggish and therefore always on his way. But I had found the Lord and I entered into Him and His church with all my heart and soul. And since I was a chosen instrument of the Lord, a light bearer, every humiliation and suffering and maltreatment I received from my uncle and his family became insignificant as my way became that of turning the other cheek. Had not my Lord and Saviour so instructed. So that I never reported anymore to my grandmother, nor ever again shuddered or ran away from it all. This maddened them, and they attacked and punched and cursed. Always as a sheep led to the slaughter I remained. Always.

The church was my refuge and only beacon of hope for a meaningful life, because in that church I found a gathering of hearts without mutual distrust, a place so stable and secure in its abiding awareness of the ties of brotherhood and oneness that for once I began to have a clear picture of what the kingdom of God was like. So I grabbed that opportunity with all eagerness and strength and zeal that sometimes I seemed to be buoyed over and above life's petty worries; those little worries that constitute the prison-yard of the mass of men and women. Because an abiding vision of the purpose of God was just before my eyes. Because the inspiration and will and strength to concretize this vision could clearly be felt and seen on my fingertips. Because the melody and tune constantly sounding in my heart filled my consciousness with nothing but inexpressible beauty; a bountiful beauty was in my heart, overflowing its banks.

Within the first month of joining the church I started reading lessons during service, and after the third month I became a preacher. That was the first time in the history of the church that a boy of that age was given that privilege, and this because in those three months I so much read or ate up the Bible that whether awake or sleeping I could quote endless portions. And the fire of the Lord was in me and the spirit of God moving through me, so that it was no big thing to stand and preach before the congregation. After all, it was the Lord who was speaking, not I. And I would stand there at the pulpit quoting and reading innumerable passages of the Bible, cursing and invoking divine wrath on all the enemies of the Lord and the enemies of His children and the church. For the Lord and His children always had enemies ever trying to pull down. Undoubtedly. Because whenever there is a step towards light, darkness always lurks around, waiting for the right opportunity to envelope. My church knew this, and so could not exist without these enemies on whom it was necessary to always invoke God's anger. So I would stand there, at the pulpit shouting and quoting verses of my favourite Psalm – Psalm thirty-five – asking God to bring ruin to the lives of our enemies, and shouting this invocation with all the emotion and strength I could gather. And the congregation would swell and sit on the edges of their seats, as I worked them to a pitch, and they would jump up and chorus a thunderous amen to my invocations.

There was power in that church. The spirit of God was moving in and through me.

Soon the church, that congregation, became too small for me. Not that it had grown smaller in number. But the power of the spirit of God surging forth from me was too much for that small church to contain. For having received the anointing of the Holy Spirit, was I not supposed to be Christ's witness in Jerusalem and all Judea and Samaria and to the ends of the earth? Our small church, with that small congregation, could not be all Jerusalem and Judea. My calling, as I definitely regarded it then, went far beyond the four walls of that very small church.

So I started going into the community to spread the word of God, trying as much as I could to gain more converts, to win more souls over to the Lord. All such missions were carried out in the early hours of the morning, between five and seven o'clock. The previous night I usually spent in the church, fasting and praying that the Holy Spirit might pour upon me to give me power to defeat all witches and wizards and all principalities and powers and evil forces that would confront me on my mission– for my mission it was. Then in the morning, the fire of the Lord blazing bright within me, I would move to the streets, accompanied by some members of the church who joined me at the church that morning.

Usually I led the way with a very long wooden cross, and, my head in the blaze of the glory of the Lord, I would shout into the silence of the morning, calling on the wicked and all witches and wizards to change their ways before the God who answereth by fire would descend to do justice with His consuming fire. The small congregation with me would at intervals clap and dance and sing praises unto the Lord.

During such missions, every old man or woman that was seen in those early hours was necessarily a wizard or a witch. For that was the time they returned to their houses after their all-night meeting during which they would have feasted on the souls of their victims. And we did see many of them, too, the fire of evil and hate raging in their hearts and eyes as they furtively shot their blazing canon-balls at us. At such times, the congregation would intensify its drumming and singing – and I knew that some cold from fear ran down their spines because it ran down mine. But I, standing on my toes and stretching my neck as far as possible, would shout at the top of my voice and hit the head of my staff on the ground; I was provided with a staff the moment I became a preacher. And I would stretch my neck and shout, praying God to destroy all evil doers who had come to tempt His children to destruction.

Incidentally, in all of those missions we never ever saw that evil woman who had poisoned my grandmother's offering and who had wanted to destroy my life before I came under the Lord's shield. But that did not declassify her as a witch before us.

As I grew stronger and stronger in the Lord, I discovered that the gulf between me and my uncle and his family widened more and more. It was inevitable, anyway. After he lost the battle to destroy me, he gave up and sank deeper and deeper into drunkenness. Many a time he would yell and yell at no one in particular. Then it was his wife and his children that he cursed, sometimes bursting into fits of violence directed at them. The wife gathered their children and took them to a church opposite mine. But that did not stop them from spitting at me whenever they had the opportunity. In fact, Peace, my uncle's eldest child once went further to cough directly on my face. I was filled with fury as she did that, but then I remembered the gentility and meekness of Jesus as he was being arrested. So I restrained myself from making her feel the strength of my arm – a move that had instinctively registered itself in my consciousness as the right response.

I was the Lord's chosen one, who had been anointed with and purified by the fire of the Holy Ghost to carry the Lord's message to the ends of the earth. I felt it did not make much sense for me to keep going into the community attempting to convert sinners to the way when my uncle and family were still wallowing in sin and I had not made any effort to convert them. For though I was sure, beyond any reasonable and unreasonable doubt, that there was no place for them in Heaven, I felt there was the need to fulfil all righteousness.

And my grandmother, too, who after that offering, returned to her paganism – though she gave me all her support in my activities in the church. I did speak to my uncle's children, though, but then Peace proved to be a real devil, hardly allowing me to talk as she laughed and made jest of me, calling me the young Moses come to lead his people out of their sinful desert world. This touched me sorely; for in some ways I truly had started seeing myself as the young Moses chosen by God for the great task of delivering the people of Israel out of the land of bondage. But it sounded a great profanity coming from her mouth. Somehow, I felt justified, purified and strengthened to carry on my work. For it was their business, not mine, if they chose to burn forever in Hell Fire. I had done my duty, and my salvation, after all, was guaranteed. I worried only about my grandmother.

But it proved not to be a matter to be easily brushed aside, for as I grew stronger and stronger in the church, my uncle and his family continued to sink deeper and deeper into sin before me. It, therefore, became extremely difficult for me to return, after church service, to that same house, that same roof under which they sheltered. Not that they bothered me much anymore. But how could I avoid being touched or somehow tainted by the enveloping force of their evil aura? How could I continue to breathe the same air into which they exhaled that most foul stench of evil? So I found myself spending more and more time in the church, doing everything I could to stay away from contact with them, to stay away from the contagion of that house. My days then were usually spent in school and nights in the church, now and then rushing into the house to pick one thing or the other. My grandmother never troubled me.

Soon I discovered that school too was a stumbling block to my activities in church. And this was beginning to worry me. I did not see any longer much that the school held out for me. And not a friendly place as the church. It was the church that redeemed me from my wicked past and gave my life a purpose. Nothing else mattered and anything that stood in the way of my progress in the church ought to be set aside. After all, had Christ not asked us to cut off any part of us that caused us to sin? There was nothing ahead for me except a life devoted to spreading the Word.

So I started missing school so that I could have more time to read my Bible and prepare for sermons. But by this time, too, I was in the last class of my secondary education, and our final examinations were not far away. I was not attending classes anymore, neither was I studying anything but the Bible. And I intensified my missionary activities, moving from my community to other villages and towns and making converts here and there for the Lord my Saviour. My absence in school was reported to the principal and he threatened to not allow me sit for the final examination if my attendance did not improve. But this did not surprise me at all, for I could see that everything had been written in the Holy Book. I was being persecuted on account of the Lord, and I knew that my reward was great in Heaven. In any case, I did not even need that examination to be a devoted servant of the Lord. There was nothing I could do with that certificate within the church. But I would sit for that examination so that I could have the certificate for keepsake. And I also knew that the whole school was going to marvel at what wonders God was going to work for me in the examinations. My principal was only swimming in the deep dark waters of sin and ignorance and knew nothing of the great power of prayer.

THE FIRE FESTIVAL

CHAPTER 7:

COMMUNION BY FIRE

When it was seven days to the beginning of the examinations, I retreated completely to the church, fasting and praying and singing praises to the Lord. For those seven days I fasted, eating and drinking nothing. The priest usually came in the evening to bless me and pray for my success. My brothers and sisters in the church also prayed for me, and some even fasted along with me, while one of my sisters-in-Christ severally shed tears of appeal to the Lord. I was deeply touched by this life of communion.

On the first day of the examinations, a special service was held for me in the morning, with the priest and the congregation jointly praying for my success. Then the priest anointed me with oil, saying:

"Go ye now into the world and be a bearer of the Word, a shinning example of His glory and infinite powers."

I left the church for the examination hall tired and weak and feeling faint. But the spirit of the Lord was with me and it guided me to that hall. I entered the hall murmuring some prayer and making a sign of the cross. The spirit of the Lord was around me. I sat down doing the same, and the feeling was strong that the spirit of God was around me. Answer sheets and question papers were distributed. Then I made a sign of the cross and prayed silently over them. Then I waited a moment for direction from the spirit. Slowly, very slowly but confidently I opened the question paper, and still I prayed.

Reading through the questions I could see that there was a mistake, there truly was a mistake somewhere; for the questions before me were different from what had been revealed to me, they certainly were not the questions I had dreamt of during my retreat. I prayed again and made a sign of the cross, then I waited for the spirit of the Lord. Still the questions were not the ones I had dreamt of, and I could make nothing out of them. Again I prayed, this time more fervently and a bit loudly, making some people to look at me. I did not wait a moment for the spirit but read the questions once again. Still they were the same and nothing had changed; for it seemed that that was what I expected. I looked round and saw that almost everybody was writing. But then I knew that the eternal Rock of Ages, the Alpha and Omega, the God who never turned His back on His chosen people in the desert, He who was, is, and always would be, He would never ever turn His back on His child who had come to Him in submission and humility. So I closed my eyes and tried to listen to the voice of the Lord. But my mind was a whirlpool of confusion, and in that confusion it seemed like the spirit had abandoned me. With considerable effort I tried to stabilize my mind. Then I listened once again, but Bible passages kept flashing into my consciousness. When this did not work, I prayed once again and then stared and stared into my question paper until the words merged into a huge darkness that hit me on the forehead, oblivion saving me the anguish and embarrassment of that moment.

I was discharged from the hospital after ten days, and by then five out of the eight subjects I enrolled for in the certificate examinations had been administered. What was the point in writing the remaining three! And then, could I really be sure that it would be different from the calamity of the first paper?

When I left the hospital, I returned to my uncle's house and for the first time in about two years spent a full day there. I truly could not tell why I decided to so spend the day. But I was somehow sure that I was not yet ready to return to the church. My brothers and sisters in Christ came to commiserate with me, praying for me and advising that I should not worry about what happened because God's time was the best. I heard all they said and tried to keep my mind blank, but my uncle kept peeping into the room, thumbing up and calling me the forsaken prophet of doom. The sting of his statement was unbearable, and after two days I fled to the church.

The ways of God are inscrutable to the little minds of men. This was consoling, but the matter was far more than that.

I resumed my preaching and tours, trying as much as I could to occupy myself with some activity and give no blank space for the beguiling questions of the devil, for those questions seemed to be hiding just below the surface of my consciousness, waiting for that moment of idleness to rear their ugly heads. I did all I could to avoid them, but there were some other problems.

Time dragged on in my consciousness, slow and bedraggled as a madman's heavy luggage of refuse. But I continued my work with the church, except that it seemed like I was not growing any stronger in the Lord.

I struggled within to stir that fire, but I realised I had no fuel whatsoever to pour. Then I struggled without through intensive activity, but there was no connection between that and the inner.

So my words and effort came out flat and empty; and my days and weeks too.

Gradually I started ruling out the possibility of a career in the church. It did not appear to be the best thing anymore; the colours of those enchanted days in the church were now fading, and through that mist I saw that I could still be active in the church while pursuing some other career outside the church. And to do this I had to pass that final certificate examination.

Was the mist fading or thickening?

With this change of focus, I started reading, now dividing my time between church activities and preparing for the examination. The realization of the necessity to pass that examination gave me a new sense of purpose which, coloured by some desperation, drove me into strenuous effort. Days and nights raced on, but I was only aware that I must study even unto death to pass that examination. How else could I move on through life?

Then it was time to enrol for the examination, but my grandmother was ill and out of trade. She had no money to take care of herself, much less give me for the enrolment. And my uncle, of course, was ruled out, for though his aggression towards me continued to lessen, he still did not regard me with kindness.

But I was going to enrol for and pass that examination: there was little else to serve as ticket into that wider world that was beginning to impress itself on my consciousness.

And so, night and day I kept thinking of what to do, kept pressing buttons here and there. And when I was becoming very desperate, an elderly woman in the church came and told me that she had discussed with the priest and that he had agreed that the church pay the fee. The priest would withdraw the needed sum from the church's account with a bank, she announced gladly.

Gladly, I rehearsed how I would show appreciation to the priest and the church, and gladly, I promised myself that I would continue to do as much work as was possible in service of the church.

Two weeks passed and the priest did not bring any money. Nor did he say anything about it. I went to that elderly woman, and she promised to remind the priest.

The priest came on the third Sunday raining fire and brimstone on everybody. He said that he saw a vision in which the whole church was surrounded by very thick darkness, and beyond that darkness was a raging inferno waiting to consume everybody. Then the voice of God came to him, the priest, where he was beyond the darkness and the fire, at the very feet of the Lord Himself. And the Lord announced to him that his church members had sinned and would be judged with the judgement of fire. But he, the priest, fell flat in prostration, interceding for his people and asking God to allow him, the priest, carry the sins and punishment of his people. He interceded for them, and the Lord heard his appeal and forgave the sins of the congregation and withdrew the judgement of fire.

And as the priest said that, the whole congregation fell flat on the floor in appreciation of his role on their behalf before God; many things, indeed, were said especially by the women in thanks and praise, if not worship, of the priest. But my mind was more on the money I was expecting, and I knew that he had brought it.

That was the end of his vision, but he added his own admonitions, saying that the whole church was on fire with gossip that he had spent the church money in his care. Then he gave a long sermon on gossip and rumour-mongering, emphasising how those who spread gossip against any man of God would be locked out on the final day of judgement and thrown into Hell fire. He ended by saying that every penny belonging to the church and left in his care was deposited in a bank and had yielded a lot of interest.

With the way he spoke, I knew that he had finally brought the money. So I warmed up, planning in my mind how I would go to each of the church elders to thank them for their kindness, and with a promise that I would continue to serve the church. But when the service ended, the priest left the church without giving me anything, nor did he even look in my direction at all – both during service and thereafter. I was confused as he walked away. Then it occurred to me that he might have forgotten. Immediately, I rushed out, calling out as I saw him approaching the exit from the compound.

"Priest! Priest!"

He turned, face unbelievably and strangely stern, almost frightening. I called up my last reserves of courage to say:

"Tuesday is the closing date, I mean the enrolment, the exam."

"So?" was his reply. After a little tensed moment, his countenance relaxed, and he added" "if it is the will of God, He will provide." Then he walked away.

God would provide if it was His will? What could be mean by that? Maybe straight from Heaven without any human agency, at least not through the priest or church. And so God would not provide if it was not His will. What else could be His will? My confusion struck me dumb. And as he walked away I just stood there, not knowing what to say or do. Somehow I walked back to the church, and as I saw members leaving in groups of twos and threes chattering and laughing away, an unforgettable picture of the lonely journey of life flashed into my consciousness, the pain of this recognition so acute and enervating that at that moment I lost all desire to live. Because as the last support on which I depended fell off and life closed in on me that very moment, I could only see my brothers and sisters in-Christ bathing in mindless innocence in the ocean of the self. And the dark despair of total abandonment and loneliness descended on me. And as I roasted in the fires of that desert, in the thick of so suffocating a need, I found no face of concern, no word of comfort, and only the behinds of people deliberately lost in chatters and consciously striding away from me.

My heart burnt to ashes.

Somehow, still, I turned, facing the altar, and the priest's vacant chair sneered at me, raucously repeating that God would provide if it was His will. And as I stared vacantly at the altar I knew that God, too, was not there anymore. And I asked, exclaiming sharply:

"Why?"

To whom would I run now, having been failed by my own brethren? And could God fail me too. Again I exclaimed.

Why?

And questions rushed up and out from the deep depths of my being, somehow choking and blinding me. And it immediately became clear that for the first time since I decided against the ways of the world to follow the Lord, I was asking questions. And I could see that all these questions had been in my mind all along; I had only chosen to ignore them, trying to believe that they never existed, or that if they did, they came from the devil. Now I was ready to listen both to the devil and to God, now I was. And I could also see that these were the same questions I almost asked after I left the hospital. They were there all along.

Again I looked at the altar, and again it occurred to me that it was not just that God had left there too; He had abandoned me, leaving me and my problem all alone. And again I asked.

Why?

Why was it that my God and my all, in Whom I trusted, why did He choose to abandon me? Where did I go wrong and why this very heavy penalty, on an issue that now mattered most to me? Had I not carried out well enough the task of spreading the Word? And if that was the case, why punish me this way? For what else could I do without enrolling for and passing that certificate examination? The church, my only home, had turned its back on me – and that meant, invariably, that God had turned His back on me too. Where then and to whom would I turn?

I turned and faced the congregation, but, of course, vacant seats stared at me, my brothers and sisters in-Christ having all gone. Standing there all alone and staring at the vacant seats, I could see the faces of my brothers and sisters in-Christ as they jumped and clapped and spoke in tongues. And I wondered if that was all that we found in brotherhood and communion. Standing there all alone, engulfed in the heat of my burning confusion, I saw again the faces of my brothers and sisters as they shared, before God and man, their dreams and visions, but I did not see my brothers and sisters genuinely sharing in the problems of others. So that in spite of all our songs of joy and sorrow and praise to the Lord, the logic was still every man to himself and God for us all.

If it is the will of God.

And I wondered again: is this the meaning of brotherhood? Of death on the cross?

A streak of hot tears rolled down my cheeks, and as I bent, it fell on the carpet and rolled towards the altar. But the priest was not there to receive it. Nor was God. So that the tears rolled just a few inches and, realizing the futility of its journey, stopped. There was nothing, no one up there for it to flow to. God was not there anymore. How was I to continue living? What to live for?

Because where there is no vision of God, the all-transcendent, where there is no vision of the god-in-man, the immanent core, all journeys are just a vacuous jostling in the blind alley of ignorance. Now that God was lost, what else was left me to aspire towards?

But I could see that I expected too much of the church, too much of people. But I did try, in the few years I was in that church, to help my brothers and sisters in-Christ, and many did enjoy many many hours of free labour from me – for that was what I had to give them. And I did give, believing that it was a service to my sisters and brothers and so a service to God. And this was precisely what I expected of those with whom I shared communion, with whom I raised a common voice of appeal towards the source of all life. What could be wrong with such expectation? What?

If it is the will of God.

So engulfed and overwhelmed as I was, I burned the more in the confusion and puzzle of why it was easy for people to share in others' joys but always hard to share in their sorrows. For I realised, though I did not seem to have registered it immediately, that as I rushed out that hot afternoon to remind the priest of the money, those who had wanted to see him and already moving towards him, on seeing me approach, took different directions than the church's main exit point to leave the premises.

As I walked back home the questions kept coming and coming, but I was now struggling to ignore them because they were choking me and I was drowning in their flood. They kept coming and coming and I struggled the more to push them back to where they came because the answers that kept suggesting themselves had the force of truth so unbearably ugly. And then it was worsened by the fact that a crazy carpenter was inside my head hitting and cracking the walls of my head with a hammer, while his brother the drummer was frenzily exercising with the walls of my heart.

My grandmother was not home when I got there – I hoped that she had not been taken to hospital. My realisation of her absence seemed to increase the carpenter's hammering and the drummer's frenzy, and more questions were thereby poured into the troubled ocean of my consciousness. For I realised that all the money collected by the church went to the priest and nobody else – even when there was supposed to be a treasurer – and nobody ever asked any questions regarding the money. Nor was any account ever given. How could this have been? And what was wrong with us all?

Maybe it was not the will of God?

Of course the church fasted and prayed fervently, asking God to provide money to build a larger church, a worthy dwelling-place for our God. A lot of money was collected over time for this purpose, but no one, except the priest, knew the total amount, what was spent and what was left. And I could see that while the new church building did not rise beyond foundation level, even after we had collected quite some money for that purpose, the priest's new and second house, which was begun soon after the first fund-raising ceremony for the new church building, kept rising and rising and was now nearly completed. Somehow, without any conscious effort to, I swam in the filthy water of the church's dirty linen, and I saw far too many things that had been happening in the church but which I always ignored, somehow turning my face to the other side. Now I could see and see and see. And the ultimate question, with a simultaneous hammering of my head, would fall:

Why?

And that question, that why, fanned the heat of my anguish, and the whole room became the burning sand of a desert. It seemed as if Hell could not possibly be more unbearable. So I went out of the room to the back of the house. There, under a tree I went, and there, steeped in the thick vapour of despair and disgust, I paced up and down, musing to myself and raising argument with Heaven and Hell and God and Satan and life and death and all that could and could not come into view. And then, in this condition, I suddenly realised that that old woman, I mean that witch that had put poison in our offering to the church, she was nearby and watching. On her face was a look I could have interpreted as that of immense pity. But this was the witch. She came up to me and said.

"My son, what is it that troubles you this much, what is it? And you won't come to me? It should not matter what they may tell you out there. You must know that you are always in my heart, and as a mother to a son I wait to share in your troubles. Come to me."

And she quickly walked away, her voice beginning to quake and tears in her eyes.

This was most unsettling an encounter, and it stirred the more the fire of my confusion and poured more fuel into my bitterness, and I was ready to die at that moment and finally be free from the madness of the meaninglessness of existence. Because large in my consciousness was the picture of a leprous and infections hand holding out the apple fruit of life, whereas the hand of light after which I had sought continued to retreat and withdraw from me. What was this life after all? What was the meaning of truth? What really was the meaning of meaning? What? And what's what?

I swirled and swirled in the heat of that confusion, search-ing for an escape channel. For here was the church- declared (or priest-declared) witch offering me that which I desperately needed, that which my priest and the community of my brothers and sisters in the Lord could not spare much of, they who weekly ate the bread and drank the wine of the sacrifice of Christ; a sac-rifice so freely given. And then the witch, offering me her hand. In my most extreme desperation.

Oh, my extreme unction!

What was wrong with her? Or was it that I was mad or stupid or what? She whom I had called my enemy and enemy of the Lord.

Because from the moment I joined the church, the moment I entered into the Lord, I could no longer eat at the old woman's house, neither could I drink nor even go there at all. And I tried as much as possible to avoid contact with her. Greeting her was only when it was inevitable. Naturally, the old woman noticed and kept asking for a long time until one day when, after she had asked, I told her to stop bothering me with that question because she ought to know that it was not possible for a child of God to eat and drink in the house of his enemy and the enemy of the Lord. She was stunned, and quietly she walked away, only turning and muttering:

"Me, your enemy?"

And now here was this witch, this enemy, declaring that I could always come to her. Which indeed was not new. But the wild confusion in my mind not only magnified this open door but also contrasted it with the closed door of my church where I had sought help and where I knew that help would always come from. But, you know, open doors could also be the wide gates unto destruction, a wide gate made open by a witch in order to lure to death. But the future which presented itself before me that critical moment, that future without passing the all-determining border of that final certificate examinations, a future with nothing but the hopelessness of a life-career with the church; that future was much more than death now. It was. And I now was beyond caring whether my salvation was in the hands of a witch or enemy of the Lord, a Lord that I was not sure that I understood anymore or that I could convincingly speak about. Salvation, after all, was what mattered – and I would go to Hell and the Devil himself if that was the only place to pick that salvation.

That night, in shame and desperation, I went to the old woman, and the following morning she gave me money for the examination

I returned to the church and time dragged by like a millipede. But I could not go on evangelisation missions anymore, I could not go into the community again to preach the gospel. I confined myself, my activities, within the four walls of the church, reading lessons and preaching with great effort: and this not yet because of a conscious decision, but because inside me was a deep dry hole, and my words always came out hollow and dry. Like the spirit was not in me anymore. Like that overshadowing cloud of glory had departed, rendering me stale, flat and unprofitable as Hamlet's world. Every word that came out of my mouth was like that.

And nobody in the church appeared to notice this change; at least nobody ever bothered to ask me, neither did anyone care to ask about the enrolment. Church activities continued as usual, but it appeared like the gamut of lives throughout the universe once again connived to mock me – as they did my lioness with a mane; because the sun still took its normal course and poured its heat and light on the world, but in it was neither warmth nor shine for me; because the birds still sang to each other and copulated; because church activities went on as usual and my priest still ruled in strength and health and awe and more financial contributions were made at each service, which was given to the priest for safe-keep, and I was there amongst them dropping whatever little I had. And no thunder rumbled.

If it is the will of God!

But thunder did rumble within me, it did because at the end of each service the priest and my brothers and sisters in-Christ would leave, but I alone would remain, turning up and down in my mind questions that now never ceased to worry. And as I was lying on the floor of the church reading my bible one Sunday afternoon, it struck me that I needed not worry myself about the priest and other evil doers in the church; for had the Lord not said that vengeance was His? But then, I mused, why did the Lord bless that priest and many others in the church with the gifts of seeing visions and dreaming dreams, knowing – as I now finally admitted that which I knew all along but simply either closed my eyes or excused it away – that these were adulterers and adulteresses, liars, fornications and cheats? It struck me there and then that the Lord probably never revealed anything to any of them.

For I remembered an occasion in the church when one young man had attempted to contradict the priest's vision, the Lord's message. A concerned and worried mother had brought her son, about twenty years old, to the church so that the priest might pray for him over some problems. After the usual church service, the priest called the young man forward and prayed for him, members of the prayer-warriors group standing round him. After the prayer, the priest declared that before God and man he had, while praying, received some message concerning the young man. The priest said that there was much in the message he would not reveal until a later time. He then said that it had been revealed to him, before God and man, that the young man had a plan to abandon a girl whom he had impregnated. But the young man would not wait for the priest to finish. He quickly stood up from his kneeling position and declared that what the priest said was a lie, that he never had the intention to abandon the girl, and that he had even started making contacts and arrangements for the marriage ceremony. And as he spoke, it was like a CNN Breaking News showing to the whole world the picture of Mary on adulterous bed. The congregation opened their mouths in disbelief, glances criss–crossing. The prayer-warriors each took a step backward, in a military fashion, and examined the devil before them. The priest smiled an all-knowing smile and, as Christ on the cross with much pity in his heart, shook his head. He fiddled with his bible a moment, fixed his gaze on the young man, and … But the young man's mother, as many mothers would sacrifice themselves to save their child, quickly rushed forward and, kneeling before the priest, asked for forgiveness because the young man did not know what he was doing. Other church members joined, kneeling and asking the priest for forgiveness, with some others shouting at the young man to kneel down and beg the priest for forgiveness. But he refused, restating that he never planned to abandon the girl. This was going to let loose in a china shop the bull in the priest, for the young man's intransigence now ignited a spasm and long bout of speaking in tongue. But the mother of the young man stood up and dragged him away.

Of course the story of the young man impregnating the girl was not a secret, and it was actually one of those common news updates in community gossip. It was not clear whether the young man was planning to marry the girl, but when the priest disclosed his vision, nobody in the church was in doubt anymore. Could you then imagine what sacrilege of the highest order it was for that young man to dare contradict the priest's vision, the Lord's message?

As I was on the floor of the church reading my bible and thinking about the whole thing, I could see that much of the visions ever disclosed to people in that church, and particularly first-time comers, were visions of witchcraft and intending problem and destruction and calamity. Always it was some vision that required a coming back to the church for some special prayer and, as in my case, a retreat. Always the vision saw a great gap in the life of the individual, a gap which the church ever after would eternally continue to endeavour to fill. Why was it always like this? But then it struck me that these were the handworks of human beings who claimed to be working for God. It was not my business to worry about them; vengeance was the Lord's.

I continued with the church, however. Only I had decided to follow no priest's sermon or command. My Bible was my guide, and I would continue to study it and work out my life through its teachings. I knew that I was in the midst of sinners, but I chose to continue with the church because I realised that, on the last day, each person would give his or her own account, not another's. I continued with the church and as the congregation sang and clapped and spoke in tongues, I knew that the glory had departed. I continued with the church, and as we shared, before God and man, our dreams and visions, I knew now that life in that church was not that elixir, was not yet that beauty for which Nietzsche's Zarathustra would want to love and perish so that it might not remain merely an image. Because the spirit was not in me anymore, and I lost the power to speak in tongues. Speak in tongues? Was it? Or that I realised that there truly was nothing to it, and I became tired of that self-deceit? Because we all believed we spoke in tongues, yet none understood the other, whereas the disciples who were said to speak in tongues during the Pentecost understood one another. How had we reduced it all to this idiocy and rank mockery?

But I continued with the church and read my bible more than ever before.

Which, indeed, made matters worse.

Because as I read the bible more often in an attempt to run away from the questions rioting deep down my consciousness, I discovered that the bible, too, was no longer the same. I discovered that I could no longer make sense of what I read – or rather that I made more sense of it than desired. It sort of made sense to the point of senselessness and meaninglessness. For the more deeply I seemed to penetrate, the more some seemingly irrational logic threw up questions for me? How come? And the same bible that I had been reading for years now? Because much that was in it, particularly the Old Testament, now appeared so stupidly primitive and brutally uncompromising to appeal to me anymore. Because the God of the bible, of the Old Testament, did not appear to be the God after Whom I had striven and hoped to serve, and this mainly because when a man sets himself apart, say to alone gain life, he deliberately and inevitably sets others apart for death, shutting that door of life against others

But we all are said to be made in the image of God.

I started with the children of Israel, God's chosen people. And I was with them in the land of Egypt in all their suffering and afflictions. I saw God appear to Moses and promise him that He would take His children, the Israelites, out of the land of bondage into the land of the Cananites, the Hittites, the Amorites, the Perizzites, the Hivites and the Jebusites; a land flowing with milk and honey. And I saw the Israelites, God's chosen people, journey out of the land of Egypt after God had descended to strike terror into the hardened hearts of the Egyptians. And I saw the children of Israel, God's chosen people, in battle with their enemies, and I saw God fighting on the side of the Israelites, His chosen people who were as sinful as their enemies.

God descended from His almighty to fight for them.

And I saw Him smiting and destroying the enemies of His chosen people. And I saw this special people who were free to sin and suffer and be forgiven, I saw them journey into this land flowing with milk and honey, and I saw them take possession of this land that did not belong to them, I saw them take possession of this land that belonged to some other creatures, even human beings (though God-forsaken), a people that God had as well expended time and energy creating as He had spent on the Israelites – the apples of God's eye.

God descended from His almighty to meddle in the petty affairs of His children. He took side.

In any case, those fighting with the chosen people of God were all children of Adam and Eve, the same parents of the people of Israel. So that they were all brothers and sisters, meaning one family.

And God descended with the sword of separatism.

And I asked: Why?

I saw God descend from that almighty to destroy the enemies of His chosen people, the Israelites, and I asked:

Why?

Why on earth should God descend so low? For hard as I tried to, I could not see any reason, acceptable reason, why God had to take side in a battle to unjustifiably dispossess and annihilate a part of His creation; I could not understand why God had to choose a special people out of the multitude of His creation; for was He not the creator and maker of everything? If I had a brother and a normal family, I certainly would not have found it funny, much less acceptable, if my father had chosen him as his special child, and I was sure that my brother too would not have found it acceptable if my father had chosen me. Why then did God choose to sharpen the edges of differences (and by implication the edges of separatism and hostility and war and the desperation of suicide-bombing) between man and his fellow man by choosing a special people? What was there in the life of one that could not be found in the other even only as a dim and latent potentiality? Was it that some and only some men were made in the image of God? What, indeed, was the meaning of that divine spark which was supposed to be glowing towards full radiance in all human beings? What was this image of God in which we were all made?

God so descended from His almighty.

There and then it struck me that I was not even a Jew, that I was a Gentile. I was not even one among God's specially chosen people. I saw it with rising confusion and a stinging bitterness that I was not one of God's own people. But it occurred to me, though, that Christ had extended that salvation to the new Israel, the church. This realisation, instead of uplifting a little, pushed me further down the deep pit of disgust; for the thought of my priest and that church of ours as part of that larger church that would enjoy eternally the inexhaustible treasures of Heaven did not in any way appear sensible.

God must make more sense than this!

Then I started wondering about the fate of my forefathers who never had any opportunity of receiving the gospel, the light of the world. And I wondered, what heinous crime, in what grue-some and unpardonable ways had they offended God or His cho-sen people that nobody was sent to preach the gospel to them? Oh, perhaps they would be judged without the law, as St. Paul said. And so with what laws then? Would it be fair to send them to Hell?

That, indeed, brought the question of Hell fire before my probing mind. Since I became saved, I had no iota of doubt that a permanent seat was awaiting me in Heaven. I was sure beyond all questioning that that eternal bliss was for me. But my grand-mother was not saved and still continued with her old ways. This meant, invariably, that she was going to burn in Hell fire forever. Then I started thinking about the nature of the eternal bliss prom-ised those who had been saved – although now, in that moment of heat as well as illumination, I could hardly explain from what they were saved. How possible was it for me to be eternal happy, know-ing that my grandmother was burning eternally in Hell? What kind of happiness would that be? Oh, maybe those in Heaven, after having crossed Lethe or tasted of ambrosia, would no lon-ger have any memory of brothers and sisters and parents and grandparents and friends. Even then, what cruel order was it that permitted any soul whatsoever to burn eternally in Hell fire? And I could see that majority of the people in my community were not Christians, and therefore were liable to Hell fire on the last day, while I and my priest and the congregation of that church would be bliss-crammed in Heaven. Again I asked: What kind of happiness would that be, what cruel and ungodly order? Why was it that any of God's creatures should ever be beyond redemption? What happened to that omnipotent and ever-merciful God? Had His ocean of mercy dried up?

God must mean something more!

Of course as I grew stronger and stronger in the Lord, I somehow moved further and further away in my heart from my grandmother. I could not show this much in action because she was the only one for me in that house. But it pained me sorely that she could not continue with me in the church after that thanksgiving, and my heart was no more with her, tucked away as it was in the holy bosom of the Lord. So that there was, somehow, something almost irksome about my grandmother's presence. But I tried very much to tolerate this because many more things in her pulled me. And when I finally asked myself what it was that made her scarce presence somewhat unsettling, I could see nothing but the fact that she worshipped idol and did not profess Christ as her Lord and personal saviour. When now I mouthed that phrase "Lord and personal saviour", it sounded stupid, vacuous and pedestrianly blind. Saviour from what? Sin? Oh, had I really been so saved, so free from dirty thoughts and foul emotions and untoward acts, had I?

Still I thought about my grandmother and I could see that her paganism, her religion, did not stop her from doing good to us, the Christians. For I recalled the fund-raising ceremony for our new church building. My grandmother was invited, and she did not fail to attend, donating from the depths of her heart her widow's mite, clapping and singing and worshipping God with us. Thinking of her, I could see how my grandmother gave out so freely to our church without feeling that she was giving to an institution that believed and worshipped a different God. And again I asked: Why was it that my grandmother's religion enabled her to tolerate and identify with and even give to us, whereas our own Christian religion branded her a sinner and unbeliever and gave her all kinds of derogatory names? We could never have given to her had she wanted us to help in her own religious activities. But here she was donating freely to us, to us that looked at her as a sinner. And, of course with no stir (much less on earthquake) of conscience, we would, and did, open our hands to receive from those whom we, sitting on the judgement seat, made sinners. And their sin, its filth, did not soil that which we were taking from them for the Lord's use. No, it did not besmirch it.

The way to God must be more sensible!

And that way I desperately searched for. And I could still see, on that first day that my grandmother took me to the church for thanksgiving, how she clapped and danced and sang freely with the congregation as if she had always been one of them. It was obvious that she did not feel she was worshipping a strange God. To her, as she once told my priest, God was still the same God everywhere, in spite of whatever name He was given or the kind of robe or garment of rituals which adorned the way to Him. So she, a pagan, went out of her way to bring me to church for prayer in a moment of need; and then she lived up to her pledge and came on my fifteenth birthday for thanksgiving, and she came and donated for our new church project. She, a pagan!

There must be something of God's way in her way.

And I looked at that way, her life-style, and I could see that she did not steal, neither did she kill. She did love God and her neighbours, including those of us who practised a different religion. Placing her life-style alongside my priest's I saw that she was a much better and loving human being than my priest. And I asked why God, on the last day, would choose my priest instead of my grandmother. The answer, though utterly distressing, was not hard to find: my priest was a Christian and my grandmother was a pagan. That's all. Not because my priest had demonstrated any true standards of godliness and purity of character more than she had. It ought to be enough qualification, in fact one ought not bother much more, that my grandmother had led a simple and honest life of loving relationship with fellow human beings. This ought to count over and above falsely professing belief and faith in godliness under the banner of Christianity. Why was it not possible to know God anywhere else but through Christianity? Why was it necessary for God to manifest the kind of variety as found in the infinite multiplicity of created beings, only to end up decreeing a constricted and constricting outlook for humanity through the Christian bible? Why were there rainy and dry seasons, summer and winter, the white man and the black, the tall and the shot, day and night, and the differing planets and stars scattered in our universe, and in other universes? If these were all manifestations of the creative activity of God, why then did He choose to abandon that pluralism, the essence of which constitutes the beauty of that creative Intelligence? Why should God abandon His own example to decree an intolerably destructive narrow way of living? Why must it be Christianity and nothing else? Why not Christianity as one of the many approaches?

As I was thinking about everything one night, I remembered the old woman whom the church had made a witch out of. And I could see now more clearly how much she loved and cared for me, how she showed me that kind of love of a mother who truly loved her child. She did treat me that way, like her own son. Where and when all else had failed me, I found an unshakeable rock of support in her. In spite of all, my foolishness, my detestable intolerance, that fundamentalist blindness. Still she cared for me.

What else is love? What godliness?

Thinking of her made me develop a torturous feeling of guilt because not even in the church (where I did expect it with all my heart) did anybody demonstrate that kind of love; not any of those numerous brothers and sisters in-Christ with whom I glibly chattered about the love of God and the supremacy of our church over others and the saintly man of God that was our priest; none among those matronly women who always told me that I was a chosen instrument of God's work; nobody from that select and saintly-looking group of church elders who always prefaced any assignment they gave me with the saying that the greatest among the children of God was he who served others. In them I found not that love, that saintliness, that desire and effort to serve others.

But I found it all in that old woman, the witch.

The way of God must make more sense!

That night, as I thought about that woman, I could neither sleep nor find any comforting escape-route; for the weight of the feeling of guilt was heavy and choking life out of me. My heart burned in the fire of that guilt, yet that heart, my being, did not disintegrate, did not crumble into the ashes of non-being, in that inferno.

And I desired neither death nor life.

Only, first thing in the morning, to go to that old woman and ask for forgiveness, explaining how the church led me into believing that she was a witch. I had little or no fear that her loving heart was still open to me and would always forgive. The problem was how to stand before her and look into her eyes and still be able to speak. But I was desperate.

I cannot tell now how I managed to get into an empty sleep, but my grandmother woke me up rather early and took me to the old woman's house where a number of people had gathered. The old woman who had been ill for sometime, I gathered, was dead, and had instructed that whatever she owned be given to me.

But for my minstrel, I had never had the experience of someone dear to me dying, and I had always wondered how I would react whenever such a thing happened. I had been saved the drama of that reaction in relation to the minstrel partly because I was still a child and partly because I did not even see the corpse. So I had always wondered how I would wail and water the soil with my tears and possibly throw myself and roll on the ground – as I saw people do.

Now that I lost that old woman – because I realised more than ever before what she meant to me –, now that somebody who had just acquired such a strong presence in my heart was dead, it all seemed different, I mean, not the way I had expected it. Now that I had every reason in the world to raise my cry of anguish high and loud to heaven, I found out, to my utter amazement, that I had no cry to cry, no will to wail, and no tears to inundate the universe with. Because the load of guilt I was carrying within multiplied in geometric progression, and I was only an atom in this very large universe of anguish. And I tried to lift up my eyes to something up there, to God, but then I realised that God had long abandoned me, that I was completely on my own and that the anguish and despair and destruction and deathless dying I could see before me were all for me and me alone, and that there was no one I could ever share them with.

What is death by drowning?

Pain and anguish and sorrow I had all known before, but none of them could capture the way I felt as I stood before the lean corpse of the old woman. It was not a matter of attempting to cry; my eyes were hot and dry, and I doubt that I even remembered the necessity to cry. A big stone, which had been somewhere in my head, descend into and sat on my heart – much like the way a very fat woman or a sumo wrestler would sit on and swallow up a tiny stool. And that was what snuffed out the power of speech and the will to stir and cry and act one way or another. I just stood there and watched her gaunt figure and pain-wrinkled face, the anguish of the whole world having been compressed into a tiny dynamite that exploded within me. I just stood before her lean corpse and pain-wrinkled face, immobile and battered into tiny incalculable shreds, the age-long promise of hell-fire eventually finding consummation within the blazing enclosure of my heart. I stood before her lean corpse and pain-wrinkled face, numbness and inertia shutting out all sight and sound but my pain and anguish.

What more is there in Hell? Can you tell?

Because once upon a time, a man shunned the warning whispers of his heart and jumped into a volcano to prove his immortality to sign-seeking compatriots.

I was that man that chose death instead of life.

Because once at the minstrel's hut, I repeatedly swept away an ant, but it kept coming back so that I let it and it crawled straight into the fire.

I was that ant that chose death instead of life.

For it was not just the case that I had chosen the path of death; I was also the cause of it for another, for the old woman. Because it became clear that she must have died with sorrow in her heart that I had not quite taken my place in her heart. I, whom she obviously took as her own, could not make up with her before she died, could not even be with her in those final moments of passing. Still it was I who called her my enemy and an enemy of the Lord. And all because my church, my priest, had made her a witch. And so the old woman died. She truly died. All my plans of profuse words of apology, of my subsequent tender and loving care to her in those greying days of hers, all that plan was just a petrol-fire burning in my heart.

Still I stood before her lean corpse and pain-wrinkled face, my eyes hot and dry and my whole body quaking under the simultaneous onslaught of heat and cold, under the growing mockery of voices within – your life could have been better if only you had shown some gratitude; because she loved you like nobody ever will, that's why you judasly kissed her and then removed the pillar on which her life depended; because you found your God, and you became too clean for non-members of your church; because your God is the God of separatism and not the Maker of all, so you judasly kissed and killed that heart of love – until somebody came and took me away.

He returned the thirty pieces of silver.

But that I could rend my clothes and wear ashes and sack-cloth. That I could. Only that days were to pass into weeks, and weeks into months of jumbled incoherence of thought and con-sciousness. These were months during which I fed, more than anything else, on sedatives. And as I fed on these, the numerous voices within fed me too and took me across time and place, cov-ering the known and unknown history of the world. My uncle was the conductor of that orchestra, showing me how, through-out millennia of earth life, I differently took the images of Satan, Set, Judas and the beast of darkness at every point eating deep into the incipient roots of civilisation, spreading filth and dark-ness and death wherever I touched. That was all I could remem-ber of the three months that I was in a psychiatric hospital, the generosity of the old woman providing for the expense.

I returned to sanity one night after I saw an image of the old woman in dazzling white, smiling and waving at me. That same night, a very violent rain washed away many houses in the land. I returned home twelve days after its flood.

And though a violent and heavy rain may suddenly stop, its flood certainly takes longer to flow away. So that the ghost of the whole experience kept haunting me every minute of the day, and a feeling of being followed made me entirely useless. I spent all day avoiding people's eyes (except my ailing grandmother) because those eyes spoke much that was unkind and accusatory, while at night I battled some fear that I could not articulate even to myself. On one of those nights I saw the old woman (whether it was a dream or not I still do not know), and once again in daz-zling brightness. In fact she was radiance possibly brighter than the sun, but that brightness did not hurt. She said to me:

"There is plenty inherited garbage in you to empty. Or if it makes more sense, you could say that you need to forgive yourself and be what you truly are".

And as my minstrel once did, she rubbed my head with her fingers of light, and the thrill did much to strengthen me.

But it was a night of confusion as I fretted to make sense of what she meant. There certainly would have been no confusion if I had been told that there was much to forgive. Because in that case there was my uncle, and his family, and my priest, and many more people who one way or another had spread the dark carpet of unpleasantness along my path. But she spoke of my forgiving myself – not others. Meaning then that there must be some ways in which I had offended or was offending myself. How could this be? Because of my past? Or the vision of what I thought I could be, that vision so close and right before me and at the same time so far away; a vision I held so tenaciously, my only rope to the side of life and fulfilment and joy in the chasm of evil and sorrow and despair. How come? Because somehow I refused to succumb to its sweeping tempest and whirlpool? Because I sought escape from the festering feast of flies on the rubbish-heap of existence, from the saltless slime-seasoned soup of death which was my life. Or was that not my life?

But there are things which are better left unsaid because either they are unsayable and can only be known or the force of their truth is so powerful as to smash our unquestioned and conventionalised living into splinters and a wreck of confusion.

Such wreck was I.

And still steeped in that confusion, I walked to the church one hot afternoon. I was not quite clear about what I was going to do there, but I knew, I was sure beyond measure, that I must go to that church. And at that moment too.

THE FIRE FESTIVAL

Chapter 8:

The Burning Bush

When I got to the church, to that place of holiness and refuge and communion, the place that was now my death and destruction, I stood in front of the building, under the stinging sun, and stared at the church, its (un)holy aloofness. I stared at the faces of my brothers and sisters who were not there at that point in time. But I stared at their faces and saw each and all of them, and very painfully, at the face of my priest. That church building stood clear of all buildings around, and it stood clear, too, in that illuminating moment of sadness and sorrow, that the church was responsible for my predicament. The church it was that led me into the problem I was facing. The church it was that made me turn my back on that loving old woman, a woman who had tried to give – and who indeed gave – where she could not have expected to receive. The old woman who truly loved me like my lioness with a mane would have. And, overflowing with the wine of the spirit, the church saw that love as poison. And that spirit intoxicated me so much that I called her my and the Lord's enemy.

Oh viper unnameable!

And she died, she truly died, with no word from me to her, no precious parting benedictions to me.

The sun was directly above me. And as I stood under its blaze, so steeped in the depths of that confusion, I asked myself if that was what religion ought to bring into people's lives; tearing apart and alienating one from the other. For if religion, any religion whatsoever, brought man closer to God, it ought to bring man closer to his fellow human being. And it occurred to me that there was no way man could be close to God without being close to his fellow man. Because closeness to God ought not mean regular and prompt attendance in church, neither was it closeness to the priest and carrying out every of his whim and bidding, nor even the act of ensuring that one was always at the forefront of every church activity. For one could do all this with a closed heart and, outside (if not even inside) the church, let loose on others the poison in heartlessness. It occurred to me, there and then, and in a blinding flash of illumination, that one could not truly find that ever-loving God without first finding one's fellows, and that our only road to God was the road to our fellow human beings – if not to all other creations of the one God.

He who serves others is the greatest.

And only thus was that peace attainable. For what peace was it if one was at peace with God – or rather if one believed so to be – and yet was not at peace with his fellow? And, again, what was the meaning of this peace with God, a peace away from and beyond one's fellows? Some place or condition in which one was sedated and became deaf to the cries of humanity in burning need, those distressing cries from our earthly inferno? Could that be peace? Where, indeed, was God to be found? Up there above and in the sky? Oh, but already science had made it clear that there was no up or down as everything was relative to where we stood. And suppose that was not the case, how were we to construct that bridge to take us to God up there? Was He just up there or was He in any way with or within us? What about the God immanent in each and all?

Where, indeed, was God to be found?

Surely beyond the church. Certainly beyond the confinement of any four walls. Not of a church. None of any creed or sect that stood apart and set itself against all others. Because one could not be in perpetual battle with the whole of creation and hope to present the booty from such battle as the ticket to that eternal peace in the bosom of the Lord. Such could not be the nature of the war which should lead to peace; because that kind of peace was too selfish to reflect the peace of the ever-loving God in whom everything lives and moves and has its being.

But, did I truly have peace while in that church?

No, I could not, indeed, say that I attained any real and lasting peace of mind in all my years in the church except the sense of worth which I seemed to have derived from being a member and seeing that I was doing much more than all my age-mates. I had borne much troubles of mind, all along, by telling myself that the way of the cross was not easy and that one had to go through all that in order to attain that peace. Now that peace appeared too illusory and costly to attract me anymore, to quench the burning desert of my discontent.

The sun was now inside my head.

And as it ate deep into the grey content of my consciousness, I saw all too clearly that the ethics of that church, as we were taught, were too selfishly inspired. For if I as a delivered and saved Christian loved or attempted to love my neighbour, it was only because I loved myself too much; I really did not love my neighbour without expectation of return – from him or from God as reward for my love. Truly, it seemed to me that we attempted to do things in the name of love only because love would earn us a ticket to heaven. In other words, we were only loving our way into heaven. One ought to love, I thought, because one believed in love, and not because one saw love as a means to a very selfish end. That appeared to be desire, a kind of lust, and in no way love. Just as a boy strong between the legs talks to a girl about his loving her. What love would be there in his heart except to empty his heat into her?

Do you not call that lust?

The purpose of religion, I told myself, ought to be to reconcile man with his fellow and with his environment, and not to tear him further apart from his kind or to forcefully but falsely attempt to create escape-routes out of his environment which he must master. Religion, and all forms of God-seeking endeavour, ought to enhance the quality of life, ought to promote peaceful coexistence amongst all human beings as well as all of creation. What was the point in arrogantly and blindly erecting discriminatory and separative structures that only sharpen the destructive points of difference and hostility? In the vineyard of God, in that creative labour towards perfection, only he who worked toward harmony of all participated in that labour divine. All else that tended to sunder the one house must be in misalignment and therefore unproductive. This was how the idea flashed into my mind that hot afternoon of the burning bush. It flashed into my mind with unprecedented lucidity; lucidity not of words, not of images, but an illumination surging forth from the deep depths of my knowing – whatever this means to you – throwing light into the dark alleys of my consciousness. So it was on that afternoon of the burning ground, in the burning bush.

Have you ever been there?

There and then I started developing a deep feeling of respect for my grandmother's religion, what the church and written history labelled paganism, heathenism and idol worship. For it seemed to me that that quality, that attribute which the church, and any religion for that matter, ought to cultivate in the arable minds of its followers (but for which the church seemed to have failed woefully) was what was most cardinal in my grandmother's religion:

Tolerance.

This was the quality lacking in the Christian church, especially tolerance not just of different denominations within Christianity but also of non-Christians. Tolerance, that ability to see and understand the need for the many different fingers of the one God, the many different approaches to our one Father, this seemed to be the most fundamental guiding philosophy of my grandmother's religion.

There and then many many more things stood clear in the crucible of my consciousness that hot afternoon of burning. And the fire burned and did not fail to consume me, and when I raised my head from its ashes I realised that I had reasoned myself into the vacuum of a meaningless and purposeless universe. But, wait a moment, was that entirely the case? Was goodness and badness, that is, was morality only to be found and practiced within the church? What about my grandmother's religion? My minstrel, ever calm and sure and smiling in all his ways, what about him? And the many more who obeyed the laws of their hearts?

Or:

Was there anything still left for me in the church, in that our church or any other church? Could I be in possession of these questions and doubt and still continue to worship in the church, could I?

Or:

Should I have accept things as they were without asking any questions and even without reflecting on them at all? Just believe and accept, without any logic, without any sense, and all would be well. Just have faith and believe. Because the ways of God and the ways of man differed so much that there was nothing for man to comprehend in God's way. So that it was simply to accept the authority of the holy book or the priest, just accept without understanding, without any questions. So, should I then continue with the church in the hope that some day I would better qualify to understand the ways of God? Or should I reject it all and then embark on a personal search for truth?

There were a million and two things on my mind, much of it being questions that I had no sure answers to. But as I walked away from the church premises that hot afternoon, I knew that I was forever walking away from that church, that I would never enter it again, nor any other like it, because I wanted to worship God. The God of that church, as of much that I read in the Christian bible, was not acceptable to me, and if I must live with any God then I had to look for Him elsewhere. Not in such church. Never again. Never.

CHAPTER 8 | THE BURNING BUSH

THE FIRE FESTIVAL

CHAPTER 9:

STUNTED FIRES

I knelt in my room that morning thinking of what to say and how to say it. True, it was water that I immediately needed, and I only had to pray to God for it. But, to the average Christian, I had become godless ever since I left the church and refused to worship in any other orthodox way. This was true in a way because I was not in doubt that I did not know what this God was or meant. What then was I to say to such a vague existence?

But, this morning, my life was at that point where either I grabbed whatever support nearby and then try leaping into freedom and more life, or I simply went down the drain and get flushed off the face of history. Because in the fever of all questing, one grabbed either more life or more death. And I had gone too far down the hollow darkness of the path of death that I was ready, and at all cost, to cling on to whatever smelled of life. So I knelt there, trying hard to say something.

"Oh God," I said, "if it is your will let us have water".

But this sounded too passive and even Christian. Besides, it did not carry a note of the urgency and desperation of Golgotha. So I tried again to reach God or whatever power could help.

"Father, no, God, please help us send down rain. You can see how badly we need it".

This too was not satisfactory, and did not even sound like a prayer. It was just like asking a mate for something – no reverence and awe in the tone. So I remained there, trying hard to think out a suitable paper. But no other form of prayer seemed to come to mind – in fact different thoughts other than that of prayer took over my mind. When I realised this, I became very angry with myself. In frustration I got up, took my gallon, managed to get a drop of water from it, and declared:

"Either receive me in thine hands today, oh Lord, or give me water."

Then, with the water, I made a mark of the cross on my forehead.

"This is my extreme unction," I told myself. And I was pleased with it. I was.

Nobody was out yet, and it appeared to me like I was the most godless of all. The raindrops had stopped falling, but the sky was still dark, with lightning flashing and thunder ravaging the silence of the morning, while the thundering accusations of evil and failure threatened to tear me apart and erupt unto the face of the earth and poison existence with my harvest of pus and rot.

But still I stood out there, in spite of the thunder; I stood out there waiting for my neighbours to come out. And I started imaging what would be going on in their different rooms. There was no doubt that Hilary would soon come out. In fact only he and his God knew what he went into that room to do, he who hardly ever wanted to hear anything about God and church and prayer, Hilary of the scathing and poisonous tongue. What was he still doing in that room now? I had no inkling of that truth.

Ruth it was who possessed the truth, the way and the life, and the burden of this possession required long hours with God in prayer and speaking in tongues. This burden also meant that she would be the last to come out. And I could see her praying feverishly for rain and husband and money and every need that was eating at her heart. How like all of us! An interminable shopping list to God who had it all in His hands and was simply waiting for our feverish appeal. Dike – oh, that unpredictable believer in the self. Must love Nietzsche's superman. Because – but a door creaked and swung open, and out came Hilary.

"Already out, eh?" he asked.

"My brother, I did not find it easy communicating with God. I just knelt in my room thinking instead of praying."

"You guys have time to waste in what you call prayer," he said.

"But what else can one do, things being this bad."

"Look, man, you've got to understand that this is the age of science and technology, not of neo-medievalism. So we don't need this God stuff anymore."

"So science and God are two contraries that have no meeting ground?"

"I don't give a shit whether God exists or not. All I know is that this is the age of science and not of any blind belief in the unprovable. We've got it all, I mean everything it takes to turn this earth into a heaven. Is it the brain, the resources? Look at this issue of water, for instance, is it not shameful beyond imagining that we should be searching for water when much of the earth's surface is nothing but water? What have we made of that? Tell me, what have we made of that abundance? Thirsty and starving in the midst of so much! And you say we should pray, as if prayer would dig boreholes from heaven straight into our mouths. Again look at the public taps. Can you remember the last time you got water from that source? And you want to pray! You disgust me, man, you do," and ended by spitting out with considerable force, as if to empty himself of that disgust, he a snake throwing me, the toad, out as I was coated with the poison of prayer.

In a way I knew that he was right; for some of these ideas had long disturbed my mind and fired much of my fruitless endeavours. And I also knew how relatively easy it was to so rake up arguments that implied standards which in our daily lives we could not live up to. True, in my quiet moments I had nursed such beautiful and seemingly straightforward ideas, but I had also discovered that it was a different story in the boiling pot of daily life. I had discovered that between thought or idea and acting out such ideas, between our wishes and dreams of life and the reality, between them was a very famished chasm that often crushed and swallowed such dreams, leaving just the carcass for the sustenance of the dreamer. And dreams, too, can be carcasses; the very stuff of that life on the periphery, on the sidelines of burning thick sorrow from where alone is found the lush green of that electric joy. For which still I seek. The burning sands of the desert of my life driving me into the belief in the God of the church; and the separatist fire of that church burnt the dream to ashes. And then it became the belief in the infinite potentials of man, the unfixated possibilities of man the measure of all things. All to the same end.

"But what is it in science that it becomes fretful and nervous at the mention of God?" I asked.

He remained silent, looking somewhat confused. At last he opened up:

"But what the hell, man, what's the use? Can we not face the challenges of living without complicating it all with this God business?"

"What's Hilary arguing over this morning?" Dike asked as he came out with two buckets.

"O, it's Eno. He says that man cannot do without his God in today's world."

"So what's wrong with that?" Dike still.

Hilary responded, open-mouthed. "You mean you, too, believe in that rubbish?"

"We have to grant that there is a lot behind the clouds that we cannot truly and fully place our fingers on yet; although this does not say that there is or isn't a God, which, indeed, is not the matter. The problem of the times is that we lack the spirit of courage to walk through the wilderness of life with our eyes open. Many surrender that will to life and power to the opium of mass culture and so float on and through the river of life. Others drown it in the delirium of alcohol and drugs in the hope to escape the banality of their lives which they rightly know to hold much promise, could they face with courage their own devil. And many more are not even living yet, as they are wholly under the dominance of their animal instincts and know little or nothing of courage which is what makes us human. Courage, that is what we lack as well as all we need. That is what sees every hero through every obstacle, and it is the spirit we need."

"Exactly, brother," shouted Hilary. "That's all I've been saying since. We don't need this God talk before we can move forward."

"But we are supposed to be talking about water and not rant over God or no God," I cut in, feeling bored with what seemed a fruitless abstraction in the midst of real need.

"It doesn't make a difference, man. We are still hoping that it will rain. Our argument can't stop the rain if at all it is going to fall." This was from Hilary.

"But we could discuss something rather more immediate," I responded, "like this problem of water, I mean, we could think of what possible ways to surmount the problem or help ourselves."

"Haven't you prayed? Let us rather eat and drink and be merry because your prayer will reach God in Heaven and all problems thereby will be solved. We don't need to worry, do we?" Hilary's caustic tongue fired.

"Try and understand me," I said, almost pleading. But he would not even let me finish.

"Forget it, man," he said, "you disgust me, going in to pray. You really disgust me these days."

"But what is wrong in praying, particularly in a situation as desperate as this?"

"Nothing, man, nothing," He was getting really worked up now. "Can't you see it's too infantile? Just like a child begging the father for some money for chocolate. I can't stand how it reduces man, and I can't endure those who smell of prayer, as you so strongly do now."

Dike came in here: "We should not take the argument too far. That won't help in any way."

"But that's all I've been trying to say since," I added, a bit relieved that Dike was somehow helping me out by pulling the argument out of that precipitous path.

Ruth came out of her house making a sign of the cross.

Hilary turned away, frowning like someone swallowing chloroquine tablets.

It was thundering and the sky was still dark, but the droplets of rain had stopped. Standing there and scanning the sky, my heart pouring forth appeal to a God I knew I was not sure of, I could not tell which way the rain would go. But somehow, I was inclined to believing that that particular day would make a difference – one-way or the other. Thinking of all the dirty things in my room awakened that nausea. How could I continue living like that? One way or another that day was going to make a difference, one way or another.

"I strongly believe that it will rain this morning," Ruth said.

"Oh, sure, you can see that it will soon start. After all, you have prayed to God, and He must answer you." This was from Hilary, and there was no concealing his bitterness in those words. Somehow Dike was on cue as he said:

"It's clear Hilary is gearing up for a fight this morning."

"I'm not gearing up for any fight, man, I'm not." He seemed a little sober now, and he added. "It's just that one is sick of everything, eking it out down low in the mud when one ought to be making it big."

"So what's stopping you?" I asked.

"You can ask that again and again."

Ruth came in: "Your problem is that you don't have faith, you don't have faith in God. And that will lead you nowhere but to despair. Don't you know that with faith you can achieve what seems impossible? With faith, Christ says, you can move mountains, and even do greater things than he did while on earth. All you need is faith. That is the word of God, and there is no reason not to believe it. Just have faith."

"And I will move mountains as you have been moving?" Hilary sneered.

"But, Ruth," I put in, "how does this faith of a thing come into an issue like our present problem?"

She must have blessed me in her heart for the lead I provided her for another short sermon.

"You see, the problem we are facing is a result of our sins. We have sinned and, as the Bible tells us, come short of the glory of God. There is no fear of God anymore in the hearts of people because sin has taken over the world. These days, people just behave the way it pleases them, forgetting that the world belongs to nobody but God alone. This is a faithless and godless generation, and God is punishing us for our sins. We have abandoned God, and He too has turned His back on us as He did to the Israelites whenever they abandoned him. Sin has overtaken the world, and we are suffering because of that."

"But is it possible that Ruth is without faith too?" Dike asked.

"Certainly not! I have faith in my God, and I have accepted Christ as my Lord and personal saviour, and I have surrendered my life to the blood of the Lamb."

"So with all your faith and surrender, why are you being punished along with the faithless and godless?" Hilary could not have allowed anybody to take this golden opportunity for a swipe.

"If it is the will of God I will have water and all that I need."

"Damn Him and His will. If it is the will of man, man will have water," Hilary still.

"May God have mercy on your soul," Ruth prayed for that faithless and godless man who was now at the brink of Hell fire.

"And send down rain," Hilary concluded, laughing. "You see, I suppose that our problem is a very simple one. And it as well needs a simple solution. It's been a long time since God died. But his carcass is still lying unburied, decomposing and smelling and polluting the air that we breathe. All we need is to dig a very deep grave and bury this carcass."

"And there will be rain thereafter?" Dike asked.

"Forget him," Ruth said, her face now swollen with anger and disgust. "Satan has taken over his soul."

"But come o," I said, "what is wrong with everybody? We have a serious problem we could lend some attention, and all we do is chatter and argue over things that help not in any way. Can't we do better than that, I mean, shouldn't we think of how we could tackle this water problem today? Or is anybody hoping on ending up with that mud water again?"

"But we are waiting for the will of God to be made manifest. We have prayed and shouldn't lose hope so quickly. God works wonders and in mysterious ways too," Ruth once again sermonized.

"We have waited for too long for His wonders, sister. Now it's man's turn to work his own wonders."

"So what do we do?"

"He is asking me what to do," turning and facing the sky. "Has his courage and heroic spirit but does not know what to do with it. And she too will ask me to kneel and pray from morning till night that manna may fall from her unknown god. And Eno too will support her. Hm! What a pack of unliberated beings I have around me."

"You the liberated successor of a dead god, what have you to show for your liberty, what have you done with it?" Dike seemed to be losing his usual patience.

"Oh, just wait and you'll soon see the supreme moment of —"

But that very moment was supremely promise-full and dangerous, that very moment. Because it was the detonation of a bomb, a thunder clap really, which slammed shut the frivolous lips of Hilary, the sense of near-extinction rippling over in the immediate aftermath of that explosion and transfixing us all. No one could speak. No one moved. And then the droplets did not drop, but rather the heavens opened in silvery torrents, striking hard against the skin.

No one moved. No one spoke.

Because if the doors of Heaven were suddenly thrown open, human beings would still turn their backs to those open gates and cling to their petty sorrows and sufferings. Because the possibility of so suddenly walking into the immaculate presence of God would be too incomprehensible that husbands would prefer to still cling to the stinging tongues of their wives, while the wives would rather moan under the tyranny of their men. Because even death itself is not a matter of a split moment; ever, in spite of all seeming, it is a gradual process of the dismantling of the burden of the flesh. Ever.

And still no one moved. Nobody spoke.

And I looked each on the face, the first movement so far. I looked, from Ruth to Hilary, to Dike who that moment seemed to break the trance to beam forth a smile once our eyes met, and my heart somehow became aglow with some life. Because something seemed to say: the water of life abundant. And then I knew that it was real, and that I had to put my containers under the eaves to collect water. And that moment, too, before I could move, another deafening thunder rumbled. And the slanting torrents ceased with it. Suddenly.

Still no one moved. Nobody spoke.

And I inhaled deeply, drawing in cupfuls of what seemed a fresh life, I drew it in and waited for its fullness to manifest. It did manifest, indeed. Only as a violent gale which threatened to blow us off the face of the earth. But we still stood there, without speech, but with evident resolve to see the end of it all. And that end was not far, because in no time a legion of devils unsealed the primordial sack of cosmic gale, and its whirlwind tore through our clothes, swept through the sky and drove the clouds away to distant lands.

Before our very eyes!

A mocking sun started peering through the remains of that cloud after a short while, and our last seeds of hope dried up in the heat of that mockery.

If men were gods. Or gods men.

Left with no other choice in the face of the unnerving silence of that moment, I murmured:

"What else can one do? What can we do now?"

Ruth it was who left immediately, sniffing as she walked away. And when she got to her door and about to enter, she burst into a bout of wailing. And as she entered, she banged the door so hard that the whole episode flashed and echoed down my consciousness.

Hilary and Dike followed, each to his room and banging his door – but theirs neither banged nor echoed in my consciousness.

I began walking back to my room. But as I reached the door and tried to open it, I could hear voices beginning to mock and accuse once again. I waited a while and listened hard through the door, but it was not clear whether the voices came from the room or elsewhere. I could still hear a loud guttural laugh. And I knew too that I would have to write my epitaph if I had to enter that room that moment. Away I walked, gallon in hand.

THE FIRE FESTIVAL

Chapter 10:

Burning Hollows

Agbe Street was its usual. A thick cloud of stench hung around everything, and everywhere was a seemingly impenetrable bustle and beehive of life. Just by, in one of those stalls along the street, a woman I knew well was emptying her bowel into a paint bucket as she was breastfeeding her baby and answering a customer who had asked for the price of some item. I nodded greetings at her, and she spat back.

I sauntered on though, registering the all-too-familiar images of that street, its colours and tone. Along in one of the stalls a woman (an infant straddled to her back) and a man were evidently exchanging currents of bodily energy as they timidly put up a make-believe show of struggling for a bottle of drink; and they appeared equally matched in their effort, though not in their look, so that the bout would last and last. And it did last while I passed by.

I sauntered on, but a sharp cry of distress pierced my heart, and when I turned I saw a man, rosary hanging down his left hand, who was just robbing a child of his biscuits. I looked about me, but nobody seemed to notice the boy's existence. Yet, hordes of people were moving to and fro. And nobody seemed to notice. Then I looked at the policeman at a nearby intersection, and he quickly chested out and saluted.

Somehow I held myself, and then the boy's cry started settling into a lull in my heart, finally rippling down. Because I was getting high on the blazing fire of a murky life. The sacrilege of the years of hopeful expectancy. The futility of these years of struggle to mould the vision out of my life, mould my life into that vision. To be or not to be is not really the question now. The baobab defies seasons of heat and dust but brings no fruit at the end. The stream twists through its winding paths hoping to but never arrives. And the fruit, always in sight of the tantalized cravings of humanity. And no more. Just the fruit always in sight and hardly ever grasped, clutched. Yet, once he pondered, as I have been doomed to ponder too, once he thought and said; everything down that earth is a wet monotony of waste; no life nor any living inspiration, and not even death as such; all is still a basket of seeds waiting for the hands of the life-multiplier. He thought it would be better with forests, valleys, land and life. In spite of all his equipment: a leaf packet of loose earth, a white hen, a pigeon and the key to the narrow razor-edged path, is it still not a marshy waste? Is this what life should be like? Have we, hollow men as we are, yet found the heart to turn this waste land into that garden of life and joy? Have we, hollow men as we are? Ah, happy is he that craves no height, never crestfallen on that treacherous and slippery path, never spilling his semen into the dry-pot of rot.

But you are the salt of the earth, you are.

Which is the tragedy of it all, of seeking after the mountain-top. Ah, happy is he that craves no height. For he who never strives and struggles towards that mountain-top never ever crashes down along its winding path. But, in truth, which way of the two is better? To sit still in the depths of your valley and seek not nor crave any height, or to walk through the burning fire of the path and lose yourself and perhaps gain something? Or nothing? Which is better?

Only he who loses himself will find it, only he.

And the boy cried out the more, the robber still in sight and now devouring the biscuits. I looked about me again, and as my eyes met with the policemen's, he gave another sharp salute, chesting out as well. And the criss-cross of movements seemed to intensify.

"O race of Polyphemous! Whence thine art of smith-craft?" I shouted.

After that, the boy's cry finally rippled down and fell dead on the mud-water of my conscience, and I sauntered on, recognizing and acknowledging it all, that street, its face.

For the face of that street was all too familiar and yet all too strange and puzzling that I truly have never stopped wondering. The face of that street, that city, had confronted me as soon as I arrived the city. And much as I tried, I could not articulate, never really define what it was that so suddenly and from nowhere stood before me, leaving me with neither power nor words. Like a lion suddenly sprang into my presence. It was years later, while studying at the University, that I began to realize what it was that puzzled me. It was while there one afternoon of heated anguish that I saw the beast, that same beast from which I ran and thought I had finally escaped from in the village. It was the same beast, only it was more beautifully clothed this time around, and it had many charming faces. I saw it running through the city and eating up, in varying degrees, the heart of every face I saw.

I saw it and the sight struck me dumb.

After a fresh attempt at the certificate examinations, I passed five out of the eight subjects I enrolled for. With this I secured my freedom from life in that village and a career in the church, and I was as well equipped for the how-much-is-your-worth world of employment and the glitter and frills of city life. So, I left the village for the city, memories of that loving old woman, the church-declared witch, fanning the fringes of my consciousness. Again it was through the old woman that I found shelter in the city, for a distant cousin of hers offered to accommodate me until I found a place of my own.

I left that village for the city not at all with any stiff upper lip but with an over-inflated balloon of hope. Because the thought of the city held this indescribable charm, it held this magic that I could not wholly define to myself. I knew that I wanted, in spite of all, I wanted to live it big and full, liberating myself from the claims of poverty and evil and irrelevance and hold in my sure hands the full-cream fullness of life.

Because finally rejecting the church as a way unto that life, or really a way of escape from it, was a very difficult matter for me. For, amongst many things, it meant that either I sank back to that consuming feeling of evil and meaninglessness that my life had been before I joined the church, or I found some other way to press forward and live a meaningful and fulfilled life – because there ever was, always was, this vision of how full and rich my life could be, a vision that was at the background of all my struggle. That other way I found in the city. But I could not tell exactly how I would attain this. All I was sure of was that the city now held the magic wand, the open sesame. I left the village for the city with this vision more or less standing out of my eyes, my certificate and testimonial placed on my forehead and the bag of my evil past trotting along some distance behind. And for some moments I thought this bag was now left behind in the village as

I moved to the city, the island of golden waters in which all thirst was quenched.

But as soon as I arrived, the city, in all its aspects, flung itself at me, saying: "I am available, all night."

I saw it all: the wonder and ingenuity in the awe-inspiring structures of modern architecture; the allure of the tarred roads and flowered side-walks and parks which showed me how humans could turn nature into the good and beautiful; the ever-arriving state-of-the-arts cars and their puffed-up-owners who worked for blue-chip companies or owned their own businesses; the powerful street-lights that transformed night into day, fear into confidence; and above all else the slime and stench which seemed to hang on to everything. In all these were so much attraction and so much repulsion, so much that made me feel like a human being and so much that made me feel like the dirtiest pig ever forced out of a mother's womb.

I am available, all night.

Again I looked and what did I see? The beggars, the unemployed, the pickpockets and layabouts, the scavengers, the homeless, the squalid buildings of the slums and the garbage that littered everywhere, the gutters over-flowing with human waste into people's houses, and above all else the courage and determination that these things emitted. And in these too were so much attraction and so much repulsion. But in all, I could not yet find that glittering charm, I could not find my place.

Again it said to me: I am available, all night.

And again I took every aspect of that city and, one by one, turned each up and down, this side and that like one turning and scanning a herbal leaf. Still I did not see myself, did not see that vision. Not that I had lost it. Rather, nothing in what I saw came close to that vision. Still I persisted, ransacking and dissecting and tearing into pieces every aspect that I saw. And still I did not see myself. And in that confused and frustrated state of disgust at my nothingness I ran to the woman I was living with and asked:

Who am I ?

But then the voice always was there and always it said the same thing:

I am available, all night.

Then I tried to avoid the streets by hiding in the room. But this seemed to worsen it, for whether I was sleeping or not, whether I was eating or not, whether I was silent or not, the one question remained:

Who am I?

I awoke one morning nearly bursting with a deluge of questions. And once again I rushed into the street and took every aspect of it and, one by one, turned each up and down, this side and that like one turning and scanning a herbal leaf. But I saw nothing that I whole-heartedly wanted, nor anything that stirred the heart even a little. But I persisted, ransacking and dissecting and tearing into pieces every aspect that I saw. Still I saw nothing that thrilled my heart. And in that confused and frustrated state of disgust at my nothingness I ran to the woman I was living with and asked.

What am I?

Then I tried to avoid the streets and the room by retreating to the graveyard where I thought I would find some solace in silence. But that seemed to worsen it, for whether I was sleeping or not, the silence of the graveyard of my mind always popped up the one question:

What am I?

I rushed out of that graveyard, hitting the streets in a fierce rage like a bull, and again took every aspect of the street one by one, turned each up and down, this side and that like one turning and scanning a herbal leaf. But in all I saw nothing that stirred my heart. And I persisted, ransacking and dissecting and tearing into pieces every aspect that I saw. Still I saw nothing that thrilled my heart. And in that confused and frustrated state of disgust at my nothingness, I ran to the woman I was living with and asked.

What do I want?

Because in all that the face of that street, the face of that city, in all its beauty and ugliness, in all its happiness and sorrow, all the cursed and the blessed, I could not find who I was, could not find what I was, what I wanted to be. The slime was disturbingly ever present, ever flowing out of all the aspects. This saddened me much that I could not stop wondering if I would ever be free from the stain of evil. Because I was now beginning to see that that baggage of evil still followed me to the city, the only place that had the promise of the way to life fully lived. There was nothing and nowhere beyond the city. And within, alive and in power and control, were those things from which I sought escape.

Or was there something wrong with me now? Was my way of seeing peculiar? Were these images in my mind and just in my mind alone, glued to the root of my consciousness, or were they truly without and could be seen just as much by some other person?

What was the matter with me?

Because I failed to find a place in the city, failed to find the answers to all the puzzles presented by life, because l failed to pin down what I truly wanted of life, I headed to the village to see my grandmother whom I missed seriously. But my grandmother was no more; death having come with dispatch, with my uncle rising to the occasion by dumping her in a shallow grave not long after she died. The villagers lamented to me that they had no chance whatsoever to pay their last respects to my grandmother, and that they were not even sure of how she died – suggesting that my uncle might have had a hand in her death.

I went to her grave and knelt beside it. I had not as yet been able to define to myself what my state of mind was. Of course, it was not that I was happy. At the same time what settled on my mind was not exactly sadness. I just wanted to pay my last respects and leave the village – I think I wanted to do that quickly and then leave the village before the reality of her death would descend on me. But kneeling beside her grave and perceiving the pungent odour of her decaying body, that reality of death, her death, enveloped me and I was filled with a sense of utter loss and loneliness. It was then I realized that my heart was heavy, indeed heavy beyond measure, and its ocean flooded my whole being but could not stream down from my eyes, that pressure threatening to tear me apart. I did not shiver. Nor did I quake. My outer expression was calm while within the ocean tried hard to tear down those walls.

It was when somebody touched me that I realized that my eyes were closed and that that ocean had even soaked my shirt. And I knew too that my grandmother had felt my agony and had now come that I might see her for the last time. There truly was no question of fear. I fully welcomed this rare happening.

Then I opened my eyes only to find that it was Peace, my Uncle's daughter. The disappointment that this was not my grandmother – and that it was even my Uncle's daughter – aroused a depth of animosity I did not think was in me. Because what I saw in her face was the face of my uncle as he lifted his mighty hand to strike me. I had lifted up my hand to strike when the girl fled, and my eyes opened to reality.

After this my feeling of loneliness increased, and a thicker cloud of sorrow enveloped me. In the deep of this dark cloud was all my life, and I realized once again that I was only a tiny ant, neither dead nor alive, but swept by the ever fluctuating tides of the ocean of life. In this ocean I ceaselessly sought and found naught to grip; and when I looked up and down, when I searched here and there, I found neither purpose nor end to the fever of existence. Because the Atlantic Ocean separated my life from that vision, a vision now so dim.

I might have been at that graveside for hours, days or even weeks – I surely cannot say because time ceased to exist for me. I was conscious only of the fact that I was in the middle of a desert, with a vast infinite nothing all about me while a desperate desire to hold on to something consumed me within. I was conscious only of that, and nothing more. The whole village was a silent and dark graveyard when I walked into the house.

My sadness and shedding of tears did not relieve me – as some say that shedding of tears does. And I lost the desire to quickly leave the village for the city. So I roamed the neighbourhood, the village, in search of someone to talk to, someone against whose vision (if he had any) I would place mine and then determine whether or not I was still a normal member of our world. I search the village for one in whose grey hairs might be found the wisdom-key to life. Because it seemed to be the curse on me that I always sought something more than what was presented to me, I always sought something which I knew deep in my guts but could not quite see anywhere. And I knew it within me, I knew it with all certainty. Somebody there must be who also knew. Such a person I sought.

But the village was bare of any willingness to partake in anything without immediate material profit, especially when it had to do with one who had just come from the city. I was born in that village. In it I grew up, and I knew that it had its own tales too. But now I saw those tales anew. And I saw that the beast not only trailed me, but that it also walked about the village in broad daylight. That abundant sense of joy that I expected everyone to share in when a member of the community succeeded in a venture was not there. Innumerable bits and pieces of the poison of gossip and envy were dropped on every doorstep and footpath. And the people did not truly care how wealth was acquired. It was enough that "our" child had made it. And honorary titles would follow. Of course, the person became "our" child only if and when he made it. Otherwise, the father would turn to the mother and ask: Have you heard from your child? And crude customs would always spew up their heads to point to the woman's place at the backyard hut, the refuse dump of irrelevance and insignificance, the dregs of written and proclaimed history, if at all, and in very tiny letters. Mule of the world, as she has been called. And she took it like that. So that the heavens would not crash. And what if they did, what if the heavens were to crash that we might see what lies behind the clouds and place it alongside our own constructed reality? What if?

The village, I knew, had its own tales, but now I saw them anew. Then I fled to the city after seven days of contemplating those tales. But I took away and along with me a certain old man's words of advice:

"The Father-creator uncreates to create, destroys to build. A place for each always is there, but each must tame, not destroy, the lions and tigers guarding the path. Seek out your place."

I returned to the city to seek out my place, and I was determined to confront the face of that city with all its colours and all its slime. Because the old man's words affirmed that long-held idea of mine that everything had its own place within the cosmic heart, I returned to that city determined to properly define who I was and identify what I wanted. Because one can know one's place if only one knows oneself. I returned to that city because when life closes its doors, there can be nothing else but death. And I wanted to claim my share of life – even if it cost me that life. I had become that desperate and in love with life; although that life was not what I had just once again left behind in the village, nor what I had seen in the city.

Before the journey to the village, all I had seen in a blinding snow-white vision and in a moment of unprecedented mental clarity and intensity was a mighty structure of life crumble from the very summit of a high mountain through a heart of darkness into the consuming stench of a pit latrine. And the setting sun had stood high and still. But now it seemed that a fragment of life emerged from this debris and took position atop a mountain of garbage. The beast, waving it before me, declared:

"You can have this. Only at the cost of your life."

I knew not what there was or would be beyond life – I mean the safe cover of the church's teaching no longer meant anything. At the same time I knew or believed that death was better than and preferable to that life without purpose and vision, that life as flotsam and jetsam on the sea of life. Better death than that life.

In search of that life, that vision, I had to start from some-where, had to find my place in that city. I started off then as a security guard.

THE FIRE FESTIVAL

CHAPTER 11:

DESERT FLARES

It was the house of the President of Aids Network, a non-governmental organization said to aid those in various kinds of need. Since it was work in service of those in need and not quite employment for profit (so I was told), I had to work for twelve hours each day and seven days a week, resuming at six in the morning and closing at six in the evening when I handed over to another guard. We had a non-negotiable salary that did not take into account transportation, housing and medical allowances. And the luxury of an annual leave would have done us much harm that we had to be spared and shielded. Although I was employed as a guard, I discovered that my duties had no limit. I was used in emptying of the refuse bin into a nearby canal, cutting of grass, washing of clothes, running of errands and all that. Of course all at no extra cost to my employer. We were rendering service.

As I spent the day doing all kinds of work, I usually returned to the house with a mind eager to study but with a body too tired and worn out to be able to prepare well for the university entrance examination that I registered for. And the date for the examination was not far anymore. Therefore I started reading during the day in my security post. It was not that there was any considerable stretch of time during which I was not called upon to perform some task or other; but I tried very hard to use the few minutes during which I was not engaged to study. And I had read for about ten minutes one day when my boss unexpectedly came home for break and saw me reading under the mango tree. He looked at me somewhat curiously and asked.

"What are you doing with those books?'

I was elated somehow because I knew he would be glad to know that I was attempting to improve myself.

"I'm reading them, sir," I replied.

"For what purpose?"

"Sir, it's for the university entrance exam. I registered for it."

His countenance immediately changed and his face dropped. Then he looked at me from head to toe, toe to head and then turned to confirm that his driver was part of it all. Of course he was very much a part of it, and his gaze was nothing but conde-scension. But I was shocked by what my boss said next.

"What makes you think that such a place is meant for people like you?'

I knew not what to say as I became utterly confused. So in that confusion I looked from my boss to his driver who did not only look but now added:

"Sir, he's beginning to get some ideas into his head, and before you know it he will start asking for a pay increase. It's better you sack him now before it gets out of hand."

And my confusion rose, some cold sweat immediately running down my body. I struggled to say something, anything no matter how stupid, but I could only mumble to myself. My boss did not give me much chance anyway as he walked into the house, the driver tailing him with a suitcase. When he came out forty-five minutes later, he said to me:

"Pack your garbage and get out of here. Come back at the end of the month for your salary. And never let me set my eyes on you again."

The driver was all smiles. He chuckled and added:

"He wants to be President like you, sir."

As I walked the two-kilometre distance back to my house, I felt like a fish thrown out of the deep sea into a wild maze of frenzied street life. Because ever since I took that job, I spent all my daylight hours at my security post, going to work before daylight and returning after nightfall. So that I was like a bat to the daily rhythm of the life of that city. Now faced with the endless criss-cross of movements under the blazing heat of the afternoon sun, I was like a baby prematurely thrown into a very dangerous world. An air of forced hostility and ruthless determination hung around every face I saw, and it appeared as if in the fever of the life in that street, tongues drooled, salivating from the great hunger and thirst for the tempering juice of life. From the cacophonous bells of hawkers peddling and thrusting their wares at passers-by, and the endless blare of horns from vehicles wounding their way through the thick bustle of that life, the street emerged large in my consciousness a demented saxophonist blowing directly into the eardrum of an infant. Because during the long months that I walked that street in the shade of twilight, I never fully came face-to-face with that street in this manner. Always it was its beginning-to-awake and retiring looks that I saw. Never its noontide bustle and boiling over as I saw it that day. And it really stood large in my consciousness, with every movement baring and almost thrusting a dagger at me. That noontide bustle bared its dagger at me, but it was my employer who thrust it into my heart, and it hurt badly even as I wobbled along that street.

I spent the rest of that week hiding in my room, occasionally looking out through the window during the day and coming out only at night. While I was not sure yet of how to handle the curious gaze and questions of neighbours, I was also trying to adjust to the day-time life of that house. But I was somehow spared all that agony by the approaching university entrance examinations. I buried myself in intensive study for three weeks following. And between the anxiety to pass the examination and the pleasure of reading I forgot all but the great need to press forward in life, to study more and more and keep improving myself. Because the more I read, the more I realized that there was much I did not know, and I was thereby fired to more and more intensive study. Nothing has yet given me that joy of intensive study. Nothing.

Anyhow, it was with such sorrow and joy that I sat for the examination.

But joy cannot endure for too long in an empty stomach. So that I had no choice but to seek some means of survival, some employment to keep me going and even possibly allow me save if only a little to start off with at the university. Because I did not know yet how I was going to pay my fees through the university. I had only seen that, if ever I was to approximate my vision of life, I had no other choice than to have a university education. I now saw that to be the only possible channel, but I did not see yet how I was going to provide the expense except that I could always do some vacation jobs to supplement whatever other aid that came to me. I was not sure of any immediate source of aid, but I was ready to approach all the rich people in the world for help. Somehow bull-headedly I believed there was such a kind person to help. I believed it. Do you?

Life, indeed, is an endless maze.

CHAPTER 11 | DESERT FLARES

A job I got, and it was as a factory staff – working at the domestic front did make me a piece of someone's nose-rag, and I was not willing to do it again. The new place was named National Cosmetics Company, and its work was the production and packaging of cosmetics. After going through a series of physical fitness tests – as if I was joining any of the military forces – I, along with fifteen others, was posted to the Compounding Section. There, apart from the Compounding Manager and the Supervisor, every other person was a casual staff.

My task was to feed with various chemicals the machine that turned them into a finished product. The supervisor, who was one-eyed, put me through an induction course that lasted two-weeks, and by the third week I was already in control, determining which chemical and in what quantity should be fed the machine. Of course it was all as I had been taught by the supervisor. And he was immensely pleased with me on account of the way I quickly mastered the whole process. Many a time he would come to me and, squinting his only eye, would ask:

"How is it going, boy?"

"Smooth," I would say

"As usual."

"Sure, as usual."

"I trust you, my boy. Keep it up. You know how much this society depends on us."

"Sure I do," still I would say, sure of what he would say next; because he never ever failed to follow the sequence.

"Every important person in the society uses our products."

"So I hear."

"It is the First Lady's choice."

"So you've told me."

"And the wives of the Governors of the States too."

"So you say."

"That's why you must keep the great tradition going."

"I'll do my best."

"You mustn't change anything."

"That's tradition."

But the curse of always taking some step away from the normal has always been mine. I was not satisfied with just feeding into the machine that which I had been taught to so do; I had to search all available libraries for materials on cosmetics production.

And then I started knowing things I was not supposed to know.

I knew, first, that our products could not stand any standard test because most of the things stated on our labels as making up each product were not used. This did not bother me much initially as I thought that I did not know enough yet to question any formula. But now I knew the worth of the chemicals we were omitting, and I could not contain my worry. So I asked the Supervisor why this was so.

"To give the best to our customers," he replied.

"But the worst is what we are giving them," I said.

"What do you mean?"

"The chemicals we are omitting are the best."

"You think so?"

"I know so. And I know too that these products without these chemicals can be harmful eventually."

"Someone has been talking to you."

"No, I've been reading, and I've found out much."

A long silence followed during which the Supervisor blinked several times. Then he said:

"But our customers know that those chemicals are not in the finished product."

"They know?" I asked in surprise.

"Of course they do, and that's how they like it."

"How come?"

"How come? May be you'll have to ask them. That's how they like it, and you are here asking me how come."

"I mean, how did you come by this crude formulation?""

Another silence followed. And again my attention was drawn to his eye as it blinked several times before maintaining a fixed gaze at me. The other eye had the lids glued together. So I could not divine the mysterious activity going on there.

"I see you will not last here, boy, "he said.

Of course I never hoped to, but to the Supervisor there was no other road-map through life than to become a permanent staff of that company. So I never mentioned to him, nor to anybody else in that company, my aspiration to further my education. That would have estranged me from them.

"Why not?" I responded.

"You ask too many questions about things that don't concern you."

"But I'm a staff here, and I ought to know why things are the way they are."

"I see you won't learn. Because you won't last here, I will tell you the story of how we got this formulation. But you must never tell it to anybody."

"Trust me," I returned.

Again some silence followed during which he worked his eye through several blinks. Then he settled to tell the story.

"Well, some years back I was so ill for some weeks that I couldn't come to work. This had never happened since I joined the company. And I had no assistant since I was always present and I preferred to do the work alone. So when I became ill and was in coma for one week, there was nobody to carry out my functions as none of the other casual staff knew the formulation for our products. I had been on the job for so long that nobody ever bothered to find out how I did it. Unfortunately, the Compounding Manager did not know too. And faced with the need to meet production target, he tried what you call our crude formulation, using only some base materials but omitting the most important chemicals and pouring in a lot of perfume. When I returned to work I noticed the error and alerted the Manager. But the First Lady and many other people had ordered for and been supplied with large quantities of that batch. So the company had to write to her to explain that there was some error in that batch, and that we needed to withdraw what was left in the market to effect correction. But the First Lady would not hear of it, having fallen in love with that formulation. And the public too. There were protests by members of the public against our attempts to return to the old formula. And when the government threatened to close us down, we had no choice. So we had to leave the whole thing like that. And our products sold like wildfire that we became the number one cosmetics company. We even got a national award, and the President himself changed our name to National Cosmetics Company, and made our products the official product for the country. Our M.D was given the highest national award."

"That's incredible," I said, almost shouting.

"But that's the truth as it is."

"It means that we are actually pouring perfume into some shit and selling to our people, and they are buying it." This was more of a reflection that I let out.

"We serve the people's need, so keep the tradition as long as you are here."

"So even the Compounding Manager did not know—"

He cut in: "Get back to work." Then he walked away.

And it does seem now that that grave which I started digging ever since I caught that indistinct but sure picture of life, that grave was somehow deepened by my experience at National Cosmetics Company. Because instead of doing my little bit, as everybody else, and moving out quietly when the admission into the university came, I rather started feeling some great discontent, and I would no longer just come each day to that company to do just my duty and duty alone. That discontent stirred some hunger in me, and I forsook the path of peace for that of trouble. That's what I seem to have always done with myself. That hunger stirred me into trouble.

For though our people were ready to, and indeed did, take rubbish, and the mass of workers in the company who were casual staff did swallow a lot of shit just to remain employed, I was not one anymore to accept whatever came my way. As at that time I had worked in the company for about six months as a casual staff (the prolonged strike by the Staff Union of Universities putting on hold admission into the universities), and there was a great many who had put in years as casual staff in that company. The Supervisor had worked as a casual staff for about ten years before he was given a permanent appointment. And that was after he had lost one eye in an accident; so that he bought his position with his eye.

The hunger for that intangible something that I could not completely define stirred within me the more as I looked at the wretched faces of the mill of casual workers in that company, many of whom were ready to equal, if not better, the Supervisor's record. Whereas labour laws did stipulate on paper that anybody who worked for as long as four months as a casual staff automatically became a permanent staff. From a habit of reading virtually everything that came my way I discovered the existence of this law, and I knew that some whispers about it were now circulating. So that there was some ground somehow prepared for cultivation.

It was not that I had any clear idea of what to do or what would result, whatever I would gain or lose. In any case I was expecting to be admitted into the university whenever the entrance examination results came out. So working there at National Cosmetics Company was not, and could not have been, permanent, But the faces I saw there daily, a great many of them seemed to have reached the end of the road and had no will anymore to accept or reject whatever came their way. They simply flowed hither and thither as the changing tastes of their bosses drove them. And they all had families to take care of, children to feed and possibly send to school. And they possibly had dreams, too. They possibly had.

Of course, I did not need many months to notice these things; I had hitherto only observed them and continued hibernating in the prison of my little concerns and needs. Now something was drawing me out of that prison. I was reading all kinds of books the way a thirsty cow gulps from a shallow stream. And Karl Marx had started stirring some roots in me when I picked up Wole Soyinka's *The Man Died*. When I finished reading that book, a rush of inspiration flooded me and some light beamed forth in my consciousness so that I saw things with a glaring lucidity as never before.

And things were never the same again. The way of gain or loss? I do not know.

When I walked into National Cosmetics Company after reading that book, I realized that my days there were over. I knew my days there were over. Because when I looked either side of me, when I looked front and back, I saw vacant faces, faces in whom the man was dead. And the sheer injustice of it all, the workers' servile acceptance of whatever came their way, it all stung my conscience, shattering that wall of indifference and inertia. As I saw it that morning, I had two choices: either I walked out of that company to seek some other place in which the upraised dust in my conscience would settle and I might find some peace to move on with my life, or I raised some dust of struggle, no matter how insignificant, in that company before being kicked out. For I knew it would easily end that way.

Again because of that indistinct vision, because of its hunger, I chose the second option. And the man in me was stirred the more to boldness and inspiration.

I started by cultivating the friendship of some of those faces in which there seemed to still be some little life to stir. And then I followed up by speaking to them individually and in groups of two and three about the need to have a union that would fight for and protect the interests of workers, bringing up the need for them to have their status in the company regularized and citing the law which so empowered them. I was surprised to see the outrage on the faces of some. Having so aroused their interest, I passed word round one day that we should have a meeting at Gents' Room – a long and secluded passage leading to the men's toilets.

Many people had shown some interest in the suggestion of having a union. So I expected a good turn-out. My only fear was that I was not sure how far word about the meeting had spread – and whether the management might have heard. But when I got to Gents' Room, I knew that the information had really spread well because everywhere was filled up. And though management seemed not to be aware – or else they would have tried to prevent the meeting –, they could become suspicious if such a gathering was noticed. I was a little worried about this possibility, but I took consolation in the fact that Gents' Room was not a place for any management staff to come near at all. And it was not so open a place anyway.

I walked in and just managed to close the door. Everybody was calmly seated, and virtually every space on the floor was occupied. And as soon as I walked in, every little murmur died down. Momentarily, I wondered if this was the sheepishness of dehumanized and brutalized prisoners or whether it was out of some sense of purpose and urgency regarding the matter that had brought us together. But there was no time to bother much as all eyes were on me. I consulted with John, a friend in the Packaging Section, and thereafter he introduced me as the person who convened the meeting. To this came the chorus:

"We know him."

I did not prepare any kind of speech, and I had not even thought much of what to say. And the fact that I had never found myself addressing such a gathering of older men increased the tension in me. But seeing the numerous faces that were looking at me with some probable high expectations, I knew that I had to do everything not to disappoint them.

"Comrades," I started, "I am very happy to have the honour to welcome everyone here. I don't know how to express myself well enough to show my happiness to all these faces gathered here. When the call was sent out, little did I imagine that as many as this would respond. I never expected that as many as this large number would agree to forfeit break for this important meeting. Once again, I am very grateful that you honoured this call. As it is now, this is no time for any long speech. So I will do my best to be brief."

I paused, drew some breath and continued.

"I know that many of us have an idea of why we are here, for I can see faces, many faces indeed, that I have had the opportunity of discussing at length with on the need for a common front. Yes, that's why we are here; to see if we can form a common and united front and platform from which we can fight."

And as many heads nodded, with some voicing out their approval of what I said, I gathered more confidence.

"Comrades," I continued, "I don't need to tell you stories of many of us here who cannot afford two meals in a day. I don't need to tell you stories of poverty and want; I don't need to tell you because daily you live these experiences. I'm not sure that I have seen any new clothes or pair of shoes on any of you since I came here. Look round and show me the person who is not wearing a patched pair of trousers or an open shoe."

And at this many people broke out in laughter, while some others nodded gravely like the sad tale of an adolescent's death was being told. A voice rose above the laughter and murmur and said:

"Even our pants are torn to shreds," more people now joining the train of laughter.

"Yes, that's true, comrades," I resumed so as to bring order and avoid extended diversion. "Many more have even discarded the luxury of wearing pants. And God help us if soon some of us won't start coming to work bare-footed. Comrades, our people in their wisdom say that it is from where someone works that they eat, but how many of us will agree that we actually are eating from our sweat in this company? Here we only work and suffer and die slowly so that our fat-bellied management will grow fatter and fly even to the moon in search of pleasure. Yet the bare necessaries of life are denied us to satisfy the lustful appetites of these lords. Comrades, we will continue to die slowly and will eventually quench in abject misery unless we do something. I am glad that we all now know that by law all of us here should have become permanent staff. And the management knows this too. But using casual workers is a very cheap method for them. And they will go any length to ensure that they spend less and less on us while we make more and more money for them. Comrades, you know as well as I do that the system here is unjust and inhuman. We know it because every sting of hunger in each of us is a testimony to the depth of deprivation which we suffer. We all know it that this company makes so much profit that international investors are struggling and ready to pay any amount to have some stake in it. We know we deserve much better wages than we are being paid. Yet we all fold our hands in resignation and watch as they enslave us and cut low the opportunities for our children."

Here I paused a little to inhale slowly and deeply in order to calm my rising anger and bitterness. It seemed I was beginning to work on some of them.

Stir that fire! Stir it!

"Comrades, do we now and then take sometime to ask ourselves questions? Do we bother to think about tomorrow? Do we at all wonder about our children, what kind of life they will live and what chances are available for them? Do we? Does it not occur to you that your life in this company is not worth a penny? Something happens to you today, and that is the end of it all; for it will only take minutes before another person takes your place. And the profit continues to flow in for the company, but there will be no single mark, even a pencil mark, on the pages of the company's history to tell of your sacrifice. Of course, there is no insurance, no medical cover and nothing to suggest that you have a family to take care of and even provide for after you might have passed on to the great beyond. And we say we are workers here. And we see these things each moment we spend here. And we only work and work and look in resignation."

The gravity of their usually placid faces told me that I was succeeding in moving them to a desired pitch. So I thought it meet to strike harder, a possible hard blow that might set ablaze the petrol-soaked compost of their anger.

"Comrades, think about your lives now if you never bothered before. Do you think that it is worth more than an ant's, more than a piece of necessary rubbish kept only insofar as there is still something in it to suck out? That is what we all are to the management of this company. And, yet, nothing can function in this company without us, nothing. Ask yourselves, comrades, whether there is any promise for you in a set-up like this. Don't you have any dreams? Never you dream of one day being able to afford three square meals, of wearing decent clothes and shoes, of being able to provide those daily needs of your loved ones? Do you ever dream of such ordinary things? So ordinary and basic, yet so far far away from our reach. And we say we work in National Cosmetics Company. We say we are members of staff of the most profitable cosmetics company in the country. And we have neither of these basic things. And we fold our hands! We fold our hands and do nothing!"

"Comrades, an old hunter in my village once told me that for anyone to live life to the fullest, he has to snatch his existence from the very grip of lions and wild beasts. I did not understand him then, but I think I am beginning to. We know the wild beasts in this company holding down our progress and happiness, and we cannot find that happiness except we snatch it from their jaws. And we can do it if we realize how much power we have when we band together. We know how easy it is to break a broomstick. But put many together and you realize the power in uniting with your kind. That is it. Our strength lies in union, and I hereby suggest that we instantly form a union to fight for improved conditions of services. Our destiny is in our hands. Either we fight now and free ourselves from slavery or we resign ourselves to the situation and forever remain dammed. The choice is ours. Thank you all for your cooperation."

I had sat down when I realized that I was sweating profusely. My shirt was even soaked. The gathering was silent and everybody seemed to be steeped in thought. The whole place was silence, but in that silence I think I saw a raging inferno. My task, my initial task, was done.

I, too, remained silent. John it was who stood up after awhile and, without any ceremony, asked those who supported the idea of a union to raise up their hands. May be I did not see well, but everybody voted in favour of a union. I was asked to be the coordinator until officers were elected, and a meeting to work out our strategies was fixed for three days' time.

The fire was raging. But the cloud. The cloud.

I came to work the following day to discover that the gates were barred against me. I was told that there was instruction from management that I should wait at the gate. Other casual workers were given a form to fill before being allowed in. I took one such form from somebody, and when I read it I saw that it required them to sign that they were not going to engage in any form of unionism in the company, that they would "remain loyal and obedient to management and would not listen to any disgruntled element who is out to disturb the peace."

Somehow I managed to laugh because it was too much the language of our illiterate military dictators who always saw any dissension, and worse a protest, as an attempt to "disturb the peace by disgruntled elements." But it was a very shallow laugh because I knew that the situation on hand was serious and demanded some quick action.

Quickly I moved around, attempting to mobilize those who had not signed by explaining the implication of signing the form. Many of them were now gathered in front of the company looking all so confused and helpless. An elderly man, hair almost all white, walked up to me.

"Son, won't I lose my job if I don't sign?"

"No, you won't as far as we all stick together."

"But some have already signed," he declared.

"The rest of us can refuse to sign."

"Then they will sack all of us and employ other people."

It seemed to me like this was just that typical psychology of the slave who has no hope in his condition, and yet would not give it up. My feeling towards him was that of repulsion as well as compassion; because that manner of thinking appeared below animal, much less human, and it as well showed the need for much help and guidance. I turned to him:

"Have you got a wife?

"Yes."

"How many children?"

"Nine."

"Are they with you here in the city?"

"No, they are in the village farming."

"So how much do you send to them in a month?"

"They take care of themselves. What I'm paid is not enough for me alone. So what do I have to send them?"

"So what will you lose if you get sacked?"

"But I don't want to lose the job."

I think it was now more of repulsion than compassion. I turned to them all:

"Comrades, I would like you to know that you are free to sign the form if you so wish. But I can promise you a good fight, and victory is certain only if we all act with one accord. Our strength lies in unity. This they know, and that's why they are trying to break us. But we should not allow them. Those of us who are here can still convince and mobilize those who have already signed, and –"

"But what if they refuse to join us?" a girl of perhaps eighteen asked. And I wondered how I had not noticed her before now. For even in her gaunt and under-nourished look, she struck this queenly beauty and a fading virginal radiance. Beauty going down the drain, the drain of city life, of our monument of concentrated selfishness.

In that moment too was a drain of my attention away from the boiling issue to that beauty before me. Many thoughts fleeted through my mind, and some longing stirred my heart. Then I said:

"We cannot waste this beau – I mean, we shouldn't waste this opportunity. Those of us here can still put up a good fight."

"And what if we fail?" someone asked.

"We cannot fail if we work as a group," I said almost feebly, the fire in me now divided.

And as I said that, I saw the security man waving a paper at me. I walked up to him and collected it. It was a sack letter, with money for the seventeen days I had worked for that month. And as the people around me saw the content of the letter, they immediately signed their forms and started going in, those who had not collected the form quickly did, signed and went in.

And as they all left me there and entered that Slough of Despond, some laughter echoed down my consciousness, and I was that alone and far-seeing Voltaire in that famous jibe of his in which he is said to have told the clergy of his time that they could not look at one another in the face without laughing.

How could I not laugh that empty laugh of bitter recognition, how could I not?

As I stood there, a kaleidoscope of impressions billowing back and forth, I saw a spectacle of fear-ridden, ignorant and helpless humanity – helpless simply because we chose not to help ourselves out of several kinds of self-imposed imprisonments. And it touched my heart sorely. Because there is no true help that can be given to those who refuse to help themselves. It touched my heart sorely. Because always the number of those who exploit and oppress others for their selfish ends is infinitesimally negligible compared to that of the oppressed. And realizing the power and strength in synergetic effort, knowing the value of accretion in swaying the balance, those who lead rule secondarily by might and primarily by division. It touched my heart sorely and to tears, and in those tears I remembered that beauty going down the drain. I did not know when, but of course she too had been drawn into the exodus into the company, where her fading radiance would finally be drained out of her. And thereafter, she would curse all men. It burnt my heart.

But tears and heart-burns are not the only strands of life. Because much as it is celebrated, and much as it sways human emotion and attention, tragedy is not all that matters. Indeed there are varying colours in the spectrum of life, and many shades and even shadows that we are not always able to fully account for. Like to think that when a seed is thrown into the ocean of life, any seed whatsoever, never does it die a final death without its own fruit. Never! Even the gentle thud of that seed will always stir ripples of life flowing forth to expanses never imagined and coming back in manifold fruitfulness.

For tragedy is not all that matters, however much the breaking news syndrome of television may suggest.

Such was it that I got my admission letter into the university that same week, and along with it too was a generous offer of full scholarship for my education. It was from an anonymous donor, and part of the condition was that I was never going to pester the administrators with questions concerning the identity of the donor. This caused me much wonder and anxiety. That such human beings as that still existed. And I was to enjoy such large generosity without ever going to have a chance to show my appreciation to my benefactor. It caused me much anxiety and questioning. But above it all, it strengthened that vision of life which was now beginning to germinate. It strengthened that vision.

THE FIRE FESTIVAL

CHAPTER 12:

THE UNNAMEABLE

I sauntered on, forcing my way through a hedge of human beings. For tragedy indeed is the dearth of vision and purpose, the blindness of ignorance which leaves a human being will-less and only floating in the unmeaning pool of the forces of denial. Tragedy is that cup of sorrow from which a man animally drinks and drinks without raising his head to ask questions. Tragedy is that which holds not that questioning search for sanity and security, the saving joy of the soul, the struggle to master our inharmonious forces, the pursuit of meaning and fulfilment and the attendant electric joy. Tragedy is that which holds not this.

But whether it is better to ride on the back of the beast and enter through the back door, the lower door, crushing everything that may stand on the way, or to listen to the silent voice of one's soul and go through the front door, suffering and enduring all the agony and sorrow till sorrow matters no more? Whether it is better to swim through an ocean of shit to pick a fragment of life

stained, or to defiantly stand in stiff rejection of all such possibility and then burn in the inward thirst for the actualization of the
visioned ideal? Whether it is better to cross that log of conscience
and live with a ruthless determination, or to accept the whispered
commands of the heart and live the life of that heart, thereby
enduring and possibly overcoming the pulls of contending forces?
In the midst of all the toys of life, one ought to be able to look
inwards and nod one's head and I exclaim: "Yes, I am real."

But how real?

Oh! Many have chosen the grave of the freedom of the intel-
lect without the melody of the heart, but too soon do they get
sucked dry in the futile fever of that shallow way. Much more,
much more are drowning in the pool of the inertia of visionless-
ness. Much more drown in that pool. Which makes it more tragic,
for the Buddha gloriously struggled for and found the middle way,
the only true way to that electric joy called bliss. He found it, and
has remained in eternal compassion for the many that still grope
in the dark. Oh, that's why He comes. Yes, He comes in the full
moon of the bull to shower blessings on the world. Oh blessed
heart of wisdom! And the Christ opened up the more that way
for the world, and that Heart of Love too is on His way back. Yes
He is. Oh Heraclitus, even with your blows, you still could not
prevent them from preferring straw to gold, from choosing the
robber to the redeemer.

Oh wonder that is called humanity!

How blindly and feverishly one searches after that joy by
thickening up the mass of clay that we are? How hard and desperately one should struggle to tame that wild beast of grabbing,
the beast that keeps sucking away the milk of our brimful world?
And that we are much more than our tongue is undeniable. Yet,
that nebulous but abiding purpose, that harmony and beauty
beyond words is possible for us all. In spite of all.

Still I sauntered on, forcing my way through a hedge of human beings.

Because man ate of the fruit of that tree, because the woman touched the face of heaven with her dirty hand, because she kept knocking against God with her pestle while pounding food, because the rope linking us with God was severed, evil then became the condition of man. All is now shards and shadows, fragments of broken godliness in enveloping evil. How one digs deeper and deeper one's grave by listening to the roaring cravings of our human side! How one may walk in indifference to these cravings so that the divine may be free and light up with its radiance one's world, light up the world! And between them is a chasm, a gulf where grains of defeat and anguish are reaped; between them is that burial-ground of many a dream. Because we hang between the animal and the superman. Nietzsche pictured us clearly.

But I sauntered on, forcing my way through a hedge of human beings, faces tight and hard with determination and desperation – much like the determined faces of suicide-bombers. The sun was now very hot, hammering away its desert-heat on the already scorched souls in the street. And nobody seemed to worry at all. They seemed to have lived for too long now with the reality of suffering to bother about a quite ordinary hot sun. When you are completely beaten and have fallen far down, nothing really matters anymore, just nothing. He that is down. But that life should be so mercilessly crammed with contradictions. To love with all one's heart only to be rejected or hated by the object of one's love; to desire with all intensity to grab in one's hand some enduring juice of life, down it in full-throated satiety and then be still, but only to have that wing of desire cut short and then crash-land unto the rock-hardness of life; to aspire truly to a moral life and possibly suffer lack thereby, only to look up and see the overflowing affluence of the petty and heartless ones along with its bloated egoism. Why is it, in any case, that it seems easier to hate than to love, to be evil than to be good? Where, tell me, where is this light of God buried deep within us, what is this image of His after which we are made? Is there or is there not cosmic support for the virtuous life, that I am so so wretched and abandoned, so hopelessly down.

Still I sauntered on, forcing my way through a hedge of human beings, faces tight and hard with determination and desperation. I sauntered on and as I looked about me I returned to the now familiar fascination with measuring and equating each person's strength, dream and zest for life according to and with the size of their container for water. For many, indeed, in that street were also in search of water. And the containers were there in varying degrees too. Of course many there were who had no containers. Either they were on some other business or had simply given up and were now only floating without any will, any desire except the waiting for the vulture of death to eat up their remains. And what would it be like if one were to overcome all illusion – as they say that all our desires are just so much illusion and verbiage? What hunger would there be? Would it then be a contact with and touch of that unadulterated truth – and what is this truth? Or would there be some more illusion to keep us keeping on? So that truth becomes progressive and relative. And that way we always are faced with one illusion after the other. And illusion becomes the rain that keeps falling on the dry desert of our lives, keeping us keeping on and even helping in throwing up more illusions. Thus, life is a series of illusions. But some of these illusions are the threads which gods and heroes weave into that reality worshipped by generations. They alone bear witness to the heavy task. And its enduring joy which they speak of. That joy. Touch me now, touch me.

Still I sauntered on.

How the curse of Tantalus hangs eternally on our heads! The burden of light on the darkened path. So we hang from the bough of our dream fruit tree, forever consumed by unquenchable thirst and hunger. And though the tree of life and joy and fulfilment that we hunger and thirst for is so laden with fruit hanging before us, we can only see but cannot pluck and taste of its blessed sweetness. And though the stream of life and happiness and contentment that we thirst and yearn after so runs through our feet, we can only see but cannot drink and rejoice in the filling satiety of that water of life. And forever we sway back and forth, wobbling after that which holds the key to our life and death. This is the condition of the human race, and the tragedy of it all: the pursuit of meaning in a seemingly meaningless world; the struggle to gain control and mastery over the forces of our lives; the taming of the animal wildness of our nature; the ever-present craving after fulfilment and the attendant joy. That we must drink fully of the cup of pain and sorrow, of the burning waters of that gulf which separates vision from actuality – this is the tragedy of it all.

Still I sauntered on, forcing my way through a hedge of human beings, the strides of determination, the force of desperation in the eyes. So was the face of that street. And as I was about to take a short cut into another street, I remembered that I was invited for a naming ceremony that morning.

He was a friend I met at a bar – those days when I had the desperation to seek escape through alcohol. This was his first child. Surely a lot of drinks and food will be there. And must have gone borrowing to do all that. To please the crowd. Walking along that shop-worn path of tradition. What's there to celebrate that a child is drawn unto this plane of sorrow and suffering by the sheer lust of two opposites? What future in a land like this, a world as ours, so lustful and dark? For either he is strong and tramples on weaker ones or he is among the class of infant humanity and is then trampled upon. A child comes crashing and crying into such a world, and we celebrate. And you want to join them. Sure, it won't all be a waste of time. At least there is the promise of a meal and some drink. Meal well cooked by women. That should hold me for a day or two. And the ceremony should have ended by now. Eating and drinking then. Perfect timing.

When I got to my friend's place, I met a gathering of people outside, some sitting while the others were standing under a rather large canopy. There was a lot of movement into and out of the house, but there was no sign anywhere of food and drink being served. It did not appear as if the actual ceremony had taken place; otherwise there would be empty bottles and plates scattered here and there. And eating would still be going on anyway.

I approached a group of bystanders and tapped one of them on the shoulder. He turned.

"Please what's happening?" I asked.

He reflected, or seemed to, on the question for some moment. Feeling that there was nothing in the question to spend an eternity cracking one's brain to answer, I explained further;

"I mean, has the ceremony been concluded?"

Again he went into a trance, and I thought I should allow him and wait for the revelation. I was not long when it became clear that he did not succeed in making that inner contact; for he turned to another among the group and said:

"My friend here is asking whether the ceremony has been concluded or not."

"The ceremony," the second person muttered and seemed too to think about it. "The ceremony, it seems that – let's find out from Jude."

And he called Jude who was with some other group nearby. The second man continued as soon as Jude joined us: "My friend says that our friend here wants to know whether the ceremony has been concluded or not. Do you know?"

"Do I know? The ceremony – but what ceremony is he asking about?"

The second man picked up from Jude. "My friend, what ceremony is our friend asking about?" he asked the first person who turned to me and asked:

"What ceremony are you asking about?"

"Why then did you come here?" I asked.

"Why did I come here?" the first asked. Then he turned to the second and asked: "Why did you come here?"

And the second, too, turned and asked Jude: "Why did you come here?"

"Why did I come here?" And after thinking it over, answered: "Of course I came here for the ceremony."

"What ceremony?" I fired at him.

"What ceremony? The ceremony, of course," he held on.

"What ceremony brought you here?" I insisted.

"The ceremony, of course. Are you new here? Or don't you know how to read signs? You see canopy mounted, chairs and tables arranged, women milling in and out of the backyard where smoke is rising to the sky, and you still ask me what ceremony."

And they all laughed.

Jude continued, "I can help you find out, but I don't see the point."

"No, thanks," I responded and walked away, now very certain that I could not find out anything useful from them.

There was something not quite normal about the whole set-up. Here and there people were gathered in groups. I observed one such group of women as they whispered conspiratorially, looked somewhat quizzically towards my friend's house, shook their heads and clapped their hands and laughed. I told myself at that point that heaven and earth must be out of joint, and I wondered the more what the matter could be. I was already approaching the entrance into the house when my friend's wife saw me, rushed towards and besought me.

"Eno! Eno! Thank God you are here. Please help me out of this shame and embarrassment. Please help me."

"What's the matter?" I asked.

Quickly she pulled me away to a removed corner at the back of the house.

"It's your friend o! For three days and three nights now he has locked himself in a room and has refused to come out. Now the ceremony cannot start without him, and the whole world is waiting. Please help me. How can I bear the shame?"

And then she turned to the heavens: "Ah God, why me, why me of all people? Why must my own be different? What have I done? Who have I offended?"

"What happened between the two of you, I mean, was there a quarrel or disagreement that led to his locking himself up?" I needed to ask this in order to draw her away from that monologue to the heavens; for it was not very much different from all I had done since the break of day. And I did not need her to reopen for me that channel yet.

"There was no quarrel, no quarrel. He said he wanted to think out a name for the baby, that he needed to find the right name. For three days he has been locked up there. And when I knocked this morning, he said he was still thinking. My sister has tried to speak with him, but he won't speak to anybody. She has left in anger, and some other relations too. I have never seen or heard of this kind of embarrassment before. Can you imagine somebody thinking of a name for three days and three nights? Why must my own be different? Who on earth have I offended that is working this evil on me? Tell me, God, who have I offended?"

Of course as she said that, she burst into tears, raising her hands and eyes once again to heaven. Thereafter, she took one end of her wrapper, wiped her face with it, and then blew her nose.

"Take me to where he is. I think he may not mind talking with me."

She led me into the house, to the room where her husband was. I knocked.

"I don't want to be disturbed. Give me more time to think," he said.

"Tam, it's me Eno, can you open the door?"

As soon as Tam unlocked and opened the door, his wife rushed in, grabbed him by the waistline of his trousers and started dragging him out. Of course her frustration also poured out:

"Useless man! Shameless thing! Either you come out now and name your child or you kill me and save me the shame. Shameless drunkard. You think impregnating a woman is what makes a man. You can't even show love to your own child. I am your slave, so –"

"Why must you rake up all –" Tam tried to say. But she would not let him, frustrated the more by her inability to drag him out of the room.

"Why must I not rake it up? Tell me why I must not when you, shameless as you are, now want to embarrass me before the whole world. I am your broomstick, so it doesn't matter what mud you use me to sweep. But this is your child. This is the least you can do for him."

"Woman, take it easy. You know how hard I have been thinking to get a suitable name. I need to think–"

"Think what? Tell me think what? What's in a name that you have to think all your life? Come out now and name your child. That's all I ask of you. I have not asked you for any money. It's just for you to come out and name your child. After that you can find a dungeon and lock up yourself there. Come out now, come out o!", and she resumed the struggle to drag him out.

"Woman, I need to think—" he managed to say before once again she cut in.

"Think what? And with what head? Is it with brain eaten up by alcohol? Any normal human being does not need to lock himself up for three days just to find a name for his child. Nobody with brain needs three days for that. What kind of man are you?"

And with that, it was like she suddenly came to the realization of a loss of great magnitude. She left him, went to a corner of the room, sat on the floor, buried her face in the wrapper and wailed inconsolably. Then she raised her eyes to heaven above, her hands and open mouth and face all turned towards God and asking what she had done to deserve that kind of man. Thereafter, she buried her face in her wrapper again and wailed and wailed.

I had started considering the possibility of escaping from the scene. But the sight of Tam's wife in that deep distress rent my escapist veil and touched me deeply. And I knew that one way or another, I was going to do, or at least attempt to do, something to help. So I walked over to her, and with all tenderness but with little or no conviction said:

"Sister, calm down and be not troubled. There is always a way round every problem. Always there is a solution to all our troubles. So why don't you leave us alone to sort this out. It's not a very difficult matter. Just give us some time, and everything will be okay."

Of course, I said all that without being sure of the truth of even a word in the whole rubbish. I simply tried to imagine what might console and give her some hope in the midst of that hopelessness. And would you believe it? It did work; for she now ceased to sob, wiped her face and said, almost solemnly:

"Thank you, thank you very much, my brother, your words are comforting, and that is how a man should talk. Your friend has never said anything like that to me. Thank you once again. I will leave because of you. And I know you won't fail me."

Then she left, but not without taking a last vicious glance at her husband. She let off some bit of the rage concentrated in that glance by hissing a rather long hiss as she walked away.

And she knew I would not fail her. So heavy a burden of trust.

"Women, they are always the same. They will never understand," Tam said as he sat on the chair and heaved a heavy sigh.

"Yes, but what is this talk about three days of searching for a name for the baby?" I asked as I sat down.

"My brother, it's not been easy at all. I have been trying very hard to find a name for the past three days. I retreated into this room so that I could think undisturbed. But here I am now in this mess. And she won't understand. Can you see my predicament?"

"I think I can. But why is it taking you this long to get a name? You don't like any of the names around, and you want to create a new one. What could be so difficult in that?"

"But you should know if nobody else does. You know that our people use words without care. And you know too that every word is a veil and an attempt to clothe an essence. And here, the life of a child is involved, and it is right that the child be covered with that name which most closely resonates to the vibration of its essential nature and destiny before being sent off into the world. You should know a bit about the science of sound. It is not for nothing that God is said to have created through the utterance of the word, that is through sound. We too should create likewise. This is my predicament."

This was very heavy matter in my ears, familiar as I was with the logic; but now logic taken too far. It rather appeared like a beer-parlour argument taken too seriously and to dagger-point.

And I know you won't fail me.

"Considering the situation as it is now, the urgency of the moment, do you think this is a practical and worthwhile effort?" I asked, convinced now that I was not the only seeker after the fantasy of dream-worlds.

"But I know it's possible, I know it. I know it's still possible for me to shout my Eureka. Only if I can meditate hard enough, I may hear it pronounced or see it flash into my consciousness. Sometimes, indeed many times, I came close to it. I know I will get it. I just need more time."

"Can you not manage, one way or the other, to go out there, pronounce a name for the child and then let the people eat and drink. Then you can return and continue with your meditation?"

"No no no," he rejoined emphatically. "That's not possible, for once that name is sounded, its exact vibration enfolds the child and it sticks. It cannot be undone thereafter, I mean I don't know how to undo it. You should understand me."

"Well, I suppose I do," I responded feebly. Of course it was practically impossible for me to have said otherwise.

"I'm glad to hear that." For the first time he smiled. "There are not many people that understand and appreciate what I'm saying."

"But you have to find a way to get the ceremony started so that people can eat and drink and go away. You shouldn't leave them out there for too long. And your wife is almost going into a frenzy with worry. Try and do something."

"You know I suggested to that woman that we should postpone this ceremony until I was sure of the right name, but she bluntly refused. She said it's the tradition that naming ceremonies must take place on the eight day, and that she didn't see any reason why her child's own should be different."

"She flows with the tide of tradition as everybody else."

"Well, that's not my business. I have to give my child the right name, and I will do that only when that right name is discovered. I don't care about anything else."

"By the way, how did she get water to prepare for this?"

"That's one of the reasons why I suggested that we should postpone the whole thing. You don't prepare for a thing like this when you are not sure of water. But she is completely crazy over having the ceremony today. So she would not hear of postponement at all. I suppose she must have fetched the stinking water from that shallow well."

Instantly that hunger which had begun to stir my entrails more and more immediately ceased. The thought of that stinking water.

"But why must it be today if it is not convenient?" I asked, somehow now beginning to be irritated.

"Help me ask her," he responded rather enthusiastically. "Help me ask her. She says it must be on the eight day. I don't know if Hell will be let loose if it's done any other day as may be convenient."

The situation appeared more than I could handle, knowing the kind of person Tam was. And the wife would be waiting expectantly, hopefully. Well, one more effort and I would leave them to their fate. After all, I still had ahead of me a whole stretch of a day of uncertainty and possible fruitless effort and mounting despair. One more effort.

"But, Tam, you know you can't continue indefinitely like this while guests are waiting. Let's try and find a way round this."

"There is nothing I can do, absolutely nothing, even if the whole world were crashing on my head. The only exception is if there is a way they can carry on with the ceremony without my having to provide a name yet," he conceded.

"I don't suppose that your wife would like to hear this at all."

"It doesn't matter how anybody feels about what I do, so long as I have tried to act in accordance with my belief. After all, she did not care about my own feelings regarding the ceremony."

"Do you not see this as the basic impulse behind all forms of fundamentalism - religious, economic, political?"

"My brother, I have not interfered with other people's rights and freedom to live as they choose. It is only with how I choose to live my life."

"Anyway, suppose I suggest names for your consideration?" I asked.

"Ah, that's not right at all. This is my first child, and I, alone and unaided, must find a name for him. It's something I must do without any form of help."

"Yes, I know," I replied, although I was sure that I did not agree. "I will only suggest names, then you can examine them and pick whichever seems right to you."

"Thanks, friend, but it won't work that way. I just have to find the name myself, and I will not compromise on such matters of principle."

"So for how long more do you think you can continue like this?" My heart was somewhat pinched by his obstinacy which appeared simultaneously ignoble and admirable.

"For as long as possible. When the people out there become tired, they will return to their homes."

"But you invited them."

"I did not invite them. I invited only three people, you being one of them. That's my wife's affair."

Some silence followed as I was sure of what next to do but did not know how to say it.

"It looks like I can't help you in any way then?"

"My brother, you've done much more than you should. This is like dying, and we each do it alone."

"In that case I have to leave then to go and continue dying my own death."

"Thanks a lot for your concern. But why not wait and let them serve you some food."

"You can imagine how awkward it will be for me to be the only person eating among that ravenous crowd. They will swallow me with their looks."

"You don't need to stay out there. You can eat here."

"I truly don't feel like. I'll see you some other time" as I walked to the door.

"Thanks once again," he said and then closed the door after me. Perhaps he was suspicious that the wife might just be lurking around.

More guests, I supposed mostly uninvited, seemed to have arrived, but Tam's wife was nowhere in sight. I had silently prayed for this, for how could I look her in the eyes to say that I had failed her. In spite of all her hope and confidence.

I hurried out of the vicinity.

THE FIRE FESTIVAL

CHAPTER 13:

THE WILD FIRES

K atakata junction was indeed a riot of wild varieties. Its thick column of traffic swam and zigzagged into innumerable directions. Vehicular traffic was at a standstill, and the traffic policeman too was at a standstill in his booth at the centre of the criss-cross of roads. A madman, completely naked, was not far from the traffic policeman, and he was controlling with his head and hands the traffic that did not move. Teenage hawkers were everywhere shouting the imagined selling-points of their wares, while under those modern towers of Babel housing a number of well-known companies, more desperate hawkers could be seen shoving their wares in front of passers-by and now and then harassing and touching the buttocks of young girls. And from those towers flowed in and out polished wood and powdered corpses of human beings. Because beneath the polish and powder were bold marks of frustration and regression into instinctual animality which is not living. The cost of being human. Or of losing our human nobility.

Still I sauntered on, forcing my way through, seeing through those faces and observing in them that same emptiness that was burning me into ashes.

How long must I continue to suffer before I find my place in this cursed life? How long? Ceaselessly but hopelessly jostling and striving after what? Maybe your life was meant to be this wretched, meant to be one of continuous suffering and anguish without meaning. And those polished woods, or even those who may have made it, what is it they have that you do not have? Many of them have struggled not even half as much as you have. Some simply try once and everything falls in place. And they see you as a low being who knows not how to struggle; for they know all and hold the key to the secrets of the universe. And worse if you need aid from them. Then you must listen to their sermon on the secrets of success, you must patiently listen to them, you low being, you wretched of the wretch wallowing in the refuse-dump of life. Fuck you!

Still I sauntered on, poking the recesses of my consciousness for an escape-route from my burning emptiness. Still I sauntered on, forcing my way through and observing in those faces that same emptiness that was burning me into ashes.

Why? Because I am not the product of love. Just the burning lust of one animal striking death into the innocent life of another. I am the cursed product of that atrocity, of that inhumanity, that below-animal brutality. Born not from love. Eternal wretchedness thereby. And all your friends are as wretched as you, all of them poverty-stricken, frustrated dreamers living a lowly existence of mud and filth and stench. What hope, what relief, what strength to draw from people as Tam? His mad search for the meaning or essence of those interlocking contradictions, how could he capture all that in a name? That animal lowness, what word to hold

it all in place? The wretchedness of it all. Maybe that's how God planned your life for you, the pact you signed before you left that zone of light for the earth, the planet of sin and sorrow and suffering where the spirit of gravity thrashes and toys with the sons of men who know not that they are the sons of God. Yes, we are toys in the play-ground of the spirit of gravity! How it thrashes us to mindless insignificance!

Show forth that signature.

Still I sauntered on, and as I approached the giant cross of the popular Redemption Centre, I realized that the press of human beings had reduced, and it seemed as if many people flowed down the adjoining Iskape Street where, anybody would easily agree, a certificate even from heaven could be forged. But it was that giant cross which stood astride my consciousness giant-like, growing and stretching into the bitter cross of my cursed life as I moved on to Golgotha, that place where my skull would finally be laid in pieces.

Because I would have conquered neither life nor death.

But the alarm raised by a woman nearby jolted me. She had grabbed a slim and hungry-looking young man by his trousers, and was shouting that he was a thief. Before I could size up the situation, someone thrust the sharp ends of a broken bottle onto the young man's forehead. Another passer-by was also quick enough to give the young man an upper cut. And many, now finding a veritable means of releasing their bottled up frustration, rushed at this outlet, and in no time thousands of fiends were let loose on the victim.

I was flushed and as well immersed in a tide of sympathy for the victim, and I was lost in observing the ingenuity and swiftness of the human heart in dealing the death blow. It struck me that – but it could have been some stone, a block of concrete or something like that which struck me hard on the head. The ground welcomed me with a bang, but I did not go blank. Through a web of feet I saw the young man, the victim, there on the ground too and soaked in his own blood. Somehow he managed to crawl through that cluster of feet out of the centre of action. It now became a free-for-all fight, each person thrusting his hand unto any face nearby, some breaking bottles on heads, any head, and virtually everybody groaning under pain and still thrusting here and there. And nobody seemed to give a damn. All that seemed to matter was just to keep on dashing out a blow. Somehow, it would always fall on some face. And that was all that was important.

At last the victim, having crawled a little away from the madness, managed to stand up. And as he seemed to be weighing his strength, someone sounded a whistle. There and then followed a sudden halt, like thunder had silenced them all.

"Here's the son of a bitch. He's escaping," declared the whistle man.

All attention, except for those who had slumped during the general commotion, now turned to their victim. And in their eyes was this knowing look that seemed to say. Oh, so you wanted to escape.

But before anybody could strike this time around, the young man took to his heels. And many followed in hot pursuit, jumping over and crashing against cars and people in the street. I was drawn along too, not knowing what I really wanted. The victim, as if realizing that he had little or no chance elsewhere, ran towards the church. As he approached the iron gates of that church, somebody who had seemed indifferent kicked the victim's feet off the ground. He fell flat but quickly got up and, in an incredible display of strength and skill, jumped over the Berlin-wall fence of the church. The mob still continued the desperate pursuit, only a handful jumping over that wall while others crashed through the gate.

I flowed with those who slid through the pedestrian portion of that gate before the mob crashed through.

The victim, sure of the safety of the church where some service seemed to be going on, continued running towards that hope. And as he was about running into that place of sure security and peace, the crowd still in mad pursuit, just as the young man was about jumping into that place of refuge, the huge door of the church – with the carved image of Jesus with outstretched hands – slammed across his forehead, the door having been ferociously closed from inside.

As that door – oh, what a huge monstrosity – as it smashed the victim's face, and as he fell backwards, something happened to me, something either entered or left me that I registered the whole experience with a kind of absorption and identification that I cannot fully explain. Again, it was like a slow motion picture.

Life's moments of agony always drag with a snail-speed cruelty.

It must have taken, in normal time reckoning, maybe about two or three seconds. But it was an eternity of anguish for me as the whole world slowed its pace a thousand times, and I watched with unbearable anguish the victim's head jerk backwards as the door rammed into him, and I watched his consequent fall from the jagged peaks of Mount Everest, through precipices and crevices, down and down and down, and I, mouth open, stretched out my hands in my imagination to arrest his fall. But down and down and down he fell, and falling through my outstretched hands – though in reality I was some distance away – he crashed with the back of his head unto the stone-hard marble veranda. And I jumped up simultaneously as he landed. And existence gathered normal pace once again. But my anguish was now deeper, and my heart was pounding.

But the crowd was now divided. Some, on seeing the way the young man fell (I supposed) withdrew, while others still closed in on him with stones, blocks, bottles and knives lifted high above their heads in readiness to strike, that's should there be any sign of life left in the victim. Meanwhile, the dancing and drumming and singing and speaking in tongues within the church seemed to increase.

I edged closer, carefully. Blood-thirsty tongues drooled. The victim was lying outstretched on his back, hands spread out in saying a final goodbye to a wicked and cruel world. It was difficult to make out his face now as blood was still coming out of his mouth (which was open), nostrils and forehead. His lower lip was split into two, and his left eye was swollen as if a ball of orange fruit had been forced into the socket.

As I stared at his lifeless body, that sense of identification with the sufferer then intensified, and my sorrow deepened as my heart pounded the more. But, somehow, I moved away from the cry of that heat, I moved away from that cry which was widening the deep wound in the depths of my being. I moved into the head and tried to rationalize and translate that identification to an attitude of indifference. Because his end simply was an inevitable part of his share of life, and each person would some day face the same end. And life's treacherous arrows may not have given him any breathing space. Maybe he too had no space in her heart. And his life may have been poisoned at the roots, like mine, and it may all have been a slow process of withering until this final and helpful act of release. Yet, he surely had dreams – illusions rather. He most likely hoped that some day he would make it – but make what? Is it to make enough money to buy those encumbrances of joy called luxuries, to buy them more because of your comrades to whom you want to measure up or even above so that they may clap for you and say flattering things about you so long as the money lasts?

What truly is it when we jostle after making it?

To acquire all that there may be to acquire (and there is hardly an end) and then save for one's tenth generation when we know not whether our milked planet would still be there the next day?

Ever seen anybody who reached that point of material satiety and then decided to grab no more?

Yet, he had hopes that some day he would make it.

But then it saddened me that he had to so end it, so callously, and at the hands of desperate failures who could hardly point to any meaningful reason for continuing to live beyond that hardly defined hope:

I will make it.

Because where there is no vision, where there is naught which matters so much that one may lay down one's life, then such a person has not started living. Better such were kept in the safety of a zoo until some vision, no matter how nebulous, began to stir them into some focused activity. Better the zoo where there is no vision. And the stream of life is polluted and poisoned where such drink. Thus spake Zarathustra, and thus affirm I.

As I stood there thinking about these things, a man, about six feet tall and with taut veins standing out on his hands, stepped out of the mob and stood astride the victim. Then he bent down, felt the victim's neck and chest with his left hand, stood up and pronounced:

"Gone to hell," which seemed to please him very much. He added: "But we ought to cut his throat to be sure he doesn't make it."

A few isolated voices said "Yes".

He bent down again, felt the neck and the chest of the victim once more, this time with his right hand, stood up and declared!

"He can't make it. Clean and out."

Then he walked away, though not before he dropped a mouthful of saliva on the face of the victim. Others started moving away too, many throwing their weapons on the victim and more muttering final curses on him – much unlike a priest during extreme unction.

I had taken my own, yes I had.

I remained there, however, not knowing exactly what to do either with myself or for the victim who was now beyond redemption. And suppose there was something I could do, some magic or miracle, I found no convincing goal for it. Because his life just might have been one long stretch of burning in the inferno of life. In death now, having slouched off his sins unto the hands of his killers, he now had a chance of tasting Heaven, of drinking from that endless ocean of joy; that place devoid of sin and sorrow and weeping and pocket-picking.

Oh, tell me more about it!

That it is all dancing and singing and praising the Lord; that there is no sickness and no hunger and no filth and no mud water and no lack whatsoever, not even of water. There is even no thirst. Only eternal joy for the elect before the almightily Inscrutable. Eternal bliss for them only. Would he qualify?

I moved closer to him, of course with no apparent motive. Just some compelling impulse. I moved closer, and watching closely, I could see that he was now breathing. I looked about me and saw that the crowd had dispersed. Only a few people watched from some distance. I looked at the young man again, and I could see that he was now breathing more noticeably. I bent down, felt his chest – sure his heart was beating. I stood up, utterly confused and yet apprehensive, and I saw that the giant door of the church was now open. A middle-aged man came out, and his flock stood behind him.

"Peace be unto you," he declared.

Again I looked up at him, then at the people behind him, a sudden rush of disgust and anger welled up within me, setting my body ablaze and releasing a million goose pimples. Again I looked at the victim, then at the Redeemers (as they were called), and more bolts of anger exploded within me, reaching and filling me up to the neck that I very badly felt like vomiting or striking someone hard on the face. Instead I jetted out a stream of saliva.

Again I looked at the Redeemers, but I found no words to say to them. I found no words for them. I spat out once again, and then struggled hard within to keep under control the raging fire.

The fire festival flames forth differing colours.

The leader of the Redeemers took a step forward and said: "Let us pray for the soul of our departed brother."

His followers came closer, forming a semi-circle around me and the victim, more people now watching from some distance.

"He hasn't gone that far," I managed to say." If you have a car, perhaps we could take him to hospital."

"You mean, he is still alive?" then he turned to his congregation and said: "Can you see the power of God? Have I not told you that nobody who comes unto Him ever loses his way? Did I not tell you?" Then he shouted a long 'praise God', and his congregation chorused a deafening 'Alleluia?' He turned to me:

"We can still pray for him. My miracle-working God will finish the work He has already started."

I was sure that the only thing that would satisfy me at that moment was to release a Mike Tyson kind of powerful upper cut on this man of God. I knew it. But still I managed to hold myself, resorting rather to words.

"If you can't do better than that, get your fucking arse out of here before someone's blood is shed."

But from nowhere somebody shouted:

"He is still alive."

And in a flash of seconds the mob I thought had disappeared now re-emerged with added weapons and instruments of killing. In that flash too, the Redeemers redeemed themselves from this satanic encounter by quickly retreating into the church and banging hard the door. A quick glance at the mob revealed to me eyes and faces of terror. Layers of sympathy enveloped and gripped me like the firm hold of a woman in labour, and I was no more in doubt. Whatever could be done should quickly be done to save this fellow sufferer of a human being. As my mind raced here and there in fast contemplation of possibilities, I saw a big stone raised by two hands high above every head and ready to demolish.

I had taken my extreme unction. So I had not much to fear as I rushed forward, shouting: "Nooooooo," and crashed into the wielder of that stone, the stone falling with a heavy thud and cracking the marble floor. Every action almost simultaneously came to a halt. All attention turned on me, many tightening their fists and others smacking their lips as if some delicious meal was being served. One looked at another and asked:

"Who's the shit?"

"Oh, a lamb and saviour come to sacrifice himself and carry away the sins of the world," a third person replied. And a general laughter, wicked and deadly, followed.

"He means to show us what stuff great men are made of," another added. "Come, Daniel, and let's see the power of your God. Kill him."

And they all rushed at me. I ducked and avoided the first blow which obviously was intended for my left eye. But almost at the same time a heavy blow almost knocked off my head from behind. Yet another, as hard as a rock on the forehead hit me and I crashed to the ground. Feet trampled and kicked me all over for a while, but high up, when I succeeded in looking in that direction, I could see fists ferociously plunging into faces. Still, some feet trampled on me, but the stage, the ring now, was high above where fists and all kinds of weapon continued to plunge unto faces. And then there was a sudden explosion, then another and another, and a bee flew past my left ear, almost tearing through the lobe. Everybody started running, somebody collapsing and falling on me, while another young man fell just by me rather heavily and without any control. I thought it was his head that first hit that marble floor.

The sight of an AK 47 rifle jolted me, and looking round I saw a group of anti-crime policemen. They had caught and were now beating some people – about five or so. I tried to stand but realised that the person who fell on me was still on my back – somehow my power to feel was cut off. I pushed him off and stood up, wobbling in the process. I noticed, as I stood up, that my shirt was soaked and stuck to my back. I looked at the body I had just pushed away and saw that he was bleeding from the heart region. The second person on the ground was bleeding from the forehead. And it was then that I started feeling some pain on my left ear. I touched it only to discover that blood was dropping. I looked about, and except for the policemen and the few people they had caught, the premises of that church was completely deserted. And there was no sound – no singing or drumming or speaking in tongues – from within the church. Across the street people watched from the safe retreats of their offices and shops. And the traffic had eased up. I was utterly confused and could not fully connect with the gravity of the situation. I turned to one of the policemen:

"Officer, officer, what –"

It was like I had invited the devil himself, for he swiftly pounced on me, slapped me several times, twisted my hands behind me and handcuffed them.

"But, Officer," I tried to protest, "I'm not –"

"Shut up, bloody idiot". And he violently pushed me from behind, and I fell. As I hit the ground with my forehead, the whole world collapsed into an awesome darkness.

Indeed, life has several levels of awareness. Because in that awesome darkness I was only a very tiny dot, a mote billowing back and forth in an ocean of darkness. So I floated until some vibration was felt, first somewhere in that darkness, then in my head (when I regained a head) and finally all over my body which was now somehow jerking as well. To this vibration was added some sound I faintly recognized as that all-too peculiar sound of my first ever ride in a motorised vehicle. My eyes opened, and after some interval of reconnecting with the normal level of existence, I managed to sit up.

I was in a moving police van with three lifeless bodies (handcuffed) and five people all sitting. Yes, the three dead bodies were handcuffed while the five who were alive were not.

But since I had lost, or was no more sure of, that saving world of my dreams, existence had ceased to present any meaningful logic. So it seemed right, illogically, that the dead were handcuffed while the living were not.

"Where are we and where are they taking us to?" I asked. They all looked away. Only one muscular figure kept looking at me. And I wondered whether he too wanted to pounce on me as the policeman had done. That would be illogically right. But he responded:

"I think they are from the famous Ganchi Station."

Then I realised that I was a dead man. Dead and done with. For what miracle would make me survive that place of death called Ganchi? We all knew it; even a day-old baby could tell you that nobody ever detained at Ganchi came out alive or sane. Now I was being taken to this most notorious a place. And I had no money to bribe my way through. Nor did I know anybody who could bail me out. Of all places, Ganchi! Truly, I was a dead man. My cursed life was about to end. I remembered and thanked Jim Reeves. I sang to myself:

This world is not my home

Lord I have no friend like you

If Heaven's not my home

Then Lord what will I do

The angels beckon me

Through Ganchi's open door

And I don't feel at home

In this rot anymore

THE FIRE FESTIVAL

CHAPTER 14:

THE BARE BONES OF TRUTH

And though I knew that the world was not my home, I realised that I was not truly in a hurry to leave it. In spite of the extreme unction. At any rate, I was sure that death through the gates of Ganchi was not a desired one. In spite of all. Not through Ganchi.

"How are we going to handle this?" Once again, I turned to my mates – because I was confused and eager and helpless. Once again they turned away. The muscular one it was who responded.

"Have you got any money?"

"Not even a farthing." I answered.

"That's a serious matter."

"I guess it is."

Just then the van pulled up and a policeman came and opened the cage-like compartment in which we were locked. He ordered us to get down, and as we did that, he added:

"Move to my right hand side if you have anything to declare."

Four people so moved, leaving only the muscular one and me in front of the police sergeant.

"You are not being smart, are you?" the sergeant asked us.

"There's nothing to be smart about this," I replied, feeling angry and desperate and irritated. "We don't have anything to declare, that's all."

He looked at me, smiled and shook his head. "Do you know where you are?"

"It can't be worse than hell," I still replied.

"Well, we'll see about that," he said. Then he came to me, searched my pockets and found only a chewing stick. This he flung with venom. He then searched the muscular one and found nothing.

"Copul," he shouted. And the corporal appeared immediately. "Take the two of them in."

Before the corporal took us away, I managed to approach one of the four and whispered my name and address to him, asking whether he could convey the news of my arrest to my neighbours. He did not utter a word in response.

At the counter the corporal took down our particulars and then searched us once again. Still nothing was found. He then commanded us not to do anything funny as he left.

Toju – that's the muscular one's name – asked:

"Ever been here before?"

"Never been arrested in all my cursed life," I replied.

"But can you use your fists?"

"Can't remember the last time I fought. But I will do anything I can. And I think I know some tricks."

"Well, the only thing to fear here is fear itself. When anyone strikes you, don't cower. Just strike back with all your strength. And don't forget to use those tricks of yours. You need them now more than ever before."

"Ever been here?" I asked.

"No, but I have been to some other stations. They are generally the same. You let them bully you, then you are finished. You must be alert as soon as we enter the cell. And whatever you see me do, do the same. No slacking, all right?"

"I'll do my best," I said.

"There's no choice now, except you want to leave here a corpse. This is Ganchi, you know."

"I've heard a lot about this place"

"Everybody has. Now you have a chance to tell others. Only if you survive it."

"Can we make a pact of friendship?" I suggested, now feeling more desperate than ever before for a solution.

"I've done what I can do for you. This is no place for words or empty promises. Either you kill somebody or you are killed. Here comes the corporal."

The corporal came to me first, searched me all over again, and, appearing satisfied, opened the cell door and pushed me in, with Toju shouting a final advice:

"Strike back and don't forget those tricks of yours."

But before I could fully enter the faintly lit room and even think of those tricks, a quick hand pulled me inside and slammed across my face, another landed on my neck and some feet kicked me on the groin. I slumped but a hand pulled me up and fists jabbed away. And instantly I saw how my life went further down that blind alley that had no exit or return routes. Each blow, each kick sent me further. I saw it all. And it alarmed me, the bare crudity and wretchedness and meaninglessness of the whole thing. I became so alarmed that I was desperate to do something. Then I remembered Toju's advice, and I started striking into the air in all directions, throwing a feeble left here and an ill-practiced right there. But all of it into the air because I could barely see yet. And that effort of mine made the fists strike at me more ferociously, for they now attacked with more vigour. And then some fist struck a really hard and mighty one on the bridge of my nose, and I fell backwards and – when I thought I was now going to rest finally in the bosom of the Lord – I crashed into a bucket of urine. The urine poured and seemed to penetrate the pores of my skin into the very depths of my being.

Have you ever felt like emptying not just your guts but even the blood stream itself? Have you?

And I realized, too, as I was down there on the floor, that dying itself was not an easy business, and that the road to Heaven was rather very long and treacherous. In that desperation I remembered one of my tricks learnt from stories of ex-detainees.

I fainted. Of course just as there was method in the madness of Hamlet.

A little interval passed, and I thought that the method was succeeding. But a hand pulled me up and, with his fist, struck an unendurable pain into my stomach. I almost shouted, but I endured it because giving in would simply stir the beehive of their fury. After all, I had fainted. The hand let go. I slumped. Still with method. Then it struck me again on the neck, and still I showed no sign of life.

It seemed they had given up.

In a moment a hand turned me, face up. And before I knew it urine was being poured into my nose. How could I hold my own anymore? How could I?

I jumped up as if the combined sting of a legion of bees had roused me. The combined assault that followed this discharged a constellation of stars from my eyes. I slumped once again, but this time without method but mad with pain. And that pain shut out everything else from my consciousness but its own deafening roar. That roar itself created, or seemed to create, a disjuncture either in my consciousness or in time. For I only recall that almost suddenly I could now see better. And the cell door opened and Toju burst in and, before anybody could reach him, was already jabbing and kicking and head-butting into the air. About four figures rushed at him, dashing out blows and kicking. He returned both, and at one full span of his right hand knocked down two people. The remaining two seemed to punch more desperately now, and one of them lunched forward and struck a hard one on Toju's right jaw. Toju staggered. Another quick one on his left jaw, this time more confidently executed, saw him finally falling.

But quickly he got up and attacked, launching headlong into the mid-section of one of his assailants, and supporting the head-butt with desperate punches. Just then there was a sudden shout; and everywhere became still. I looked, for the first time, at the other end of the cell from where the shout came, and I saw a man of about forty sitting with regal poise on a chair; with three people standing and fanning him, one on his right, another on the left, and the third from behind. To his right was a caricature of a lower degree royal personage who was also being fanned, but by one person only. The two royal personages were smoking, and from the way it was wrapped, I knew it was Indian hemp. I could perceive only urine.

I watched, still on my knees. Toju was standing.

"Yes sir," someone shouted and swiftly stepped forward and stood before the two men. He was one of those who had engaged Toju.

"Brigade Commandant, have you sampled enough of them?" the second degree royalty asked.

"My unflinching support and loyalty to the government of His Excellency Presido of the Sovereign Peoples' Republic of Ganchi I declare," the Brigade Commandant replied. "Your honour sir, our able and respected 2 1.C. I have sampled enough of the intending citizens. Permission, sir, to give verdict."

"Permission granted," the Second-in-Command said.

"Your Excellency the Presido of our dear Sovereign Peoples' Republic of Ganchi, and your honour sir, our able 21.C., my eternal loyalty to your beneficent reign. May you rule forever. I have sampled the two of them, and I find them fit to be citizens of this great republic. One is strong enough to join the combatants, while the other is fit only as your Excellency's domestic officer. Permission, sir, to present them before His Excellency."

The Second-in-Command (2 1. C) stood up, took three steps forward, turned and faced the Presido, and then said;

"Your Excellency Sir, Presido of the Peoples' Republic of Ganchi, our own and only Presido who alone in the history of the world has foiled ten coup attempts, our own dear Presido who single-handedly took on five disgruntled dissidents with his bare hands and triumphed over them."

"Yes father, you are the one," voices chorused.

'My unflinching support and eternal loyalty to your government," the Second-in-Command continued, while the voices followed after him.

"Our unflinching support and eternal loyalty to your government."

But that was not enough for one among the crowd who stepped out, fell in prostration and shouted;

"Oh, father, do with me as you please, for you are good."

Again the chorus:

"Oh father, do with us as you please, for you are good."

"Permit me, your Excellency," continued the Second-in-Command, "to permit your Brigade Commandant to present the two intending citizens of this great republic. My loyalty and eternal support I declare once again."

At a wave of the Presido's left hand, the person fanning him on the left stopped. The Presido did the same for the person fanning him on the right, and the man stopped fanning and sat down. It was now only the person – or more appropriately the fan – behind that continued to work; and he was a boy who could not have been more than sixteen years old.

The Presido, who had barely opened his eyes all along as he smoked away, now graciously raised his head and opened his eyes, a roll of hemp in his mouth. And as he did that, three people rushed forward, prostrated before him and declared:

"Yes Father, you are merciful and kind." Then they stood up and stepped back.

The Presido looked left, right and then centre. Then he observed the roll of hemp in his mouth – like he had just become conscious of it – inhaled for about five seconds, held the smoke in relish before finally puffing out. And with that the whole republic echoed "Yes father." Then he muttered:

"Permission granted," smoke coiling out of his mouth as he spoke. And as he said that the whole cell erupted in a thunderous applause, many falling before him and proclaiming:

"Blessed am I to be alive to see this day."

"Not even from the Capitol has ever emerged such a beautiful speech."

"Oh, father is great!"

"You are merciful."

"May you reign forever."

The Second-in-Command then nodded approval at the Brigade Commandant who then asked Toju and me to come forward. I lazily stood up, but before I could take the first step, two people rushed at me and shoved me. Another approached Toju, possibly with the same intention, but Toju acted swiftly and gave him an upper-cut. That settled the matter. Toju then walked forward and joined me.

The Brigade Commandant turned to the Second-in-Command: "The Presido of the Peoples' Republic of Ganchi. Your honour, sir, able 2 1.C, permission to permit the Minister of State for Information to perform his duty."

The Second-in-Command stood up again and came before the Presido:

"Your Excellency the Presido of the Peoples' Republic of Ganchi, my support and eternal loyalty I declare. Permit me, your Excellency, to permit the Brigade Commandant to permit the Minister of State for Information to perform his duties on the intending citizens of our great republic. Once again I declare my eternal loyalty to your Excellency."

The Presido did not waste much time this time around, neither did he deem it necessary to open his gracious mouth. He only nodded approval, and everybody clapped, a few shouting "yes father." Then the Second-in-Command nodded approval at the Brigade Commandant who in turn nodded approval at one of those who shouted "yes father."

He stepped out, cleared his throat and looked at me somewhat curiously. I turned to Toju to avoid what I considered the wicked fire of those eyes. And I think that I also sought to enlist Toju's aid, or at least a signal on what to do. But his gaze was straight. The Minister of State for Information turned and faced the Presido. He did not immediately speak. He rather looked intently at the Presido, ardour in those wicked eyes of his, smile of admiration, nay, of worship, on his face and the whole Republic waiting in pin-drop silence. Then he took one calculated step and lay flat before the Presido, lifting the Presido's feet and placing them on his head – his head became the Presido's footstool – and declared:

"My Most Revered One, my shield and provider, most merciful and kind, the youngest ever to be initiated into the noble business of snatching our due from the pen robbers, the only one so far who stormed the army barracks, took from the feared Commanding Officer himself and returned unscathed, the great lion and provider of the tribe of the needy, most loving and adorable one, father, you are the only one."

And the chorus was indeed loud: "Oh father, you are the only one."

"Bless us, father, that our strength may never fail us," the Minister continued.

And still they chorused:" Yes father, bless us that our strength may never fail us." They all lay flat before the Presido.

Much as a king satiated and bloated with pride in the reaches and riches of his vast empire, our Presido nodded his head with royal elegance. Then he took a rather long inhalation of the hemp, held it for perhaps about a minute and poured it on the Minister's head. The Minister seemed immensely pleased as he raised his head, swallowed as much of the smoke as he could, and declared:

"You are merciful, father."

The chorus did not fail.

The Minister then stood up. His chorus stood too. But he had not had enough:

"The only one who held up traffic for hours and took with impunity while the police ran for cover; the one and only Presido whose unparalleled achievements will cover pages more voluminous than Shakespeare's Complete Works."

Voices hailed and hands applauded and bodies fell again in prostration.

"There is no one like you." The chorus followed up.

"My utmost support and loyalty I declare not just in this world but also in the world beyond," the Minister still declared. The chorus still echoed.

"Your honour, our able 2-1.C., and to you, too, our gallant Brigade Commandant." Then he turned to Toju and me.

"I am His Excellency's Minister of State for Information, a position I occupy not because of any personal merit, but because of the grace and kindness of our Presido. This is the Peoples' Republic of Ganchi, and it is sustained by the might and love of our dear Presido. As you leave the outside and false world into this our dear republic of truth, you will need to throw into the dustbin those elegant lies and pretences of civility which hide the barbarity of that outside world. Life here is lived with a brutal candour and clarity. Everything here is by His Excellency's grace and whatever you say or do must accord with his wishes. So the most important task for you is to learn to read His Excellency's wishes at every point in time. We all have learnt to do this over time, and you have no choice about that. The only exception is Prof over there," as he pointed to the extreme end of the room.

It was then I realized that what had seemed a silhouette was a human being. He was sitting in the lotus position at that point where the two ends of the wall met and joined, and he maintained a tranquil repose, like one in the seventh heaven. His large head seemed ready to fall any moment, and it took no effort at all to count his ribs. Yet he had this strange dignified poise and a seemingly imperturbable calm. But – the Minister was still talking.

"I shall now call on the Minister for State on Information to carry on from here."

And with that he turned to the Brigade Commandant and asked for permission to permit the Minister for State on Information to perform his duties. Then the Brigade Commandant asked for permission from the Second-in-Command who in turn asked the Presido. The Presido nodded approval, and the approval was nodded down the hierarchy. The Minister for State on Information stepped forward, faced us and started.

"I am His Excellency's Minister for State on –" but the Presido cleared his throat. The Minister broke off, turned swiftly to the Presido and prostrated.

"My most merciful and revered leader, your Excellency, my kind and beloved Presido of the sovereign Peoples' Republic of Ganchi, my support and unflinching loyalty now and even after the hour of my death."

His Excellency nodded, and the Minister stood up and continued; "Our able 2 I.C, the indefatigable Brigade Commandant, and my prolific and ever versatile Minister of State for Information, my respect to you all." Then he turned to us:

"I'm His Excellency's humble Minister for State on Information. Before you become full-fledged citizens of this great republic, it is necessary for me to do my duty which is to let you know the structure on which our republic stands. Here, as you may have noticed, we try to raise the banner of truth to its highest pedestal and without any adornment or make-up. It is survival of the fittest, and might is always right. Experience has taught us that all human organizations practice this philosophy; the only difference between these organizations and our great republic is that they are not honest, as we are, enough to proclaim the truth of this philosophy. And we proclaim it from the rooftop. Later, you may have a chance of listening to Prof expound this philosophy. For now, it is helpful to bear in mind that our Presido is Presido because with his bare hands he ripped open the stomach of the previous Presido. Also always remember that our dear Presido is the toughest and the best, and no regime can be better than his. That is why we don't entertain any stupid ideas that go contrary to his will. I need not waste energy as you will learn."

Here he turned to the Minister of State for Information and said: " Permit me, honourable Minister of State for Information, to permit the honourable Minister of State on Special Matters to collect the naturalization fee from the intending citizens."

The request then passed from the Minister of State for Information through the Brigade Commandant and the Second-in-Command to the Presido. The Presido nodded approval, and this passed down the line to the Minister of State on Special Matters who prostrated before the Presido. But before he could say anything the Presido ordered:

"Cut it out and collect the fee."

The whole cell exploded in a bout of clapping and shouts of "Yes father." The Minister then stood up and turned to us.

"Come here, you" he ordered me.

I moved closer, though wondering why they must always start with me instead of with Toju. For his response and conduct would have given me some idea of what to do if it got to my turn.

"Let's see what you have as your naturalization fee," the Minister directed.

I did not know what to do or say, so I turned to see if there would be any sign from Toju. He looked indifferent and – but the Minister slapped me, a hot stinging slap. And as I rubbed that side of cheek, the Minister followed it up, this time on the other wide.

"Are you a loyal subject of His Excellency the Presido of the Peoples' Republic of Ganchi?" he asked and slapped me again.

"Yes I am," I found myself saying.

"Then pay your naturalization fee," he ordered.

"But I don't have any money," I replied.

It was a blinding slap that followed.

"But I have no money with me," I repeated. I then became a punching bag as he attacked me and punched away furiously. When I had received enough, my knees gave in and I slumped on the floor. But that was not all. Two people rushed at me, dragged and held me up for the Minister to finish his job.

"You have no money, eh," and he punched again and again and again.

"Make him shit it out," he commanded the two.

Immediately, they removed my trouser and shirt, and some-one brought a bucket of waste. They sat me on it.

"Shit it out," the Minister still slapped. Then he ordered the two to leave me. And as they did that, I fell out of the bucket.

"Oh, you don't want to do it yourself?" the Minister asked me.

"Fuck it out of him," the Presido ordered.

And the cell was rent again with joy and applause and "yes father, you are merciful."

The Minister of State for Special Matters was almost in a frenzy. "The stick!" he shouted.

Again a general shout of joy followed as someone brought the stick to the Minister.

"Stick his arse out to heaven," he gleefully ordered.

And – but their animal joy, that animal joy overflowed once again in shrieks and all sorts. Lips were evidently smacked.

Three people rushed at me now, dragged me up and forced me to bend down, my head between my legs and my anus facing up. The Minister then stuck out his tongue, licked his lips methodically and smacked them. There followed a general smacking of lips and rejoicing and applause. The Minister then ran his hand up and down the stick, and raised it to strike right into my anus. The festive expectancy was unimaginably superfluous.

I looked at Toju. He was still standing and looking somewhat indifferent to the situation. It was then that I realized the complete hopelessness of the situation. But then I summoned up all energy within me and was about to shout and plead for mercy from the almighty Presido when Toju declared:

"Touch him at the cost of your life."

And everywhere became still. The Minister's hand hung in the air with the stick, and the three people holding me let go, mouths open. I stood erect now, not knowing from where I suddenly go that kind of strength. The Minister finally dropped his hand and turned to Toju.

"Can this be true?" the Minister for State on Information queried.

"A challenge to the authority of His Excellency the Presido of our dear republic?" the Minister of State for Information added.

"Let him who can dare," Toju challenged still, immovable in his elephant-confidence.

At this His Excellency the Presido stood up and threw away the wrap of hemp he had been smoking. The boy fanning him continued to fan the chair. The Brigade Commandant then fell before the Presido and pleaded.

"Your Excellency, grant me the privilege and honour to handle this. It is too little for your Excellency's might. Grant me the honour, oh father!"

But the Second-in-Command wanted not just the honour but also to prove his office. He declared:

"My most mighty one, honour and grace are the droppings of hard-won victory over the dragon, and they rightly belong only to you. But I would rather be dead than remain alive and watch you lower that honour by taking on so inconsequential a fly as this. May my little office handle this little affair?"

But the Presido waved them both away. Then he took one long stride forward and stopped. The capacity-full stadium erupted once again in applause, with many shouting.

"Oh father, you are the best."

"A disgruntled element come to test the might of my republic or just an ignorant child trying the explosive anger of his father" the Presido asked, looking intently at Toju.

Another round of applause followed this, but the Presido shouted it down. The cell became still. Then he resumed:

"A serious contender for my honour or a child seeking fun in the hole of a scorpion?"

"I play no games, much less with someone's life," Toju responded, still looking immovable. "But if you doubt me, then touch my friend for measure."

"Your friend to my honour." Then the Presido laughed. A general chorus of laughter followed. "Shut up you fools. I want no sound anymore from any idiot."

"In all the years that I have snatched my survival picking pockets, I have come to learn not to toy with a few things. One of such is friendship. Let him dare touch my friend who can eat fire," Toju declared.

The Presido took one, two, three steps and stood directly before Toju. They were roughly the same height, but the Presido was sturdier and more muscular. And as they stood face-to-face and looked straight into each other's eyes, everybody else retreated to the wall. But I was still by the bucket now feeling much stronger but worried about what was going to happen next. For here was someone who had now taken over my burden, one who had possibly saved my life. Here he was face-to-face with that Presido who was said to have committed all kinds of evil, and who could any time put an end to the life of my saviour and friend – a friend whose sacrificial action now told much more than anything he said or could have said at my earlier proposal for a pact of friendship.

Again, it stirred the fire in my heart that something so noble could still be found within the human heart. It stirred my heart to tears.

But that cell was no place for tears either of joy or agony; for there was little or nothing of the colour of joy in all that took place there, whereas agony was its cream so thick as to smother every other sensation; and even too thick for tears.

"My wrath is only on him who impinges on my honour," the Presido declared and struck a swift right hand at Toju. But Toju was alert as he blocked the assault with his left hand. The two hands hung in the air.

"I don't –" Toju tried to say but the Presido struck another quick one into Toju's stomach. And it was on target. Toju recoiled momentarily and then returned a series of blows. The Presido too struck left and right in quick succession, while Toju threw in his own too. They struck away at each other, they struck and struck and struck until Toju scored an upper-cut which somehow unbalanced the Presido. This infuriated him and he now attacked more ferociously, teeth clenched and all the muscles in his body standing out, the veins like electric cables. Toju returned left and right too, but the Presido was now beside himself as he closed his eyes, teeth still clenched, and struck and struck. Toju seemed to want to take advantage of the Presido closing his eyes, but the Presido struck into every direction almost at the same time that there was no opening of any sort. And as he struck, he yelled a wild animal shout and swung round swiftly and kicked Toju somewhere around the neck. Toju fell on his knees, but quickly got up, staggering. He seemed to have been taken by surprise. The Presido yelled again, and this time the whole pack of animals in the cell yelled along with him. It was a very strange kind of sound, maddening and disorienting. On the wave of that madness the Presido launched forward, punched and punched and then swung round and kicked Toju again on the same spot.

Toju fell again, somewhat hopelessly now. But even as he fell and tried to stagger back to his feet, he still threw feeble punches here and there; which was nothing to the Presido who now yelled continuously and punched and punched away until Toju collapsed on the floor.

But the Presido was thirsty for blood, for he wagged his tongue as a dog's tail and slobbered. He jumped on Toju and let loose a hail of blows. Toju did not return any. Then the Presido dragged Toju to the wall and stood him against it. Toju could not stand. Then the Presido made a shrill meaningless sound; but that sound was not so meaningless to two among the pack who rushed to Toju, dragged him up and held him against the wall. The Presido thereafter moved back to the opposite wall, yelled again. The cell yelled with him. The whole cell was mad for blood.

As I was mad with concern over Toju who did not seem to be in this world again. Frantically, I searched my mind for what to do to save the situation – for it was for my sake he was now about to be killed. And it seemed better, much more honourable, that I should be killed along with him than thereafter face an eternity of the flaming pangs of conscience for my inaction at this critical moment. He who had taken my burden off my shoulders and was now paying dearly for his heartful action.

I would rather die with him than face the fires of conscience thereafter.

But I could not think out anything practical – I mean a way to use either words or my fists to some advantage. And I realized that as I struggled fruitlessly to think out a solution, I was continuously chiming God God God... Not that I knew who or what this God was, or precisely what I wanted from Him or Her. But I realized that the song in my consciousness was just God God God. ... And I knew it – but you ought to understand what I'm saying – I knew it that this song flowed from my heart, but when I tried to reason about it, I found no meaning or sense in the whole rubbish. Then my heart said aloud:

"Please God help!"

But the Presido yelled a continuous one now, and the pack yelled along, and he ran forward and ran his head as a bull into Toju's stomach. Toju sagged the more, but they pulled him up and held him still against the wall. My heart was now pounding wildly and about to jump out of my body.

"Please God help! Please God help! Please God help!"

Still I did not hear from or see this God.

And, lo! That most revered one, most merciful and kind Presido, he now yelled another loud but different yell and lifted up his right hand, his finger's outstretched like a cartoonist's image of a witch's. The wild and joyful uproar that followed this was unprecedented, and many shouted.

"Oh yes, father, do it, for you are merciful and kind."

I realized he was going to rip open Toju's stomach. I knew it. I became uncontrollably desperate as I searched feverishly for what to do.

The Presido was now ready to launch forward for that blood-letting blow. I closed my eyes in order not to see this, but my heart knocked open those eyes.

"Please God help Please God help! Please God help!"

The Presido yelled and launched forward again, his hand out-stretched in front, and the whole cell yelled along with him. And as he launched forward, I swiftly grabbed a bucket of shit and poured the waste across his path. His right leg it was that stepped into it, and he slipped and fell heavily with the back of his head.

The ensuing silence in the cell could freeze a bottle of hot water. I watched the Presido, just like everybody else, to see what he would do. Time stilled into an eternity of intense anxiety. But only minutes slipped away during those anxious moments, just as the life of the Presido seemed to have slipped away. For he showed no sign of life. And, all at once, something seemed to dawn on everybody as all eyes moved from the Presido to me and back to him. And though none spoke out, I could see their words:

"Let us wake from this dream, let us wake."

Which gave me some courage to approach the Presido. As I examined him, he started blinking his eyes. I almost retreated in fright, but I remembered one of those things I had watched on *Wrestlemania*. Quickly I pulled up the Presido – and that took stupendous effort – then pushed his neck into my armpit and fell heavily with him, hitting his head on the floor, I got up and dragged him up once again, but he sagged like a wet sack. That, however, could not deter me. So once again I pulled him up (and that took virtually all the strength in me that I almost collapsed), did like heretofore and hit much harder his head on the floor. I repeated the same procedure three times more before I then examined him. He was far gone.

Then I took some steps away from him and looked round the cell. Prof was still in his contemplative silence undisturbed by all that was going on – and it appeared that had some bomb exploded in that cell, he would still remain undisturbed. Everybody else was more or less as still as Prof. Only that their eyes seemed ready, from fixedly staring at me, to burn me to ashes. But I was saved because there was little or no fire in those eyes. I walked to Toju who was now resting against the wall.

"How bad is it with you, my true friend?"

"I'm alright," he whispered more or less. "You have done well. You saved me."

"But you saved my life, and you suffered because of me."

"You've done well, very well. You are now the Presido, you are Presido," he whispered and staggered up. Then he took my right hand, raised it and declared.

"Long live the new Presido of the Peoples' Republic of Ganchi!"

That was what broke that long spell which had engulfed everyone but Toju and me; for now they all prostrated before me and shouted.

"Long live the new Presido of the Peoples' Republic of Ganchi. Our honour and loyalty to you, our new Presido."

And that was when it dawned fully on me that by defeating the Presido, I had become the new Presido. That was the unwritten but irrevocable law of that jungle – that the greater demonstrated and proven power must be in control. Somehow it seemed right; for why should power be given to the weakling and the novice. He would simply drawn himself in its alcohol.

That cell was now a universe under me, and I smiled within as I watched them all lying in prostration before me. But much unlike you might expect, it was not the laugh of victory and that extra-large egotism of power. Some soldiers within me took up arms against the charade before me. It was a repulsive sight.

"Rise everyone," I ordered as a king.

They all got up and sat on the floor. Only Toju and I remained standing. But the mockery had to proceed at any rate. In spite of the soldiers on rampage within, I took Toju's left hand, raised it up and declared.

"Long live the Second-in-Command!"

They applauded and chorused.

"Our support and eternal loyalty to your Excellency the Presido of the Peoples' Republic of Ganchi, and to our able 2.1.C."

The Second–in-Command to the former Presido stood up, quickly removed his shirt and pair of trousers and prostrated before me.

"Your Excellency," he started, "the one and only Presido to defeat the longest ruling enemy of the people, the one and only Presido who has single-handedly released us from the bondage of a man of bottomless cruelty, the one and only Presido whose face radiates the mercy and kindness that we all desire with all our hearts and souls, my unflinching and unalloyed support to you forever and ever. And to our able 2-1.C., most power-packed and wise in the ways of our republic and of the world, honour to you. Your Excellency my Presido, it is not fitting that your Excellency should stand naked before his subjects. Instead of your Excellency being naked, let it rather be me your humble servant. Permit me, your Excellency, to clothe you in these wretched rags of mine."

I had completely forgotten that I was naked. I ran a cursory look down my naked body, and then looked up. The former Minister of State on Special Matters was flat on the floor before me, completely naked. He too had his song:

"Your Excellency, Sir, the most merciful and most kind, the one and only Presido whose overflowing jar of mercy keeps us going, my support and eternal loyalty I declare. Your Excellency, the honour of your person is too pure and holy to have any association with the filthy and the dishonourable, much less of being clothed in a pair of wretched rags of dishonour. Permit me, your

Excellency, to have the honour of clothing you with these more befitting clothes of mine."

I smiled a smile I did not fully understand. Perhaps that kind that you smile when the whole world seems to be under your feet, and you realize that in spite of the immense fever, that there is nothing to it. And you smile at the emptiness, the emptiness of all that has no heart at its centre, that does not emerge from the heart. That was how and why I smiled at that moment. I wanted to talk, say a few things, maybe heartfelt, to them, but the smile was still on my lips, and I could not thus speak from the heart. So I looked down, closed my eyes and shook, somewhat violently, my head; the goal being to shake off that smile. I succeeded in some measure. And when I opened my eyes, the former Minister of State for Information and Minister for State on Information were flat on the ground before me. Of course both of them were naked, and their clothes were on my feet.

"No no no!" I said, shaking my head out of irritation. "Can't take anymore of this. Please stand."

But they remained flat on the floor. And it struck me that it perhaps had to do, if only partially, with wrong choice of words on my part. Wrong register.

"I order you to stand up now," I said.

Of course before I knew it they were all up.

"Tell me your names, four of you. First the former 2-1.C."

"Your Excellency, most merciful and—"

"Just your name, your name only," I cut in as more and more of the soldiers in me were on rampage.

"Your Excellency, my name is Uba, and I was —"

"No more but your name," I said. "You, Special Matters?"

"Your Excellency, my name is Abu. Thank you for your kindness, your Excellency."

"Of State for Information?"

"Your Excellency, my loyalty I declare now and all the days of my life. My name is Une."

"And you for State on Information?"

"Your Excellency –"

"Just your name."

"Your Excellency, my name is Enu."

Again I surveyed them one after the other, and pictures of the human condition in its most abject wretchedness and debasement flitted across my consciousness. As Presido I would have liked to address them. But I would like to do that only as a Bill Clinton, that is with confidence and poise and charm and beauty of the heart during a State of the Union address. But I had none of that, and I was faced only with a pack of animal-human beings to whom the only appropriate address would be on the state of our wretchedness. But to what end?

"I thank you all for the honour and professed loyalty," I said. "You say I'm your new Presido, I know, but I will not dispossess any man of that which rightly belongs to him. Let me have my own clothes."

"Fetch his Excellency's clothes," Uba ordered.

And there ensued a mad scramble for my clothes. After some moment of struggle during which blows and kicks were exchanged, two people finally grabbed my trousers and a third my shirt. But Uba snatched the clothes from them and presented them to me.

Slowly, I put them on, Uba and Abu struggling to be of use. But I refused any help whatsoever.

"Shall we sit, your Excellency?" Toju now.

And I burst into perhaps the only hearty laughter since I entered that dome of death called a cell. I could not help asking:

"You mean you too will play this foolery of excellencying me?"

"As your Excellency wishes."

"Even if others have to address me by that, you don't. In any case I don't want anybody using this excellency stuff for me."

"As you say then," was Toju's response.

And as we were about to sit on the floor, Uba and Abu rushed to the former Presido's chair, grabbed it and quickly dragged it to me. I shook my head to affirm my rejection as Toju looked at me.

"Take that at least," he urged. "You are now the Presido and there ought to be some difference. Take it."

I sat on the chair while Toju sat by me on the floor. Then I ordered them all to sit. They did.

Something was stirring in me. It was, and I knew that if only for a while I wanted to be still, just be still, without any concerns, not about me, anybody else or even about our mad world. But something was stirring in me, and I cried in my heart. I cried because I knew I could not be, much as I wanted to. I just could not. What was wrong with me?

I turned to Toju.

"I could not have believed it, had I been told the story, that this level of animal-like fist-throwing and bootlicking kind of life was possible with human beings, more so of our so-called civilized modern age. But here it is well established and in full bloom as a way of life. I find it unimaginable and totally unacceptable, and I don't see how we are going to continue like this. Changes have to be made so that we can live like human beings. I need your support for this and for many more."

He seemed to reflect on it for a while. Then he said:

"In health and in sickness I promise my support. But do you think that such changes can work here?"

"I don't see why they shouldn't. After all, these people have not always been like this. They were forced into this by the need to survive. I think we can as well create a situation where they don't need this level of dehumanization in order to survive."

"Can such idea work in a police cell?"

"A police cell, as well as any other environment and situation, can be humanized. It is what we make it."

"Well, let's see how far."

"My name is Eno," I started, "and henceforth I wish to be called by and only by that name. I want no more of this Excellency stuff. Is this clear?"

"Yes, your Excellency," they chorused.

I could not help laughing. Toju too, advising, "you'll need to give them more time to get used to the idea."

It was well to give them time to get used to the stuff, but there was some other stuff I was becoming conscious of and which I knew that, given even eternity, I could not get used to. Somebody was fanning me from behind, and when I turned I saw it was just that boy who had been fanning the former Presido. He was just fanning, his gaze fixed on the chair and his expression showing only a determined commitment to a task besides which nothing else mattered in the world.

"Find some place and sit," I said.

But he did not move. Neither did he stop fanning. He just continued as if I had said nothing to him, as if I did not exist.

"Stop fanning me and go and sit down," I ordered.

But the boy continued like before.

"Sit down," Toju shouted.

The boy continued. I stared in disbelief.

"Your Excellency," Uba stood up, "Your Excellency, I know, I can explain, I know what is wrong."

"What is wrong? That I ask him to sit and he refuses?"

"I mean, I know what is wrong with the boy."

"What is wrong with him?" Toju now.

"He cannot stop fanning. That's how he is," Uba explained.

"What do you mean by that? What are you trying to say?"

"Your Excellency–"

"Stop this excellency business and call me by my name," I cut in. "Tell me, if you say you know, why the boy cannot stop fanning."

"I don't know the full story, but –"

"Who knows the full story?" I interrupted.

"Nobody here except the former Presido," Uba continued.

"In that case tell us the part you know."

"Well, the boy is deaf and dumb, but he was not like this before. Nobody here knows the full story because he arrived here before us. He was a member of the former Presido's robbery gang. The gang went to a bank on an operation, and actually succeeded at the bank. But it ran into a police ambush, and a shoot-out ensued. Forty lives were lost in the encounter; twenty pedestrians, fifteen policemen and five of the robbers. The Presido escaped but eight of his men were arrested, and they made statements which led to the arrest of the Presido. He was then thrown into this same cell as the other members of his gang who had been arrested. One after another they died rather expectedly but unmysteriously. Only one of them survived, and that's this boy. They said the Presido loved him and allowed him to remain alive. But he burst the boy's ear drums. It's not totally clear how he became dumb. Some say the Presido administered an oath on him never to speak, while others say that it was the result of repeated assaults on the boy's throat by the Presido. Since I came here, the boy has done nothing than fan the Presido. The only time he ever takes a break is when he falls asleep, usually once a week, and he sleeps standing."

"Which Presido did this to him?" I asked.

"Same as the one you've just silenced."

It was then I recalled that he was still on the floor. I looked at him, but he was as still as a dead body.

"I hope he is still alive," I turned to Toju.

"He deserves nothing but a slow and painful death," he replied. "But the devil may not be dead yet. Anyway, I will take care of him if he ever wakes up."

But I was not ready to take chances with that Presido, I mean, suppose he was not dead and maybe suddenly got up. Where was the strength in me to match his? So I asked that his hands be tied behind him.

Quickly this was done.

"What's your name?" I tried what I now knew was impossible. He did not even look at me. He just continued fanning. I moved some distance away from the chair, but the boy continued fanning, his eyes fixed on the chair. Then I asked that the chair be moved. This being done, the boy followed the chair, fanning it with fanatical devotion. It occurred to me that the boy might even be seeing the image of his Presido on that chair; so that to him his dedication to his Presido remained unquestionable.

My mouth was full.

"Can you see what I've been talking about," I turned to the waiting eyes. "Can you see what I'm saying about where this kind of animal life can lead one to? Can you see how someone, with all the nearly limitless latent potentials of a human being, has been reduced to this condition of non-being? Can you see? And a small boy for that matter! But let's leave this boy's matter for now. Tell me, whoever knows, what do we do with this devil?" as I pointed to the former Presido.

"Cut his throat as he has cut many people's throats", the chorus was unanimous.

"Did you see him do it or is this just one of those many stories?" Toju came in here, and adequately gave expression to what was on my mind.

"The only surviving member of his gang is this boy. The rest died here", Enu now.

"Only last week he killed a student who was arrested and thrown in here for participating in a protest march. The student had nothing to give, and in addition was rude and abused everybody". Uba added.

"So what did the police do?" I asked.

"Nothing", Uba still. "I mean nothing that we are aware of. They removed the body without any questions. And that's more the reason why we should cut his throat. We should cut his throat, or else he may recover and live to kill many more people."

"Yes, he surely deserves to die, but I don't feel comfortable with this business of throat-cutting. I do not see how I can lift my hand to do that", I said.

"But you do not have to do it. I will be happy to do it myself. I will do it with song in my mouth. If we don't do it now, he could come back and do something worse to us. The rule of his life was that either you killed and prospered thereby or you were killed. Prof captured this philosophy so well that the Presido gave him leave to do as he liked. If you don't mind, we can listen to him a little".

Of course he was there at that far corner where two walls met, there he was, immovable and in voluptuous contemplation.

"Is he a real Prof or just the Prof of the cell?" Toju asked.

"He was a professor at the University."

"Really? So how did he end up in a place like this?" I put in.

Uba had the gist on his fingertips:

"His coming here is connected with the last abortive military coup. During the few hours when the coupists took over the radio station, Prof – like everybody else – thought the coupists had succeeded in removing that government. So Prof, in a sermon at the Church that morning, criticized the government, claiming that it was the misadministration of that government that produced the coup. But the coup, as we all know, failed hours later, and Prof was arrested and thrown here. They say he was silent for the first twelve days – and many people thought he had become dumb. But on the thirteenth day he spoke and the first word he is said to have uttered seven times is Canimanism, and the philosophy he has been expounding ever since then is known by that name. If you would like to hear him, I can seek his face."

Of course philosophy of any kind had always attracted me, and I would not miss the chance to hear this new philosophy – even if it was born from the slime-life of this cell. I inquiringly turned toward Toju.

"If it pleases you," he responded.

I nodded approval.

"Let's hear him," Toju directed.

Uba then went to Prof, and instead of touching him to wake him from his trance-like state, knocked three times on the floor. Then he waited for about a minute during which nothing happened. Again, he knocked, this time five times, and then waited a little longer. Still Prof did not stir. Then he knocked a third time and now seven times. He did not wait for long before Prof now slowly opened his eyes, and without looking round, focused his gaze at me. There was some disquieting fire in those eyes, and this was worsened by the fact that he stared without blinking. From the way he looked with a near-perfect composure, one would think that he was the king of the whole world rather than a starved and insane detainee at Ganchi. But he was Shakespeare's Roman soothsayer:

"I warned him to beware of the ides of March", he said as he continued to look at me.

But it struck me that that day was the 15th, though not of March.

"You have naught to fear if you eat the bread and drink the wine of Canimanism."

"We disturbed you in order to hear that philosophy", I said.

Which, indeed, was a great sacrilege; for Prof frowned and tightened his face as if he suddenly went into some intense pain. Eyes, of course, were closed.

"You don't talk while he's talking. You only listen," Uba whispered.

But Prof had returned to that world of his, far far away from the roar and grime of that cell. He was like someone in a trance. And we waited and waited and he would neither open his eyes nor speak. Again Uba knocked seven times before Prof slowly opened his eyes.

"The beauty of ideas, from planes of mind high, what a waste to cast to dogs," he started. But silence followed this for sometime, though his eyes were now open. He resumed.

"Canimanism is a philosophy of conquest because the beauty of all life lies in conquest. The glory of the animal kingdom is the conquest of instinct; that of the animal-man, the herds of the human family, the conquest of emotion; and of the philosopher-king that of the mind. Conquest, indeed, is the watchword and you conquer not but by making war. Glory, therefore, to the war-makers and mongers. War must be perpetuated if the race is to advance. The greatest and fastest progress recorded by the human race is the result of war. A man who does not set himself at war with himself has not yet started living and is unworthy of the appellation 'human'. Make war wherever you are, for it must be perpetuated if there is to be beauty in living."

"Listen not to the honeyed tongues of vipers who speak of the greatest good for the greatest number. They have no courage to face their own emptiness, so they hide in the sea of mass life and splutter and mumble therefrom. They scatter droplets of honey along the wide road of the masses in order to draw to themselves the dog-devotion of unthinking followership. Seize your sword and strike down him who stands between you and your goal. The race has always been and always will be for the fittest, and the glory of the race lies far more in producing one philosopher-king than in satisfying the lustful thirst of the sleeping millions. War is the watchword of progress."

"Morality is ever the vomit of the fickle-hearted, they who are feverish and sick of life and so want to take the fire of war out of all life. But no man ever conquers without first burning in that fire. Strike then below the belt if it serves the purpose of the philosopher-king. Why should it count that millions have to roast in the oven so that the superman may have his way? Why must a man of war vacillate in the halls of morality and allow the blind millions to perish in their very blindness when he could have led them unto that flame that produces the philosopher-king? The race ever is for the fittest, and war is the only road to progress. Therefore, seize your sword and strike down. Else, the one-eyed man will strike you down and drink your blood and gloat over it and be worshipped."

"This is poison coated with honey", I said with purpose.

And Prof frowned, recoiled and froze into his contemplative trance as a snail into its shell.

"He will not speak again", Uba said, "at least not today anymore."

We waited for sometime anyhow, but Prof had left our world.

"That's a Nazist reading of Nietzsche," I said.

"Who is he?" Uba asked.

Toju was blank; so his expression announced.

And I realized that I was actually talking to myself.

"There is something in that philosophy which sounds true, I mean from my experience of life in the street. Yet, something in me does not like it. I don't know." Toju now.

"That philosophy is poison coated with honey," I repeated. "You must not think about it, and I advise that you just carry on with your life as if you never heard this."

Of course as all that was going on, much was brewing in my mind. I was there with them in the cell, but that thing, that silent but nagging voice within which always stirred my failed life to trouble, that voice was actively at work again and would not let me be. In the cellar of my mind, then, were many bottles of ideas, and quickly I opened and tasted from as many as I could. There always is something to choose. I addressed them:

"I would like to know the names of the rest of you, and what offence you committed that brought you here. But that has to be later. For now I want to make some suggestions regarding how we live here. And note that I said 'suggestions', meaning that we are free to accept them or not."

"We will accept our Presido's suggestions", someone said among the yet unidentified.

I wanted to but thought it of no use pursuing the argument. I simply went ahead:

"We all know that Ganchi is the most notorious station in the world. But it is so because we the detainees have made it so. Granted that the authorities are not doing what they are supposed to do, we still can make here a liveable place. The first thing I would like to suggest is that we stop attacking and beating new detainees. We should find some better ways to welcome them, and we should allow them to contribute whatever they have to our republic. The second suggestion is that we should agree to empty these buckets of shit each day. It is not healthy for us to keep depositing mound upon mound each day when we can easily empty the buckets. These are things we can do for ourselves, and I will start the process by being the first to empty the buckets."

But they all shouted noooooo, somebody adding:
"Our Presido must not touch shit. We will do it."

"I thank you all. But I insist on starting the process because as your Presido, I am here to serve you and not to sit cross-legged on a burnished Olympian throne."

And this threw the whole cell into a wild applause and all kinds of hearty comments:

"My Presido is a man of words."

"He swims in words as fishes in the sea."

"My Presido is the only genuine Prof; all the others are fake".

"Ah, my Presido, I doff my short for you," which, indeed, he did.

And many more such. Which was not what moved me. A joyousness stirred in my heart because heartiness, some life, was now beginning to stir in them, they who had appeared to know nothing else than either fisticuffs or boot-licking of the Presido. More than I can express now, I was encouraged, and much now brewed in my heart.

The heart is a wonderful cellar. Does its wine flow through you to others, does it?

"The third and final suggestion for now," I resumed, "is that all positions, from the Presido down to the lowest post, should be attained through election and not through combat. These are my suggestions for now, and I would like to know your views."

Toju it was who responded first.

"I would not have considered at all such proposals some hours before now. But having gone through this experience with the former Presido and considering how you saved my life, I have come to realize the importance of cooperation and group effort. There was no way I could have survived that encounter with the former Presido. The sum total of what we each can achieve as individuals can never measure up to what we as a group can. If, for instance, the Presido wakes up and finds that we all are ready to do battle with him, that is as a team, he will have no choice than to join us because no matter how powerful an individual, his strength can never match that of a group. So I will try henceforth to work for cooperation among all, and I support these proposals."

Applause followed this. A few more people spoke, with only one dissenting voice arguing that the proposal was too idealistic to work in such environment as that cell. However, the suggestions were adopted – nineteen people for, and two against. Of course Prof was not part of the whole thing.

But I remembered or rather an idea struck me, and I added.

"One other important thing I forgot to include in my pro-posal is that whenever any of us is released from here, he should try whatever he can to help those who may still remain. Do we accept this?"

Everybody assented, and as we congratulated one another and shook hands, the cell door opened, and a policeman pushed in his head.

"Who is Eno?" he asked. And, without waiting for a reply, ordered." Get your things and come out."

"What have I done now?" I queried. "I'm alright here."

The policeman, or his head rather, laughed a deep guttural one and said: "You sure you're alright in the head? Anyway the D.P.O. has ordered us to release you."

"Release! Release!" And I walked down to him.

"Yes, you're released. But you will see the D.P.O. first."

I was about to start rejoicing when I remembered Toju.

"But we are two. What about the second person?"

"The D.P.O. is waiting," he said.

I turned and looked at Toju. He was already seated on the Presido's chair, smiling.

"I'm alright here as Presido, even if only for a while. It's better than the risk of picking pockets. And be sure that I will carry out our decisions."

"But we –" I tried to say. But the policeman gently pulled me out and banged the door.

I could not understand this gentility. But I did when I met the D.P.O.

"I'm sorry, Eno, but you did not tell us you were a journalist", he explained, a national newspaper spread on his table.

I could not quite swim along with him. I was puzzled.

"Is this not your name here? And even your photograph?" He too was puzzled.

I looked at the paper, and then I could now connect. I now and then did freelance writing for that newspaper, and a story I had sent in about a month back was published that day. This, some would say, was divine intervention.

"Well, yes, it's me, and I write for that newspaper," I assured him.

"We're extremely sorry that you got mixed up in this. But you should have told us that you were a journalist. Please accept my sincere apologies."

He waited to hear me, but I found nothing to say because I was still confused about who I truly was – considering this privileged treatment being given to an imagined journalist who had a voice across the country and therefore could tell a tale about Ganchi.

"I apologise once again, my friend Eno", he continued. "I hope you are alright – I mean you were not hurt in there?"

Of course they knew about it all. But say something:

"No, not at all."

"I'm glad about that. Please regard me as a friend, and feel free to come to me any time. The Corporal will ensure you have all your things back."

I was at the door and about to open it when his infested hand touched my shoulder. I shuddered. He withdrew it, surprise on his face.

"I'm – I apologise once again. But just one last thing." And then he almost whispered: "Please, nothing about this in the newspaper."

"Nothing," I said.

He sighed. "Thank you my friend. And come to me any time."

I walked down the street with a blank mind, but that street, with all its cursed and blessed features, instantly acquired a new colour of inestimable beauty. May be it was because of my just-regained freedom; I was overwhelmed by some kind of light joy, and I carefreely walked down the street in that elated mood, my movement almost swift.

But I could not so swiftly push out of my mind that D.P.O. who said he was my friend; a one-sided friendship. Nor that Toju was now Presido, pickpocket turned Presido of the People's Republic of Ganchi. Just like you – frustrated and failed and unemployed a-minute-to-graduate-but-expelled young man. You should appear in the Failed Persons Tribunal and give account of your evil life. You should.

And that was how my light joy was drowned, a condition which was worsened when I saw a child walking down the street with a bucket – I was supposed to be searching for water. Then my spirit fell completely low, really low, and I fell deeper into that void where the waters of abundant life were just a myth. And I burned in the fever for that water. Because I was not a stone. Because I wanted the feel of that assuring hand.

But no hand touched me, and only the unattractive face of hopelessness unveiled itself in my consciousness. And it did not just unveil its face; it also sang:

Welcome to my world
Where all is in shards
Welcome to our mud
Welcome to my rot.

I was used to that, but also my extreme unction had its own logic. So I fought back with my own song:

Today today
Today today
My Saviour will answer me

Today today.

Because I was no stone.

Somehow the song lifted me in some way, lifted me up to a world faintly magnetic and as well illusory.

CHAPTER 14 | THE BARE BONES OF TRUTH

THE FIRE FESTIVAL

CHAPTER 15:

THE TOWER OF ILLUSION

A s the University too had lifted me into its own world, charming, magnetic and illusory. And as soon as I walked into that tower of illusion, I was swallowed completely by that charm, its promise of life. I swam rather away from the shallow ends to the deepest depths of that sea so that I would be cleansed enough to finally succeed in raising my head above the consuming stench of my life. There was nothing anybody could have said to make me believe that the beast was also here in full nakedness, nothing that could have been said to make me accept that it was not yet *Uhuru*. Some persons, however, sensing the hunger of my soul through the fire in my eyes, did whisper warnings. But I thought that the whole thing was said in bad faith; for where else could that purifying and thirst quenching word be found. I was to wait a few years before I burst through the cloud. And the word, which had seemed so near, was never so far, so far far out.

The promise, which the University dangled before my eyes, so consumed me that I buried myself in the written thoughts of ages, communing with that world in which the thoughts of ages both past and present merge into a seamless eternal now. I left my room for lectures in the morning everyday of the week but weekends, and from lectures to the library where I would read till close-down. Then I would return to my room where I would have my dinner and then read into the early hours of the following morning. During weekends, I practically opened the library with the staff, just as I closed with them. And my cave, my favourite corner in that library, was a spot on the penthouse of the seven-story building. You could count on your fingers the number of people that ever bothered to climb the stairs up to that Penthouse. It was a hermit's mountain-top retreat, and each day I was there I blessed those who ever conceived the idea of such a retreat from the maddening crowed. The crowd truly maddens!

I still am searching for the joys of the hours spent there.

This, in truth, was my routine. And it seemed like I could now shout it from the mountaintop that I was a human being. And this because for the first time I found people who adequately expressed my emotions and fears, emotions and fears that many times had made me place question marks on my sanity – because often I saw that other people were not truly free of that baggage of filth which I dragged along; only that they did not seem to care, or they did not even know. Now, the more I read, the more I found better articulations of hitherto tormentous and unexpressed ideas. Life, indeed, had never been so good, I mean to know that many people across time and place thought and felt and battled with the same ideas and emotions that had been sapping the roots of my being. What more could one do but gulp down this breath of life?

Which indeed I did in order to strengthen the roots of my shrivelling being.

But the fruits of that endeavour were falling farther than that: I set a record of distinction in all my major and elective courses, and being the best result, won the faculty prize which meant subsidized tuition. In addition to my scholarship.

Was this life, my life?

Of course I had not been working that hard either to pass or to fail. I was just discovering much and enjoying myself. But now that I knew that much more benefit than I had imagined also went with such effort, I decided to work even harder in the second semester.

Therefore, when the semester started, I tried to resume the former routine of study. But to my surprise the fire of zeal was not so fierce any more. I struggled and struggled to at least maintain that routine – if I could not improve on it – but I realized that I needed a raging inferno to burn out the lethargy that was increasingly settling on me.

I knew not how to start off that inferno.

And when I succeeded in forcing myself to read, the material casually sipped in without stirring any fire.

Still I knew not how to start the fire.

And at times I would come to the library and stare and stare at a book in front of me for hours. At other times I would shout abuses at some idea or position which appeared stupid. As interest in reading gradually waned, I now spent much of my time wandering around the campus and haunting quiet and desolate places for the peace that I could not find within; and such places seemed to hold some promise. And much that had hitherto interested now only irritated me. Human contact was far worse – what with those bland, indifferent or animal-innocent faces with mouths that frittered away only lip-deep words! What agony to hold myself and not strike at someone. Away from the maddening crowd! Far far away!

I had not quite made many friends, and the only person I so regarded, Ifeh, I consciously avoided. But he always sought me out, and we always managed to get on some harmonious track. He was an aspiring writer – as I was – and we had met at Literafest, a department organized weeklong literary fiesta. So with him I could let off some of the steam of those crushing puzzles of life and perhaps was thereby saved that second semester which drifted on that boring and barren course. There was no fire in me, or if there was, it was either at a very low ebb or it burnt the wrong end of me.

Vacation was a great relief. As death could be!

The second year started on the same note, and perhaps might have so ended but for Ifeh who did all he could to draw me into writing once again.

For I had started writing in the tense interval between my dismissal from National Cosmetics and when I entered the University. I just realized that I could write just as well. So when I entered the University, I assured myself that I would have completed one book at the end of my study. But the world of ideas, that world of great thinking minds which I discovered during the first semester, kept impressing the idea into me that I needed to read a lot more in order to write a good book. Yet, that first semester was a period of relative creative success compared with the second semester when I would often brood over a line or phrase for hours or days.

My discussions with Ifeh centred mainly on literature and philosophy. And we did spend much time arguing. But through this interaction, I kept hold on the vision and managed not to fall into bottomless darkness. It was on account of this thread, my hold to it, that I succeeded in discovering the pedestal from which to leap.

Which, in truth, was my contact with Socrates.

His name actually was Maso, but not many people knew him by that. He was a lecturer in the department of Philosophy, and his class was the largest in the faculty. Even at that, many people were glad to have the opportunity to look and listen through the window wherever and whenever he lectured. How he became known as Socrates was not clear, but anybody who knew him and who had read about the Greek Socrates would agree that he was the Socrates of the University; although I did fervently wish that he would not be forced by ignorant and reactionary forces to down hemlock.

It was for me that the University reserved that full cup of hemlock, not for Socrates.

I had heard about him in my first year, and I had decided to register for his course as one of my elective courses come second year. This I did, and though I found, during that first semester, little or nothing to stir me in the lectures I attended, I however managed to continue attending. And I used to wonder why many of those who called themselves lecturers could not find some other occupation than teaching; their cold and lethargic existence was enough to quench the fire in any thirsty student. I did not see that they stirred, or even hoped to stir, anything in the students who were mostly eager to stenograph and then regurgitate at examinations.

I managed, however, to continue attending those lectures, my only prayer being that they would not succeed in drowning in me some incipient embers.

Embers which were suddenly fanned into a full blaze the first day I entered Socrates' class. That day he taught for about three hours, giving notes and quotations without looking into any text. But it was not really that. His words were not just words as had dropped from the mouths of all the lecturers I had met before then – words all too cold and lifeless and therefore meaningless. Words as flowed forth from the mouth of Socrates were not just words; they had a power of high intensity radiation, a life pleasantly magnetic and uplifting, and a meaning whose combined radiation and magnetism shook the depths of my inertia – but what does all this mean to you? What?

But they fanned my fire into a blaze.

And as I watched him teach and demonstrate, as I watched him walk from one end of the lecture hall to another, I found it difficult to believe that something of that worth was standing before me – or that this mirage from my dream world was an actuality. But he was right there with the full force of a living presence, a radiant joy and vitality pouring forth from him to us.

Did others see him as I saw him, did they see that much in him? Or was it my own madness?

But that radiant joy and vitality touched me with a dynamic immediacy, and some seed which had been lying deep within the recesses of my consciousness spontaneously sprouted and shot forth. And I knew, deep within and with an unquestioning certainty, that many things were possible with me.

As with any other human being.

Nietzsche's concept of the unfixated possibilities of growth inherent in man was the central thrust of Socrates' lecture that day. And when I got to the library that evening, I combed the catalogue and borrowed all the books I found by and on Nietzsche. The next seven days I did little else but study the books, discovering and sharing in those manifold possibilities of man – indeed the rope between animal and god; I identified very much with the possibilities of man to assert his freedom or the alternative of submission to an animal existence; I shared much in that will unto power which, when balanced by the will-to-be-good, was the will-to-be-god in each and all of us; and his praise of the spirit of adventure, that spirit to dare, which leads into uncharted seas, that creative impulse without which progress and innovation in all sphere of life is not possible.

And much more. And much more.

It was an invigorating dive into a regenerative world of ideas. By the time I finished reading the books and stepped out of my room, strong and my spirit incredibly high, I went, head in the clouds, straight to Socrates' office where we exchanged ideas for more than four hours. At the end of it all, Socrates succeeded in persuading me to join the Reformers' Academy, a study group of which he was the head.

My cup of hemlock started filling up.

It was a group of about fifty members, many being students while few were university workers. Expectedly Socrates was the founder. The group started with no ideological affiliations as such, nor did it have any set beliefs. What it aimed at was to study different philosophies and schools of thought across time and place, and then come out with its own ideas for social reformation.

We divided ourselves into groups of three, each group assigned a specific subject to study and present before the general house. Whenever such presentations were made, questions were raised and more contributions made. Therefore, if it was agreed that the study had worthwhile contributions to human uplift and the spread of good-will, it was circulated to each member for more focused study. Copies were also sent to the media.

The fire of this period was, in truth, intense.

So much that at the end of that second semester, I did not go home during the vacation. I stayed in school studying and discussing with Socrates; for two of us were in the same study group, and it seemed that the progress of the Academy depended on how hard we worked. All through the vacation, I stayed with Socrates in his house, constantly studying and exchanging ideas. Much mental cloud was cleared for me. And we interacted like mates, like two souls who had known each other for millennia; sharing everything freely and giving ourselves to each other.

It was a period of fire.

As it was of great discovery. Because for the first time I could feel the concrete-reality of an aspect of that vision which always nudged. I could see that one could truly completely give oneself to the other – without fear, without suspicion, without hate but all in trust and love. I found in full livingness a very important part of that vision – the great healing value of human company, the invigorating power of loving living, of sharing and trusting. I, hitherto, had felt and seen this only in the nebulous world of my dreams. But now it had a full form, the full moon of love.

Oh, this fire was radiant, yes it was.

And I started building, as I was always wont to build, a castle-dream of a world in which each person would love everybody else; a world in which there would be no hate, no injustice and no wickedness; a world in which, in an effort to uplift the race, one could attempt to walk across any needed slim-rope of chance without fear, walk across any stretch of taut rope in confidence because one knew that whichever way one fell there always would be hands waiting to rescue. I started dreaming of a world in which everybody was unhappy because some human being somewhere was in the grip of sorrow; a world in which everybody was hungry and thirsty because one fellow human being was hungry and thirsty; a world in which everybody else agonized and lamented because someone somewhere was in agony and lamentation.

Because these were the unspoken terms on which Socrates and I seemed to relate. And that seemed to be the deep hunger of my soul; a hunger which is the root of sadness or joy.

That blessed Man of sorrow and suffering!

By the end of the vacation, we had been able to come up with a draft of a guiding philosophy for the Academy. This draft was adopted, after some additions, by the group. Thereafter, we broke up into new groups and committees for further studies, now concentrating more on topics as non-violence, social reformation, love, selfless service, justice and truth; such topics being the pillar of our philosophy of life. As we carried on with our studies, we also invited non-members to give lectures on some of these subjects, while engaging the services of the leader of the Judo Club for our physical training exercises. For the goal was a sound mind in a healthy and fit body.

Were we crazy?

And every member was to relate to every other member not just as colleagues but as beings whom one could trust and depend on. Each person was encouraged to share, willingly, whatever he had with him who needed but did not have.

Do you think we were not crazy?

But we found out, as is mostly the case, that there was considerable gap between these words and their actual practice. Obviously, effort was made by some, though few, to practise these ideals, but the many parasited on them and only received without giving. And Socrates would always calmly explain that this must be expected, and that it needed not disturb those who were true to our ideals - or at least attempting to be.

As these things happened, I discovered that I could hardly attend lectures. It was not that, had I so chosen, I could not make out time for lectures. The fact was that I found the classroom dry and unchallenging. And the dogmatism of it all, just like that of orthodox religion, that one-eyed myopic kind of seeing, it made me feel as if I was being straitjacketed.

Knowledge must free, not limit or hamstring.

However, I kept abreast with what was going on in the department through Ifeh. And owing to my voracious and interdisciplinary studies at the Academy, I did not find the examinations difficult. Many were surprised that I still took the first position in the faculty.

I resumed the second semester of that third year so engrossed in study and work for the Academy I usually forgot to take my meals. And Socrates was not so regular as he used to be, so that it seemed as if the task of the leadership of the group was on my shoulders. So I laboured very hard to meet the needs at that level. But, at some stage, I had to take up this matter with Socrates.

"Comrade," I confronted him one day in his office, "I hope it doesn't sound as if I'm complaining. But I suppose that with you there is little or no fear of speaking out."

"Feel free, brother", he returned.

"You are no more regular in the Academy as you used to be, and I can't help wondering what is happening."

"Two things basically," he responded. "The first is that with or without me, the movement must stand on its own. The aim, as you well know, is to train a group that will not rely on the person-ality of any individual. It must draw its strength from the general pool generated by the contribution of each individual member. I am the founder, but I must not be too strongly visible so that the group may establish this group life and power independent of me. Therefore, I am attempting to gradually sever the umbilical cord. This should not sound strange to you."

"No, it doesn't, and I think I understand."

"The other point is that I have some thorns on my feet to remove. I need to remove these in order that I may walk more strongly and contribute my share of the work. That's how far I can explain that for now. But you need not be bothered about this, and you may as well forget that I mentioned this to you. What's important to keep in mind is that the movement is growing and consequently has ahead days of trial in form of turbulence. Such experience is not to be lamented or feared because it holds much promise of learning; which, after all, is all that matters. And every true reformer has to pass through that flame in order to bring forth that pearl which endures and shines forth the light on to the world. And do not just accept all that I have just said because it is said by your beloved brother. Above everything, submit it to the smithy of your heart."

So I carried on with the work like that, hardly having any breathing space from the ever-widening range of our activities. Ifeh, whom I had tried but failed to persuade into joining the Academy, kept coming for our usual give-and-take of ideas. Through this I was able to keep alive my interest in creative writing such that I resumed work on a collection of poems.

But the work of the Academy ranked above everything else – because it was something I believed in with all my heart; it was that kind of thing one could lay down one's life. And, because of this, it filled a need, a hole, an emptiness in my life. It did, the Academy.

And from a strictly study group, we progressed to discussing matters affecting the university and even taking positions on these matters. Our positions were usually made known to the public through press releases, much of which I wrote. Our initial releases were unsurprisingly greeted with the usual scepticism and indifference of students who are eager more for bread than for ideas – you know that scepticism which always says: Oh, they are all the same. But after six such releases and we embarked on a three-day hunger strike in solidarity with an expelled student, it became clear that we had become widely accepted. Ours then became the voice of the people, although I always ensured that it did not get muddled up in the noise of the people but only poured some clarifying light.

Much later, after that full cup had been downed, I was to think that the whole mistake started when we decided to start taking positions on issues on campus and letting the public know through the press releases. Because it was after we had become known through these press releases that many aggrieved persons started coming to us to help them fight for justice. Most of these problems were either with the school authorities or the students' union which was little else than an extension of the Vice

Chancellor's office. This, inevitably, brought us in direct confrontation with the authorities, in spite of our non-violent method.

But confrontation need not be violent.

We took up so many matters and we became so popular that when it happened that a group of fraternity members attacked and matcheted a student, the whole school did not expect only a press release from us; they expected us, as many told me, to act.

Indeed the matter proved a very contentious one during debate in the Academy. What seemed to make it complex was that I could identify two members of that fraternity whom I had seen in complete regalia on the morning of the incident. I was returning to the room after studying for the night – that was when I saw them. So that the debate was whether or not I should appear before the Disciplinary Committee investigating the matter to give evidence. Many argued that we would be inviting the kind of trouble we were not equipped to battle if I went ahead to expose the culprits, while more felt that this was a perfect chance to practise much that we had been reading and preaching about truth and justice. At the end, majority voted that I should appear before the committee.

But would they go with me down to Calvary, to Golgotha?

We prepared the evidence we had, the most concrete being a recorded interview with a member of that fraternity (incidentally the Vice Chancellor's son) in which he admitted that he was among the gang and that he tried everything he could to prevent the attack. How we were able to get that confession on tape was the idea of Tom, a strong member of the Academy. I took care of the actual interview, with the Vice Chancellor's son not knowing that the conversation was being recorded on tape.

So I appeared before the committee, told them all that I saw and knew, and then deposited the interview. The Chairman, a Professor of Law, turned and said to me:

"We do appreciate your selfless and painstaking effort in getting this evidence. But, if I may ask, do you think that the world out there is like that?"

I was not quite sure of what he meant or even whether he expected an answer from me. So I simply stared at him. He too stared, shook his head knowingly and said:

"You children of these days think you know everything. By the time you are thrown into the streets, you will begin to know the truth about life."

When I came out of Senate Chambers where the committee was sitting, I was shocked to see a crowd of students waiting. Word had gone round, I was to learn, that the Reformers' Academy had incriminating evidence. That seemed, for whatever reason, to be what the students expected from us. And it did not matter whether the task required some superhuman power. The Reformers were capable – that was what many said. So that as soon as I came out of Senate Chambers, somebody shouted from among the crowd:

"Greatest students! Behold our hope."

And many rushed towards me. Before I realised what was happening, I was high up on somebody's shoulders with hands propping and everybody singing praises of me. As the procession marched on towards my hall of residence, it swelled in number as more and more people joined.

I was not quite comfortable having somebody carry me on his shoulders. So I asked the person who had chosen that task to put me down. I was rather firm and insistent before he agreed. And just as he was doing that, before I could even step on the ground, another head had pushed in between my legs and lifted me up once again on his shoulders. Of course he was the fastest among the many contending heads. How would I convince them that I preferred to walk?

As I could neither convince myself that I should be wholly happy with some twists in the unfolding story. I truly had not expected it, and I was not sure of how this would be understood among my comrades in the Academy; for I had taken it, as many others had, that everything we were doing was being done in the name of Reformers' Academy. And so it was anyway. Even the press releases I wrote never carried my name as the writer. It was just once that one such release bore my name. And that was the mistake of the Secretary who typed my name on it. In any case, the house did unanimously agree, when I suggested an amendment to have my name removed, that it did not matter. Now it was my praise that was being sung, not that of the Academy. I did not like this portent.

Just as I was now beginning to think of and fear the Professor's portentous statement about my being thrown into the streets. Because I risked everything to aid the course of justice? Because an untouchable, the V.C.'s son, was involved? And then a so-called Professor of Law would so speak, so shamelessly unmindful of that law.

Was he *professing* the Law?

I was so carried high and away on the wings of such thoughts fanned by the emotion-stirring processional songs that when we got to my hall of residence and I was now allowed to stand on my feet, I did not know exactly what to say to the mass of students who were expectantly looking at me. All eyes were on me, murmurs dying down as I stood on some platform. I could start my own battle with that Professor here and now.

"Fellow students, I would like to thank you, on behalf of the Reformers' Academy, for your support and cooperation. We in the Academy believe in the brotherhood of all, in justice, love of all, non-violence and truth. It was because of this that the Academy mandated me to appear before the committee."

"We are all behind you," someone shouted.

"At all times," another added.

"Even into the lion's den," a third assured.

"Comrades," I continued, "in line with the wishes of the mass of students and the mandate of the Academy, I have presented the evidence before the committee."

"You are the sun of our lives," again from the crowd.

And many more such that I had to cut into in order to continue.

"But I must tell you all that from what the Committee Chairman said, this may just be the beginning of our struggle."

"We will fight to the end," again they started.

"Aluta continua!"

"Tell us what he said."

"Yes, tell us what he said."

"Sure I will tell you," I assured them. And indeed I did.

"What did he mean by that?" someone queried.

"Did he mean that as an insult on our generation?" another followed.

"But theirs is the wasted generation," someone shouted. And voices shouted the more, some abusing while others were insisting that we should immediately march in protest to the Senate Chambers and disrupt the proceedings. I waited until they had somehow emptied some of the fire of anger in them. Then they quietened down some bit.

"Dear comrades," I now continued, "it should not surprise you much that the professor should have said what he said. It is a typical reflection of the smug ineptitude of their generation; their generation that had it so good. Of course, you all know that they are the blessed generation who had everything going for them, they who had it so good because a mountain-size cake of opportunities was presented them. You may each ask yourselves what they have left for us, they who had it so good. We all know how deep into this mountain they have burrowed, eating up all there is to eat and leaving for us that enervating emptiness of suffering and hopelessness; that is all their gift; they who did not face so much mass impoverishment and displacement; they who did not experience the frustration of the academic calendar being torn and scattered into unimaginable bits; they who did not have to devise all kinds of feeding formula because they could not afford three meals in a day; they who did not have to walk and wander through our cities for years without jobs; they who did not, as employed graduates, starve and walk long distances to work because their salary was too paltry to feed and transport, much less appropriately clothe, them; they who did not have to deny their nationality and themselves in order to escape from the country into lands of greener pasture; they who had it so good, what are they leaving for us; tell me, my people, what are they leaving for us?"

And voices shouted: corruption, moral stench, depraved values, godfatherism, mediocrity, self-serving leadership, and many more things jumbled up in that market of voices. But I continued.

"What can they say now, that generation of wastes that has taught us that money, at the expense of good name and integrity, is the most important asset in life? What can they tell us now, that generation of destroyers that has erected staggering and formidable structures of moral depravity which block and frustrate any genuine and honest endeavour; what can they tell us now? Can they truly look into the fire in our eyes and then beat their chests without any uprising and repulsion in their hearts? Can they do that?"

I paused to swallow saliva. Nobody stirred. Add more fuel, add it, I told myself.

"Fairy tales they are now of how students used to enjoy well-balanced meals in the universities; of how students and authorities could plan ten years ahead because academic calendars were always stable; of how the dining tables of knowledge overflowed in abundance for those who truly sought to know; of how prospective employers used to come to the universities to scramble for graduating students; of how a graduate-worker could buy a car within a few months after getting a job. All that is the story of the blessed generation of our leaders, and these things were possible because some human beings – and not angels from Heaven – laid down structures that made possible these blessings of life to these blessed ones of the wasted generation. What structures have they laid, that generation of destroyers, what structures have they laid down for those of us coming after them? What is it, dear co-sufferers, that they are leaving for us? What can you see?"

I paused once again, and solemn faces stared. I could still work on them without bursting the sack of their anger yet – although a beautiful face was now sobbing close by, and the tears were just a free flowing river. It would be more useful to burst that sack in the next phase of the struggle, not now when it was not yet clear how the university authorities through that committee would descend on me. Burst not the sack yet. Only push it up a little more, and then leave it hanging.

"At no time in the history of this land have the ordinary people had to suffer so much dislocation, unemployment, hunger and deprivation. Let no one deceive oneself that life after school presents any blue-chip cards. Out there only those who have connections and godfathers get the few good jobs – because such jobs are always created, whether there is need or not. The rest of us, who believe in merit and hard work and excellence, and who struggle to keep the flame of knowledge burning, many of us end up frustrated or scavenging at the huge heap of menial and ill-fitting jobs, many more roving our cities in vain, and a few retreating to distant villages where, they very well know, their certificates have no meaning, much less relevance. What a shame!"

"What a shame!" they roared.

"We can see now, or so this cursed generation of destructive leaders wants us to believe, that it is better to receive than to give; that it is better to tell lies than to speak and live by the truth; that it is better to make as much money as possible, and by all means too, than to live a noble and honest life; that it is indeed bad, if not a crime, to be good while it is good and heroic and admirable to see slime and call it gold. Many now wonder what it means when some mad people mutter the mad phrase; 'die for one's country.' But above everything (and this is the truth we all know deep down our hearts) is that all this is just the vomit of a generation of destroyers, a band of wild beasts let loose into the innocent and fruit-laden garden of our country, of our earth. What an inheritance!"

"What a shame!" still they roared.

Again I paused to allow it all go down very well. Many shouted abuses here and there at that generation. More tightened their faces. And on another beautiful face tears rolled down. Her face was tight, gaze immovably fixed on me, and she cared not to wipe her flowing tears. How beautiful persons always struck deep chords in me! And looking at that face that moment, I knew that all I needed to go down to Golgotha was available, and I knew too that for sure one or two people could walk that long journey with me. They could.

Fulfilment is all about beauty and harmony in living.

"We are the cursed seedlings of a generation of destroyers," I shouted more powerfully now. "But it is no tragedy that we are the drained dregs of a time who must hunger and thirst and suffer in the desert created by our predecessors and leaders; it is no tragedy that we are the slime of the time who must suffer and panic and watch our dreams fizzle away. It is no tragedy that we must bite our fingers and lips in agony and bitterness that our predecessors do not give a damn whether we have air to breathe or not. It is no tragedy that we are the inheritors, from our predecessors of the wasted generation, of the inferno of abject lack and utter deprivation. The tragedy, dear fellow sufferers, lies in whether we are going to follow their footpaths and cast only images of desertification and death and thereby bequeath a worse inferno to those who are coming after us. The tragedy, dear ones, lies in whether we are going to fold our hands and sheepishly watch them destroy our future or whether we are going to carve out a more dignifying and noble path for ourselves and children, whether we are going to retire to sleep and wait for the heavens to come down in their own time and do justice or whether we choose to take our destiny in our own hands and therefore confront headlong and through struggle these destroyers and murderers."

"That is it, dear co-sufferers, that is the choice before us. Shall we watch and allow them destroy our future or shall we revolt and carve out a path for ourselves and even for succeeding generations. That is it, dear ones, whether or not we are going to search for, rediscover and re-establish that saving path of light shining through the deepest darkness of the history of humanity; a path we all know to be hallowed and sanctified by the heavens."

"But out of this moral debris must rise life glorious and true and beautiful, whether they like it or no; out of this darkness must shine light; out of this deep and dark pit a rope to climb out; out of this decay a cleansing. This earth belongs to us all, and we must claim and play our part in it. Out of this debris, fellow sufferers, must rise new life wholesome, if from us that now bear the burden of tomorrow on our shoulders. Thank you all for your love."

For a moment nothing happened. The stillness was such that you could almost hear the breathing of the person next to you. And all eyes, hardly blinking, were on me, and I could see the fire in those eyes. And I could look into them with no shiver in or violence to my heart because it simply was a deep sharing and communion of souls – in spite of our individual weaknesses. And in that communion, in that silent moment we spoke without words and signed without pen a pact. It was all written in the heart of each and all of us. Because there was naught that we asked for except the chance to live and strike our chord within the symphony of life, that chord as emerging from the deep whispers of our hearts, the fire of the heart. Because reduced to its basic essence, this is the dream, even if unrealized, of every life.

The silence that sounds, that silence.

It was a solitary clap of the hands that broke it. And a thunderous applause followed and lasted and lasted and lasted that I wondered whether it would ever stop. But it did stop. A voice raised a song of battle and we all sang and cursed the perpetuators of injustice and corruption and sundry vices. Another raised a song of solidarity, and we sang and swore that we would fight even with the last drops of our blood. Tears were also shed here and there, and in its bucket was a mixture of joy and sorrow. The fire of the heart was the spring. And in the silence and well of that spring, someone suggested that we should march to Senate Chambers and demand for justice.

"Dear comrades," I took over, "it gladdens my heart to know that we have all chosen the path of struggle, however arduous and trying it is. We have chosen the right course. But to achieve good results in our struggle, we must be calculative and constructive in our thinking. Now is not an auspicious time to march to the Chambers. Let us wait till the Committee comes out with its verdict. Then we shall know in what direction to move. What is important is for you to always answer us whenever we call on you."

"Call on us even if it's midnight, we'll answer."

"We are behind you always."

"Aluta continua."

"I assure you all," I continued "that the Reformers' Academy is and always will be ready. For now, let's disperse, but having it in mind that a lot of struggle is ahead of us. Thank you all."

Again a solemn song was raised, and we sang and dispersed.

When I got to the room and sat on the bed to collect myself and know what next to do, I realised that the fire was far from being out. My mind was in a wild and jumpy state, different scenes of the day's activities moved up and down the market-scene of my consciousness, and different faces from the crowd zoomed in and out. I then decided to go to the library and try and still my mind through studying something of interest.

But those smiling faces of presenters on CNN must tell you of their agonies too.

Because I could not do much in the library as every minute one person or another would come to greet and congratulate me on all I was doing on campus. And it usually was about what I, not the Academy, was doing. The stream of compliments became too much that I could stay no longer in the library. I took my books and went to Socrates' house where I spent the rest of the day.

I returned at night to my room and found a note for me on the door. I opened it and it read:

BLOOD ON YOUR HEAD

And the paper was smeared with blood – or what looked like it.

I knew it was from that fraternity, and I knew too that the danger was real. Immediately I took it to Socrates who then sent round a notice of an emergency meeting of the Academy for the following day. Thereafter I returned to the room, confident that the four members of the Academy squatting in my room were enough security for the night. I might not be attacked in the room, knowing that I had that number of people around me.

The four of them were back to the room when I got back. I showed them the threat letter and we all agreed it would be safer and wiser for me not to make any movements that night anymore. And we were to be extra-vigilant.

I tried to rest on the bed, but obviously this was no time for rest. My mind ran here and there in search of some solution and approach to the situation. And realizing that it would be difficult to think clearly with my mind in that state, I decided to read any of the books that always held my attention and admiration. Therefore I picked *Strides Toward Freedom* by Luther King, and, resting my head on the pillow, started reading. I had not read for long when it occurred to me to lock the door. When I dropped the book and got up from the bed, I realized that I was alone in the room. I came out of the room but could not find any of my companions. I returned to the room and stayed.

A sense of urgency and danger tugged at me and I became rather very worried as I could not immediately make sense of what was happening. I came out of the room once again, but I found no sign of any of them around. It was then that it occurred to me that I might have been abandoned. I returned to the room and locked the door.

I sat on the bed, and, looking round, realized the enormity of the danger I was facing. And my mind now started beating, started beating very hard and fast. I got up from the bed and started pacing about the room. I had read about sacrifice and martyrdom before now, and I had somehow thought that I was ready for these. But now being so close to danger and possible death, I was sure that I had a different idea about martyrdom and sacrifice – I mean I now knew I would not, as a lamb led to the slaughter, surrender. For one thing, I was sure that I was not ready to let a gang of ignorant and beastly boys destroy my life for nothing. I had read and spoken much on the principle of non-violence, and the Academy had adopted it as its method of struggle. But as I was abandoned in that room that night, and faced with the danger that the threat promised, I knew that if only for one moment I was going to forget that principle. I had every right to defend myself against that kind of senseless destruction. I knew what those fraternity boys had done to many students, I knew of many senseless slaughters, and of many more that had been maimed. But if I was going to be maimed, I was now sure that I would have to maim first, that I would have to kill first if I was going to be killed.

That was my resolution at that moment of intense burning as the fire of danger burned before me and threatened to consume my whole being. And just now that I was also burning with intense zest for life, that life that was now taking some definite shape.

So I went ahead gathering all available instruments of violence that I could lay my hands on when I heard a knock on the door. My heart almost jumped out of my body.

"Who are you?" I shouted.

But it was only Socrates. I opened the door and he came in. He did not even look round to ask.

"They have disappeared?"

"Yes," I responded.

"You know not your friends yet at Bethlehem. Only those who reach Calvary with you can truly be called your friends. But, above all, always remember that they are your little brothers to whom you must demonstrate the meaning and quality of love."

"I see all that more clearly now," I responded. "But I won't deny that I'm rather surprised. If someone out there among the students in general did this, I would find it easily excusable; these are comrades, or are supposed to be. And –"

"No cloak or garment we put on ever changes what we are within. The cloak of a comrade in the Academy or anywhere else could just be as much a disguise for a rogue as it is for a saint. Look therefore for the colour of the heart in all. But, if I need repeat, they are your brothers who need the strength of character you can demonstrate more than you may think you need them. Give them that, no matter the situation."

Then he seemed to notice all the weapons I had gathered. I waited to hear his comment, but there was none.

"Self-defence," I explained. "I put them together after I realized that I had been abandoned."

"Principles and philosophies can be hydra-head and are truly worked out only in moments of tension as this. But it may be helpful to bear in mind that much in life is relative."

This was typical of Socrates when he wanted neither to praise nor blame. I did not find it comforting at all.

"Why don't you visit Luther and Gandhi while I commune with Jesus the Christ," he suggested.

And that was how we spent the night reading. Of course I dosed off several times, and each time I woke up I saw Socrates either reading or ruminating. When it was daybreak, he left for his house. And I started preparing for the day when Ifeh came in.

"I hear you are now their target?" he asked as he came in.

"Well, somebody always has to be. But from where did you hear?"

"I spent the night at the Reading Room, and it was there I saw one of your room-mates who then told me," he replied.

This was interesting to me. I pushed further. "Did he come there to read too?"

"I had thought so. But he slept throughout. In fact he was still sleeping when I left at about 5.30."

What more confirmation did I need that they deliberately abandoned me?

"So I guess the whole school now knows that I'm a wanted man," I said. "Anyway, it's a small matter."

"It's no small matter; it's no small matter at all. You have to take every measure to protect yourself. These guys are bad and dangerous, and you know that. I think you should report to the security."

"So what can they do, being unarmed?" I asked.

"At least let it be known that you did report, I mean, in case anything happens."

"Well, I'll see to that. But how do you stand before your muse?"

"Oh, not so highly favoured. Mainly average rate of production, and lacking verve. Sometimes I work on just a line throughout the night."

"Is it that dry?"

"Yes it is. The only consolation is that infrequently pages just flow and flow as a stream from its source, and usually with little or nothing to correct. But this is not the rule."

"I wish I could create a little more time for writing. I'll have to find a way round that."

"That reminds me", he said. "You have to find time to see Prof and settle the matter of 444. He insists you must have at least seventy percent attendance in class before you can sit for the exam."

"Is that not The African Novel?"

"Yes."

"But why are these Profs like this? Must I attend his class? Is it not more important that I am able to turn in good material at the end of the day than to attend all lectures and really learn nothing?"

"I think you'll have to wait till you see him so that you may ask him that. My concern is that you should find a way to settle with him so that you can write the exam."

"I'll try," I replied, as I indeed intended to.

"I've got to go," as he stood up. "Will you not at least for once surprise us with your holy presence in class today?"

"I'm not sure yet, but I might try if I succeed in sorting out some things early enough."

When he left, I had a hurried breakfast of bread and water, and thereafter went to the library to check some materials. Then I tried but could not find Socrates anywhere. I managed and attended a class after which I went to see Prof. I was in difficulty what to explain to him was responsible for my long absence in class. And he was known to be very tough and strict. Even as I knocked on his door, I still did not know what to say to him.

"Ah, Eno," he reached out to me with so much familiarity that overwhelmed me. "I've been looking for you. But I will be very brief with you as I am already late for a meeting."

His smile and warmth melted away my anxiety. He began.

"The goal of education, as I understand it, is to produce fruitful and functional members of society. That education does not necessarily consist in sitting in classroom listening to somebody who supposedly knows. Much knowledge, that is real knowledge, is self-taught and self-directed. You seem to be aware of these facts as you appear to be walking in that direction. Such gives me much joy. So I waive the rule of seventy percent attendance before you can sit for my course. But I also worry that you must learn a sense of balance, a balance between vision and what is possible. Our environment is thick and heavy with corruption and all kinds of evil. That is more the reason why you need a sense of proportion. Else, the evil you are attempting to fight will sweep you off your feet and flush you down the drain. There are many who appreciate your effort. But you must move with caution. You can always find a friend here. Good luck."

The encounter made me wild with anxiety to narrate to Socrates, but I could not find him anywhere. That Prof whom we all respected and feared, that he, of all people, observed and appreciated our activities in the Academy, this was information most invigorating and heart-thrilling. And if everyone else turned their backs on the struggle and the cause, if those reactionary forces finally overwhelmed and destroyed me, I would rest assured in the grave that somebody of worth appreciated our vision and effort.

In the whirlpool of the excitement of that encounter and my fruitless effort to reach Socrates, I forgot all about that threat letter and the emergency meeting until the alarm of my wristwatch went off. The recollection of this dangerous situation in which I was somewhat deflated my sack of strength. But I lost it not entirely. Something of it still held on to the fringes of my consciousness, tugging somehow.

I hurried down to the room to get the necessary Academy files as well as the letter. When I got there, I saw another note for me on the door. Since I did not have much time before the meeting would start, I decided to waste no time in finding out the content of the note. I simply picked and dropped it on the table. Then I collected the needed files and left. But some metres away from the room it occurred to me that that note could be another threat from the fraternity. It would be necessary then to present it at the meeting. So I returned to the room and, opening it, saw that it was from Socrates. It read:

My brother,

I have been invited by the National Security Agency for discussion over our Academy. I don't expect it's anything serious. Whatever the case, it is a phase of the struggle, and this, insofar as is possible, I must handle alone – if only for now. Please breathe not a word of this matter to anyone in order not to demoralize the other brothers. But if you don't see me after twenty-four hours, mobilize support here and in the media.

I walk this road with deep conviction that we are never alone in the struggle for a sane society and beautiful living. Many, uncountable indeed, there are who cannot speak and whose unspoken thoughts and dreams of life we articulate. Their thoughts and goodwill always add to the power of our work. A long and inclusive view of the evolutionary growth of humanity easily reveals that there is a goal, a plan and some order towards which all life is moving. This cannot be the product of accident but of some intelligence, some Super Intelligence too immense and therefore inscrutable to the little mind of man. But any honest and inclusive view always reveals something of this Super Intelligence. And as little as we are able to grasp of this plan, we must endeavour to align ourselves, our vision, with its purpose. Experience teaches me that this Super Intelligence is always on the side of justice and truth and love.

Let this conviction guide you today and all the days of your life. Stand fearless and firm in the radiance of this vision, and let not the pettiness of your brothers, who may not as yet see what you see, let that not dampen your spirit. Always there are little ones to give the uplifting hand of understanding and love balanced by wisdom; for we too are pulled unto the platform raised by great men who are ahead of us. Thus is the chain of life, and it links from the minutest life to that Super Intelligence. Therefore I ask you to love them all, no matter the circumstances.

I will call on you when I return.

Your brother,
Maso.

Of course this was the voice of Socrates, and in spite of how simple he tried to make the matter, I could not help worrying.

Because a so-called 'discussion' or 'chat' with the NSA could always turn to months or even years of detention without trial. And from that detention stories of incurable ailments could emerge, leading to the death of the detainee – supposedly on account of that ailment. And I wondered how we had become some threat to the security of the state to warrant focus by the NSA. So far virtually all our activities were within the university community. Except that not long ago we mobilized the Market Women Association in making traders clean up the market which had become notorious because of how dirty it was. We also participated in the clean-up, a thing that surprised many of the traders; that we, from the so-called elitist (and highbrow) intellectual community could so mingle with and aid them in such a dirty activity.

After the exercise, Socrates addressed them, promising that we would come back as there were many things we could do together. And whoever arranged it we did not know, but a reporter from National Watch, a national weekly magazine, was present and covered everything, even interviewing Socrates about the Reformers' Academy. Almost a week after, the magazine had it as its cover story, and it was titled "The Reforming Reformers," with a picture of Socrates emptying filth into the refuse bin. Perhaps this was what drew the attention of the NSA to us.

But there was no time for me to worry about these things as I was already late for the meeting. I hurried on.

The meeting had started by the time I got to the venue. I walked in and greeted in the usual Academy manner, but the only response I got seemed to be a murmur. They were not happy I was late, I thought. I apologized, found some place and sat down. But for Socrates, it seemed that the best heads were present.

"We had just started the meeting when you came in," Ted explained. "We were already worried. But it's good that finally you are here, for it is a very crucial meeting. Do you have any word from Comrade Socrates?"

"Yes, he left a note explaining that he had some emergency out of town to attend to," I replied.

"Thank you, Comrade, that message is noted, and the meeting has to move on." Ted continued, looking round ostensibly for support. And many nodded. He went on: "Shortly before you arrived, it was decided that I should preside. I wonder if you have any objection to that?"

"Not at all. It's okay by me."

"Well then, I guess we can fully start off," Ted continued.

"The notice of meeting indicates that a threat letter was sent to Comrade Eno. So we are gathered to look into the matter and then decide what action to take in tackling the problem. But I suppose it would be nice and possibly enlightening to have Comrade Eno tell us all he knows about the letter. Comrade, you have the floor."

I stood up and narrated how I came back from the library and saw the note, and how I immediately went to Socrates' house to brief him. I also expressed my conviction that it came from that fraternity, and that it was not unconnected with my recent appearance before the Disciplinary Committee to expose the perpetuators of that attack. Then I gave the letter to Ted to pass round. Many simply passed it to the next person without looking at it.

"Thank you, Comrade," Ted took over after I had sat down. "We have heard it all from the horse's mouth, and I'm sure that many of us have something to contribute. The floor is open."

David, a very vocal but often confused number, raised his hand to speak. Ted signalled approval.

"Thank you very much," David started after clearing his throat. "The struggle for truth and justice is one that is age-old as man himself, and the quest for knowledge and fullness of mind can never cease as long as man is still on the surface of this our earth. Perhaps, this may suggest that man realizes, or assumes to realize, the importance of the ideal of a just and humanely ordered world. We all know that the Academy shares this vision of the world. We wouldn't be here if we did not believe, or at least profess to believe, in this vision. But I sincerely wish that things were that easy and straightforward, that we could all truly so relate with one another without treachery hiding in our hearts. But I would not like to waste your time."

Then he took a quick look at me – a most unfriendly look that did not in any way suggest that he was confused about what to do. But he continued:

"Comrades, I know that some of you are wondering why I speak like this. Please don't worry much. If you knew what I know, you probably would do worse. Comrades, I won't waste your time any longer by telling you stories. Betrayal! That is the word. There is betrayal, and it is good that everybody should know about it at this point before we go jumping into the fire not prepared by or for us."

He took out a handkerchief and wiped his sweating face. I was wondering if there was a way I too could wipe some suspicion off my consciousness. But he continued:

"We all know what this Academy stands for, and we also know how we've all suffered and persevered. All this was because we had a common vision, a collective goal which all of us worked towards. Yes, our collective goal it was, not the desire and goal and scheming of one individual. And we have succeeded this far because we have been working as a group. I believe that many of you will agree with me that this has been the secret of our success. Our success has been possible not because we have been working as individuals in search of personal glory, as individuals seeking to reap alone where everybody has contributed. Am I with you, Comrades?"

"Very much, carry on", was the chorus. The long over-hanging chill now finally settled on me.

"Thank you all," David continued as he cast a quick glance in my direction and even seemed to eye me, sort of saying: You are finished.

"Ordinarily," he resumed, "it ought not be much trouble mapping out a strategy to contain these fraternity boys and their threat, I mean supposing we were all wholeheartedly working as a group. This kind of challenge even ought to be something to welcome since it provides us an opportunity to practically try out our philosophy of non-violent resistance. It would have been easy for us to march all out in our own way against them. But that's if all things were equal, as they say. It would have been possible if all of us still lived in the ignorance of the past. Today, I know, and some other members know too, that things have changed. So we have to be careful in jumping into issues, especially when they have to do with the people's hero."

In spite of the chill that had settled on me, that last expression – the people's hero – stung me like a bee. Because although I had smelt rat, it was now that I got the direction of David's indirection and long-winded speech.

"Thank you very much, comrade," Ted said, and looking round, added, "the floor is still open, and I ask for more contributions."

It was obvious I had to begin my fight here. I stood up.

"I thank Comrade David for everything he said. It's some fine piece of speech," as I trod the path of sarcasm. Could I help it? "But in order to save time, we could be a little more direct and straightforward. It –"

"What more do you want to hear?" Tom attacked, standing up at the same time. I was surprised into silence. It was unexpected, I mean from him. They had prepared themselves.

"That under your selfish design but through the collective labour of us all, you have risen to fame and glory, and now it is Eno the hope of tomorrow. Before it used to be the Reformers. But no, it was too belittling for you to share in the collective glory. What you gained from that was too small for your mighty self. So that now it's Eno everywhere and no more the Reformers. We know it's all your design, and we were so stupid to have trusted you, thinking you were selflessly working for the progress of the Academy. So stupid we have been in trusting and giving you that much room. What about those virtues of humility and truth and selflessness that you so effortlessly reel out? And why –"

"Why not stop this ridiculous display and come direct with your accusation," I cut in out of growing incredulity and stupefaction.

"Oh, here comes our hero in innocence and humility. What is it you don't know?" Tom asked.

"Whatever it is you have in mind, better speak out and stop this unnecessary beating about the bush. What kind of mischief is this?"

"Comrades," Ted, who had been watching all this while, took over, "this emergency meeting was called so that we could decide on what to do about the threat letter sent to Comrade Eno. But I can see that there are deep grievances we must address along with this matter. In line with our belief in democratic practice, I ask that whoever has any resentment should speak out now. Comrade Tom, please tell us what your complaint is. And I may need to caution that only one person at a time should speak, and only after the consent of the presiding officer has been obtained. We are all familiar with this rule, we have always been guided by it, and we still must continue to be so guided. So speak on, Comrade Tom."

Tom conferred with David before continuing.

"Comrades, I feel happy this moment as I look at the faces present here. I feel happy because I can see that many of the faces here, in fact about eighty percent, are all pioneer members of this movement. This means that many of us here know how this Academy started, or rather how we started it from the scratch. I know that you all have contributed in varying degrees to the success of this movement. I know how much many of you have suffered and sweated so that our Academy would not fail. The outcome of that sweat of yours is the success we have achieved today. Again this success has been possible because you all sacrificed personal interest to the vision and ideals of our beloved movement. Today the Academy has grown, it has grown far wider than I personally ever imagined. But this has been because of the commitment and sacrifice of us all, not that of one man. Now that success, that result of years of collective labour is what one man, a man who did not even labour and sweat with us from the beginning, that collective labour is what he is trying to channel to personal ends."

At this point he deliberately stopped and looked round for approval. And he was not disappointed as many heads nodded in affirmation. But I was calm on the surface – for I had repeatedly cautioned myself to watch with complete detachment this stage-play. So I was calm on the surface, but a riot of a battalion of soldiers was going on within, urging me to say very many things. Somehow, I succeeded in retreating to some fairly well insulated region.

"I have always admired and respected Comrade Eno for his immense contribution to the Academy," he resumed. "I know, as I believe that many of you will agree, that apart from Comrade Maso, Comrade Eno's untiring effort in building this movement is unequalled. I have always paid him glowing tribute on account of this. I know too that many of you have been doing the same. This was because we thought that everything was being done in the interest of the Academy. But recent events have shown that there was some ulterior motive behind all this so-called selfless labour in the service of the group. There has always been a hidden agenda. When we applauded and prayed for him as he went about the work, little did we think that he was only struggling in order to see a platform for a very personal goal. But we gave him the chance, trusting him. So we left so many things to him without asking questions. But, Comrades, you know it too well that power corrupts, and absolute power corrupts absolutely."

He took a break here to again confer with David who nodded vigorously. They had planned everything before now. Still I remained calm, though the volcano raging within was now threatening to erupt.

"Comrades," he resumed, "I am not here to tell you stories of all his so-called selfless activities, I will say nothing of the numerous press releases aimed at nothing but the exploitation of popular sentiments, I will say no more of that catalogue of cares of students who would have suffered either expulsion or rustication had our knight-errant not come into the scene to fight. Of course I will not say anything of his heroic appearance before the Disciplinary Committee to ensure that the course of justice was not hindered. You all know these stories, but I'm almost sure you did not know, nor even suspected, the motive behind all that heroism. Oh, forget all that sweet-sounding talk about truth at all times, about justice and selfless service and humility. Never take him, or anybody else, serious when he talks about everybody sorrowing on account of the sorrow of some other member of the human family – that specious logic of the brotherhood of all. Events have exposed all that to be sheer intellectual mouth-clapping dishonesty. The rhetoric of that trap–"

"What the hell is happening?" I shouted at Ted, because the sack in me was full and I had to let out something or I would burst. "Are you going to allow this mischievous rubbish to continue? Or has everybody suddenly gone crazy? What is the crime in all I've been doing, and what have I done that was not approved by the Academy? What devil has entered –"

"Please Comrade Eno," Ted now stood up, "I'm in charge, and–"

"Yes you are in charge, but is that why you should allow this fucking–"

But he would not let me.

"Nothing and nobody is fucking. Sit down, Comrade Eno, and let's get done with this matter."

I was now very sure that this was a rehearsed text, but it was too ridiculous to be real. Yet it was real. Each time I looked round, the unreality of the situation released a sharp pain in my heart and that pain made me realize that everything was real. And each time that unreal reality pierced and tore my heart into more and more shreds. I looked at Ted, fixed my gaze straight into his eyes. But I think the fire of that gaze burned him, for he lowered his face. Some relief came to me as a result of that. There was still some heart in him, and in the silence of that heart he had many questions to answer. I was relieved a bit.

"Please carry on, Comrade Tom," Ted directed.

"Thank you comrade. I was about to round off before that interruption. Well, my dear comrades, that is the matter as it is, that is as it appears on the surface. That's how he is, a selfless self-sacrificing hero. But many of us do not know what is beyond that surface, what is at the bottom. And that, my dear comrades, that hard truth is that our hero, the hope of tomorrow, our own Moses, our Jesus, the Mahatma and Luther King of our time, has been flying high on the wings of the Reformers' Academy to become the President of the Students Union. This is the truth of the matter, and I have my evidence. Thank you."

As he concluded with that allegation, some cold shiver ran down my body, releasing goose pimples all over me. I had not seen, all along, that there was any concrete accusation that could be raked up against me. For what was there to argue against me in all I had done so far? And none of that work, none of the activities had been carried out without the mandate of the Academy. There were, though, only a few emergencies I had to attend to without waiting to inform and get approval from the movement; and this simply because such cases needed immediate response. But then, on such matters I always consulted Socrates. Nobody ever complained – except, of course, behind me.

So what could they rake up against me?

But when he mentioned the bid for the student's Union Presidency, I instantly turned and looked at David who simultaneously looked at me. He stared at me, smiling somewhat tauntingly before turning away. And from the heads that nodded approval and the eyes that sought to burn me out of existence, I knew that the story had already gone round.

But the things that can hide in the human heart.

The idea of contesting for elective positions in the Union was suggested to me by Socrates. I could not exactly consent because I felt it would divert our attention from the original purpose of studying to fashion a suitable and practical ideology for our society. We however agreed that the matter should be presented in a meeting. And I remembered that not long ago I did mention this matter to David, he being one of those believed to be serious members. While expressing my reservation I told him that the issue would soon be thrown open for debate. I recalled that he specifically asked me if I would like to contest for any position, to which I replied that I was not sure yet, but that it was unlikely. Somehow the matter never came up for discussion in any meeting.

Ted, who was now standing, took over. "Thank you very much, comrade, for that very frank disclosure."

Frank disclosure! I shouted. But it was only within.

"It takes a man of courage to stand face to face with his brother and tell him the bitter truth. Thank you once again. I believe some of us have something to add to that. Yes, Comrade David, you should–"

"Tom has said it all," David interrupted.

"Well then, who else has anything to contribute before I call on Comrade Eno to tell his own side of the story?"

Nobody showed willingness to say anything – which was quite unusual.

"Comrade, you have the floor," he told me and sat down.

Looking at the cold and hostile faces of my comrades in that room, I became sure that there was little or nothing I could say to them; the guillotine had already been applied, and there was nothing to shift these stone-minds. And I saw that I had taken many chances, believing that it was possible to make saints out of human beings – in spite of the darkness of the heart. I had not thought it possible that the beast could so cheaply find its way into that circle of what I had called innocents, that circle where a common realization (was there any such?) of brother-hood seemed to have welded us, in spite of all, into that ideal of oneness proclaimed by all true religions of the world. And to think that David and Tom were at the forefront of this; they who had appeared promising. It was all a very unpleasant dream. But then reality loomed large and loud, and with a painful pull on my heart.

The things that can hide in the heart.

What was wrong, anyway, in running for any position in the Union? One would have thought that it would help in spreading the ideals of our group, provide a field for testing out those ideals and possibly affect more lives thereby. But the hard and hostile, if not strange, faces I saw there on that day and at that moment of fire, the faces I saw there did not seem to see it that way. And I could not help biting my lips in pain and anguish that all our labour and effort had come to this. Because the whole thing threw up, rather rudely, unto the face the question of whether all our effort at building one family of love and trust and goodwill and sharing, whether such effort was not the nauseating vomit of ideal and impractical dreamers.

But that darkness that can hide the fire of the heart.

For many among them in that room at that moment were direct beneficiaries of our philosophy as they turned Socrates' house into a sanctuary and place of refuge from hunger and all kinds of lack. I, too, in my own little way, had tried to give not just as Socrates generally taught but as he had given to me.

And there is this something that is inexplicably holy and filling about giving. There is some joy attendant. Perhaps why they say that blessed is the hand that giveth.

Of course four of these members (though absent from the meeting) were squatting in my room, while seven were staying with Socrates. To these, perhaps all the Academy meant was just to have people to grab from. Nothing about the reciprocity and mutuality of love.

"Comrade Eno, don't you want to respond to the matter?" Ted asked.

But the bitterness of gull was in my mouth, and its fire raged in my heart. I was sure I was already down the pit and could fall no further. Shouldn't I help them dig deeper? But I would hit them too where it would pain. To God I would. Like Caesar's Antony.

"Thank you very much, Comrade Ted, for giving me such a wonderful opportunity," I started. "And I thank you all, comrades, for your anxiety to hear me speak which I see so clearly on your faces. I do understand the fact that it is because of the way you hold me in your hearts. I also understand why Comrades David and Tom so courageously spoke out their observations; you know as well as I do that they are honest men who mean no harm.

And that is why I do not fully understand why you still want me to speak. Comrades David and Tom are honest men who mean no harm. As honest men, they cannot but have spoken the truth, the whole truth and nothing but the truth. So what more is there beyond truth that I can now tell you? They told you they had the evidence, and you too, brothers of mine, saw the mountain of evidence they presented. What more then do you expect to hear from me? Or is it just the question of the horse's mouth, of my thirty pieces of silver? As honest men, they are incapable of mischief; they cannot bear false witness against their neighbour, much less their own comrade and beloved brother. So why don't you believe them wholeheartedly and let me be? Or you want to watch and listen for the last time to how I play the game of deception? Is that why you still want to hear me?"

"Enough of this sarcasm. Why don't you shut up and sit down if you have nothing to say," someone shouted.

"Oh, let his Excellency talk," another added. "He already feels like a president."

"Not yet. He is only trying to convince us to vote for him," a third said. Some laughed while some others murmured. But Ted managed to take control by intervening.

"Comrades, shall we give him a chance to speak?"

They became quiet. I continued:

"Thank you, Comrade Ted, and thank you all comrades for all your support and understanding and cooperation. You are such a wonderful set of people that I won't dare bore you with any more lectures. I will just make a few comments, and I beg you to give me your attention."

There was little or no need for that because they were all silent and listening. But I was trying to organize myself.

"All my days in this Academy I have done little more than talk. And to think that I did all that with my motive stowed away in a secret personal vault, why should I ever lecture you anymore?

CHAPTER 15 | THE TOWER OF ILLUSION

Only that I have been asked to defend myself, and you know, as well as I do, that there is no point in that. However, I still beg you to listen to me, and I know that being intelligent people, you will understand and give me a chance. But please don't forget to block your mind, though your ears hear me, against the poison and contagion of my logic. Or if you leave open your minds, don't forget to throw everything I say to the winds; or if you could find a worse place like a pit latrine or the bowels of a decomposing corpse, throw it there so that nobody will ever get to it."

I paused to gauge the temperature. The fire of my words was raging. Stir it the more and hit them hard. Stir it into a harmattan fire. Because their hearts are clogged with pettiness and are hardened against you. All that talk of brotherhood is just water poured on a rock. Love has no place yet in their hearts. Only in their mouths, which is no more than love of their stomachs and their pockets. Stir more the fire!

"Comrades David and Tom are honest men who mean no harm, and you all know now that I cannot compare with them in matters of honesty. Because honest men they are. And you all know too how much they have done towards the growth of this movement, you cannot count (I'm sure) how many times they've had to go out of their ways to make sacrifices all in the interest of the Academy. And they have been so plain and open that none of us here should ever doubt their intention – the way that you should doubt mine. We ought to believe them even when there is no basis or evidence for whatever claims they may make. We, as reasoning and intelligent beings, ought to swallow everything they say hook, line and sinker. They are honest men who mean no harm, and we ought to name streets after them."

"Now more specifically, you all know, now that our heroes of the moment have unearthed that secret vault of mine, that it has been black all this time while I proclaimed it all white. You all know, now that our truly selfless and honest comrades have

275

suffered for us all (hope nobody doubts them), that I am sharing my room with four comrades who are all absent here so that their votes can secure me the presidency of the Union. You all know, too, that I spent incalculable hours of research in the library not really to broaden my scope and then attempt to straighten out some of the bases of our philosophy, but simply to become so learned in the art of speech-making so that I would be able to convince even stones to vote for me. You all know, still, that if not for my selfish effort, that girl who accidentally burnt part of the female hostel would have been expelled from the University. And I know that you all know so many things now; that I took the very dangerous risk of exposing the culprits of that cult attack because I knew that my reward of the presidency of the Union would come thereby; that I now and then spent my personal money in running the affairs of the Academy because I knew that the presidency of the union, once assumed, would yield a million times; that I donated my little personal collection of books to the Academy not because I believed every member should have unfettered access to such materials but because I knew that the votes of the books were badly needed to become the President; and that indeed I aspire to become President and I never told David that it was unlikely that I would be involved; and that you now know many many things I thought were hidden under the sun."

"Comrades, aspiring to become president of the Students' Union is such an unpardonable crime that anyone who calls himself a member of the Reformers' Academy who murmurs such aspiration should be executed by firing squad. Politics and social reformation are on such different planes that anybody who attempts to use one as a means to the other, or even tries to merge the two, should be summarily sent to hell to burn without redemption. And that is why I particularly want to thank you all, good-natured and understanding people, for your cooperation and kindness. I promise that I won't dream again. I would also like to thank Comrades David and Tom, honest and harmless heroes of the hour. I thank you all once again for being tolerant. You know, only tolerant and reasonable people like you will realize that we have abandoned our main purpose of gathering here today. Thank you very much."

As I sat down and looked round, I saw that faces were swollen. And the fire in those eyes too, I could feel it all over me. It can't be worse, I thought.

"Presiding Officer, it's over to you", I said as they all seemed lost, and there was no evident attempt on his part to say or do something.

"Oh, thank you, comrade," he responded. "Who has any more contributions to make?"

"Eh," David started, lips shaking. "I don't know how you all feel, but in all my years I have never seen this level of insolence and disrespect as shown to us by Comrade Eno. As a result, I am of the opinion that we should allow him to solve this problem which he has brought upon himself. The Academy should not be involved in the outcome of a man's inordinate ambition. I would like to move a motion on that."

As he sat down, Kin, who hardly spoke in any of our meetings, raised his hand.

"Yes, Comrade Kin, you want to second the motion?" Ted asked.

"No, not quite or so quickly. I would like to make some comments before we carry on with the issue of motion."

"But we have finished debate. It's just to vote," David pushed.

"We have not even debated the matter," Kin insisted. "And I have things I must say if we are to vote on the issue."

"But we are through with that, and there is no point dragging us back," Tom added.

"Comrades," someone shouted", Let the Presiding Officer decide on this."

As I watched what was happening, I was almost certain that Kin would not go along with them. That meant one person on my side, which almost made me feel bad for the way I spoke. But his was just a rare voice, like a tiny fruit in a wilderness of rubbish. And he was never a pushover. He was not the kind to contribute to every matter, but each time he spoke he made strong impact and carried almost everybody along – that is when and where logic and that so uncommon commonsense are allowed to prevail. David and Tom must have suspected that he would not support them. And Ted, too, who did not waste any time in announcing his decision.

"Comrades," he started, "I'm happy that comrade Kin is eager to contribute to this issue. We all know how highly valued his contributions always are. And fair play may seem to suggest that we allow each interested member to speak. But, Comrades, what does it pay anybody drawing the hands of the clock back? It might favour somebody, though, but it won't be fair on others. So for this reason, I do rule that we are through with that debate. Comrade David has proposed a motion, and the only thing left is to vote."

"Who are the 'we' that have debated the issue? And where was it debated? At this meeting or in some other nocturnal gathering? And suppose I want to oppose the motion, don't I have a right to explain why?" Kin asked.

And at that point many fuming volcanoes erupted, some shouting abuses at Kin while others poked fingers at and sought many answers from me. I remained seated, the final manifestation of that surging tide somehow toughening me. The disappointment was, or seemed to be, over. And I watched my comrades with some sort of admiration; admiration because they did not seem to have let themselves too far out – as Hemingway's

Old Man – into that gulf, that gulf of supposed trust and truth and oneness and brotherhood. It was as if they had been waiting all along for that single moment when somebody would raise an accusing finger that would fit into the phantom of their expectation, that way of seeing which is only a blind way of fitting any noble endeavour into the mould of our own particular individual failings and inabilities: And we would easily say of all others; they are all the same. Simply because we do not see ourselves as being capable of making any difference. So wherever we fail, all others must fail too.

And all this, in spite of all that we had professed to believe in, in spite of all the hurdles we had, or seemed to have, crossed together, hurdles which I thought had forged and strengthened our belief in universal love and brotherhood, belief in solidarity and unity, in a world where all lives flowed into a communal pool. So all of it is the dream of a demented mystic shut away from the stinging realities of life? All this just the illusion of the high priests of the Gods who proclaimed and sought the binding chords of communal living? A mirage of the all-too-far-seeing giants of every age and clime who saw and proclaimed one vision for humanity – the vision of oneness and brotherhood?

But this little hole of a dream, this illusory hut of trust and oneness had been developed into a house of many mansions by my contact and interaction with Socrates. Because that contact lit up in my consciousness much that I had sensed vaguely and hoped to see in real life. That contact enabled me to move away from the shallow fringes and plunge into the depths of the visioned life.

For they have not started living yet who find nothing in life that pulls the deepest strings of their heart that they can commit all that they are to; they know not yet that raging joy! It was so simple and true between Socrates and me. It was, the thought of which presently intensified my anguish.

But Kin's anguish was somewhat different as he still demanded:

"I deserve a chance to state my position before –"

But, of course, they would not let him.

"You deserve nothing."

"Except to be thrown out if you make any more noise."

Kin, however, still wanted to say something when I called him and said:

"They will injure themselves more than they will injure you or me," remembering Socrates of Athens.

He looked at me thoughtfully, then round the assembled comrades and finally sat down. But he was not a chronic dreamer, as I was. So he rose and demanded;

"But how can we call –"

Tom rose in fury and shouted:

"Comrade Ted, I cannot stand here and watch this disregard for constituted authority. This intransigent attitude of Comrade Kin's is a gross violation of long-standing rules of the Academy. I cannot take that from any man because this movement is for all of us. Comrades," now addressing everybody, "I am walking out on this house and from this meeting. If you believe that what you are seeing here is in order, you may stay behind, but if you don't, you may come with me."

Then he walked out, and virtually everybody else followed, some shouting hurrah while others cursed those who thought they could ride on the back of the Academy to attain godhead.

I looked at Kin who, of course, stayed back, and when our eyes met he shook his head, most likely in disappointment. I managed to release a false smile, and turned to Ted's seat. He was there, but quickly turned away as the beam of my gaze touched him.

"Glory to those who can stare into the sunbeam of their conscience and remain steady," I said and walked away.

It was already dark and the few functional street lights had been switched on. As I passed through Bill Clinton Square, I

noticed that the place was unusually quiet. Only about three people were at the snooker spot, and only a handful at the line of
shops where drinks and food were sold.

I passed through Soyinka Street, down to Mandela Lane,
hurrying to get to Socrates' house as soon as possible. And as I
walked on, I tried to shut out of my consciousness everything that
had just happened. I wished I could fly straight to Socrates' house
to see if he was back. But I could not, and as I walked along that
Lane, I could not help noticing another unusual; some column of
ant-like movement. And I wondered. I was jolted into awareness
by a passer-by who asked another if he was starting his examinations the following day. I had completely forgotten. Examinations
were starting the following day.

When I got to Socrates' house, I was told that he had not
returned. That homely house immediately became unbearably
empty and boring, and I could not waste a second longer there.

As I walked down the street, a sudden and immense feeling
of loneliness and fear took over me. It struck me in a way I had
never thought or felt that I was completely alone, that I was utterly
deserted, and that there was nothing I could do to change the situation. The Academy was, of course, a pot of fire burning in my
heart, and Socrates, with whom I might have shared my burden,
was nowhere around. And then, my fear and feeling of loneliness were heightened by a thought which asked: Suppose you are
never to see Socrates again? Some cold shiver ran down my entire
being with that thought. I walked down the street, treading with
fear and sorrow. The night instantly acquired a very frightening
hue and sound, and every little object or person I saw became
some potential danger. I could see the words shining through the
darkness:

BLOOD ON YOUR HEAD

So that I increased my pace, frequently looking backwards and side-ways to see if anybody came too close. And the distance between Socrates' house and my room became a forty-year journey that I happily walked into my room, heaving a great sigh. With much relief I walked into that room.

And it was somewhat completely bare of any human presence. My room-mates, expectedly, were not there.

I flung on the table the file I took to the meeting, and then lay on the bed. Immediately an image of Ku Klux Klan members burning a cross in front of Luther King's house rose before my eyes. Then it was a bomb explosion; and then an image of Jesus the Christ on the cross as he said: "Father, Father, why hast thou forsaken me?" A familiar voice then started: "That under your design but—"

I jumped out of the bed and went to Ifeh's room where I spent the night trying to see what preparations I could make for the examinations. I could not share my agony with him because he had never really shown interest in the Academy and in matters of social struggle outside literature. His interest in writing was as a possible profession, and he was somehow committed to not diluting it with what he called the muck and slime of daily living – while I approached the matter from the other extreme which saw literature as meaningful only if it emerged from that muck and slime of everyday life. So we stood at two different ends.

As we stood that night too during which I burned in the fires of agony and could find no sleep, while Ifeh snored away like a baby in the mother's arms. Much as I tried to keep my mind away from the events of the day, I realized that I could think of little else. And the thought of Socrates' safety was beginning to gnaw away at my heart. But I repeatedly told myself that there was nothing I could do about the matter that night. Then I tried to soak myself in the thought of and preparation for that examinations. In all I was soaked in nothing else but my agony. So that all through that night I frequently jumped out of the dark pool of the moment to stare at the books before me, which then led me unavoidably back to that pool.

Daybreak was of greatest moment as I realized that, truly, the night hides with a knife. Because as the sun gradually unveiled its face, piercing and dissipating the darkness of the night, the over-hanging atmosphere of danger lightened and I experienced some measure of momentary relief. But more than this, it seemed, was the fact that I could now go to the Academy's lawyer to see what could be done regarding Socrates.

I was a little surprised to hear him say that Socrates had duly briefed him on the matter – obviously he too did not quite trust the NSA, although he did not so sound in his note to me. But the lawyer asked me not to worry since he was already taking neces-sary steps. I was to check back on him in three days' time if I did not see Socrates within that interval.

Those three days were spent in the purgatory of anxiety and loneliness and a certain feeling of weightlessness. Because it appeared like my life was a rudderless ship that could not find any anchor in the tempest of the high sea of life. Because it was like I always stood on some quicksand of vision which always gave in and pulled down to rock-bottom wretchedness of life. Wretched as I always was. Because I felt completely naked and utterly ashamed in the noon-tide bustle of the market-square of life where every eye stared mockingly.

But purgatory is supposed to be a place of transition holding some hope. So I hung on the thin and slippery thread of that hope, the passing of each day increasing the tension and making the thread thinner. The examinations also helped a little as I sat for three of my courses. And it pleased to know that somehow and from some place in the deep of my being I always found something to say. It was like someone was always there to stir that well (the result of accumulated intensive study), to rake up the answers to the questions. It pleased my heart to know this, and it lightened the burden of my sorrow.

As did the lawyer's calm assurance, when I saw him at the end of three days, that Socrates was alright and would be back in two days. He, the lawyer, would be personally present to bring back Socrates. Socrates had only been delayed a little, the lawyer explained, because the Chief Security Officer suddenly had to travel. The CSO wanted to have a 'friendly' chat with Socrates, and that would only be possible in two days' time, after which Socrates would return.

On the promised day, I shuttled all day long between Socrates' house and the lawyer's office. And when the lawyer's office was locked at nightfall, with neither him nor Socrates in sight, a thick darkness of sorrow – not anxiety – fell on me, and that chord of sanity and normalcy snapped. I roamed the streets of the university all through the night, in utter abandon, and with no purpose or direction in mind. At dawn and at about nine o'clock, I returned to the lawyer's.

He was back. But then, there was no anxiety in me anymore. I listlessly walked into his office and found him surrounded by his staff and many more people. His dishevelled outlook and the unnatural hollowness of his gaze sounded the note of doomsday. But my own doomsday had been experienced earlier.

A staff of the lawyer's took me to a room and explained that Socrates had indeed been released late in the evening of the previous day, and he and the lawyer had left the Security office at nightfall. About thirty minutes into their journey, a car overtook theirs and forced them to stop. Two men came out and shot Socrates on the head.

Of course, the chord had already snapped the previous day. So as I heard what happened, there was little or no thrill down the line of my being. But I still think that I took a dive into a deeper depth as I wobbled away from that office, away from the world into the dark graveyard of the fringes of consciousness and sanity, asking the beast to come and finally take me away. And it did come, the beast, but it spoke not to me. It simply stared into my eyes, and the peace of defeat and purposelessness and blindness settled on me. We stared at each other, neither grinning at the other nor attempting to conquer. Some sort of peace settled between us, a joyless peace that stirred no life.

It was a peaceless peace.

Socrates was shot on the forehead. What is it in the heart of man that is capable of such thought? What kind of fire is it that burns in such heart? Or is there truly any fire of the heart in such thought, in such action? Is there?

He was shot on the forehead, Socrates, noblest of the noble, the saving stream of love, nourishing all life whom he contacted. Socrates, that perfect blend of the fires of heart and mind, living the life of love balanced by wisdom. And that could not save him from the darkness of man's heart. It led him to the altar of the beast. And they slaughtered him.

Senselessly!

Was that action animal, or human, or divine? What was in it to lift any life onto its next level? What was the poison in that stream of love which he so selflessly poured forth, what was the poison in it to make any man unsheathe the sword? Hemlock in the hands of the unseeing herd?

Ignorance is the greatest disease of life, and those who wish to hold down progress inundate with their darkness the incipient streams of that life-giving knowledge.

In that stream of darkness the beast and I stared at each other, as uncountable whats and whys and wheres struck at my heart, attempting to inflame a heart that had no more life in it. But standing between us, between the beast and me, was the radiant and magnetic light on the face of the psychiatrist who asked me several questions. And it bothered me much that he did not deem it necessary to ask any from the beast who constantly flashed a key in the psychiatrist's face. I do not recall my responses to the psychiatrist's questions, but I still can see vividly that moment when he placed the cool and soft palms of his hands against mine and beamed on me and from his forehead rays of light brighter and more radiant than the sun's. Instantly something stirred in me, and I made up my mind that I would do whatever he asked me to do, even if it cost me my life. And that was the rope with which I climbed out of that pit.

They say I was there for about two months. When I was discharged, I was put on disgustingly fat drugs. But I always took them because between that psychiatrist and me was a wordless agreement. I was determined to fulfil my part.

CHAPTER 15 | THE TOWER OF ILLUSION

THE FIRE FESTIVAL

CHAPTER 16:

THE FIRE OF LOVE

t was a new session, and I was now in my final year, though I was to carry-over two courses from the third year. As events gathered normal pace and colour in my sight, I took a lot of quiet moments to identify a point, any point whatsoever, to anchor my existence. Because the fire of Socrates' slaughter and of events at about that time burnt down much of my castle. But being an incurable believer in that world of my dreams, I still sought it, I still sought its fuel to fill up my empty tank if I was to carry on with the journey of life. I took a lot of quiet moments.

Often at night I would take a stroll down to the Faculty where I would climb to the last floor and bathe in the colours and life of the night sky. And the cool breeze blowing through the unhaunted roof garden of that floor touched some roots in me, stirring remembrances of things past and of everything good that would come. Its images and colours once again started hanging around my vision. It was in this roof garden that I was some night of full moon when she came, Julia.

Like a soothing breeze you just suddenly become aware of.

"We are never completely alone, much as may seem to suggest so," she said as she walked up to me.

I turned and looked at her, then turned away, wondering what it was that gave her that heavenly poise and radiance and thereby making her unreal. But I turned away.

She was to come another night.

"Evil is an undeniable part of creation, but through the values we live by we can either empower or overpower it. The voice of conscience is the way of light."

Her words struck a note which sounded true in my heart, the truth not of dogma but of something personally known deep down the guts. I found myself enchanted by these words. How could one so steal into another's heart and reveal what was buried there? Radiation of the heart? Resonance?

Still I turned away, but with so much effort and violence on my heart.

And still she came another night.

"This world of strife is the most fertile for the beauty of harmony through conflict and the consequent attainment of godhead. There is no other worthwhile goal than that beauty, and there is no true conquest outside the battle-ground."

I could not turn away. An impulse pushed me to query:

"Is that why He dropped him in such a sable wild?"

"To plumb the depths of experience and thereby gain wisdom. That wisdom is the balancing arm of His love that ever is," she replied.

And I knew that this was a song not so unfamiliar that I could without thought sing with her. And I did:

"But then, He blessed us with the rage of hunger."

"That rage is the fire of motion, the dynamic force of growth. His love ever is in that fire."

"But He seems to speak no more, especially after the blaze of the burning bush."

"Ever His voice sounds, ever in that silence that sounds. But this is possible only in the deep of our being, in that silent sphere above the noise of the earth. His love ever points us there, always. You know how to find that silence."

She came closer now, closer than she ever did, and, looking into my eyes, asked:

"Have you not discovered His love yet? Can you not see that holding centre of all life?"

"It's difficult to say now, but I seem to have known it only in dreams."

"Vision is the raw material. Know you not the secret of translation?"

"All my efforts crash against the rocks on the way to that secret."

"Know you not the staying power of the indestructible, the immortal, that which we truly are? You must empty completely that basket of aeons of wrong choosing before you step on to the mountaintop. Can you not steer against the current long enough?"

Again as vision I could not fault what she said: its truth I seemed to have tended in the nursery of my life, but it never grew to fruition. Except, of course, as it crashed against that rock.

"I know naught anymore," I said.

"The way is the synergy of the middle pillar, that narrow razor-edge path. We must all learn to walk this path."

Then she took my hands in hers, and as her soft palms touched mine it was as if the whole tension of all my life instantly surged up to my heart, ready to tear through it. And still she edged closer, looking straight into my eyes. But the heat of it all, the fire that seemed to burn from those eyes, who indeed could withstand it? So I closed my eyes. That did not help matters much because as I felt, in a moment, her lips touch mine in a kiss, a petrol fire was ignited all over me – though it hurt me not – and the volcano erupted and I shook and quivered and quaked. On and on and on until all the tension of my life seemed to completely disappear through the pores in heat and sweat. And then total calm, calm ineffable enfolded me. It was the final repose of a soul that had for long burnt in Hell; the heavy sigh of a life that had finally beaten death to it: the ecstatic bliss of the mystic identification not just with but as the Father; the stillness of that being who had finally been accepted into the bosom of the Almighty.

So wretched as we are, so wretched, what indeed are words to translate the inner radiance of that life, the life divine? Such is the wretchedness of words to truly translate and reflect the wordless. Because it is wordless.

In all it was a feeling of life, a livingness I had never known. Not and never in anything I had ever experienced. So why should I be in a hurry to lose that? I chose to open not my eyes.

"One wrung breaks, you step on another," she whispered.

"Yes yes!" I returned almost unconsciously.

"Countless are the false and wrong steps up to that dream mountain of joy."

"Countless, countless," still I returned.

"Yet, climb we must, the fire of life burning in us."

It was only now that I could say words of my own: "But it is full of risk."

"All life is a risk, and every success story is woven with uncountable plots of failure. There is no worthwhile growth without risk."

"But why does the beast win almost all the time?" I could now ask.

"There is much that seems but is it. Only if we can see truly, only if we can stand apart from our tongues and stomachs and the noise and roar of the moment."

"My life has been nothing but a series of failures."

"You fight and lose, re-assemble your tools, replan and re-attack with the benefit of experience. All life is a continuous battle."

"You've been to hell?"

"I speak mostly of things I experienced."

"What kind? Betrayal?"

"Yes, with its deep lesson of love for the betraying hand. It is only ignorance that makes us bestow that kiss of betrayal."

"Was that why He prayed for forgiveness even in the agony of the cross?"

"Yes, but even that love has to wield the sword too."

"What more do you expect?"

"Life, my contribution to its uplift."

"You've not dropped any seeds yet?"

"Just some, but not yet in full measure."

"You believe in the illusion of a heaven here?"

"Not in the illusion, but the reality. Is it illusion you experience with me now?"

"You sound more than human, super-human, godlike."

'But that's precisely what we are. Only if we realized this."

We stood there, hand in hand, and stared into each other's eyes – yes, I could now stare into the full radiance of the moons of her eyes. And it was all the ecstatic shock in the victory over the seemingly invincible, that ecstasy and fullness of a pleasant dream. It was a swift flash of time as I stared and stared at the glow of life that flowed from her eyes. I froze in the satiety of that resplendent moment, unutterably still. Again she was to open up first, as she seemed to hold the keys to the mystery of existence.

"You seem to be standing on the Everest of Peace."

"It's much more, much more. But is this real?"

"Yes. And we can make it more real."

"How?"

"By letting it last and last."

"What more can there be, what more worth?"

"The anchor of love holds the universe. This is its diluted manifestation. With it we can make the most fortified of all castles."

"Do I have anything else?"

"All my life I have struggled for nothing else."

"So will you be my mother?"

"You need not ask: to nurture life to full blossom is the hunger of my life."

"And my father?"

"That informing purpose is weighty, but we must be its concrete manifestation."

"And my sister?"

"The fires of experience have shown us to be one and the same."

"And my brother?"

"By our actions we must show it to the world."

Moments in eternity, moments beyond time passed. But it was the same night. As always, she opened up: "What, truly, will you be to me?"

"A mother and a father and a sister and a brother."

"Is that all?"

"And a friend."

"And no more?"

But I could not think of anything anymore to say. It all seemed to have been exhausted. So I stared in admiration and confusion. She came to the rescue:

"In the full measure of each count, each of the above will have fulfilled its task and will fall away. Indestructible ties are knotted in the true love of the soul. Can you look into yourself and see if there is any such?"

I did not speak, but I said to myself, silently: For what have I burnt in the fires of life?

She heard me, though I did not speak out. And I knew that she hard. And I became aware, too, of her reply which was not spoken out. She said. Even after death do us unite?

Together we said, neither speaking out: forever and ever and ever and ever.

And each knew what was in the other's heart. We knew. And we were sure.

The peace of that anchor quelled all the riotous wildness of those days, and all the voices that always mocked and tormented suddenly disappeared. Through her – rather in her – I found or re-found a purpose to work or to play, to eat or to hunger, to live or to die. Through her a new life emerged, bubbling with freshness and energy and strength. It was too good to be part of my walk through life, but it had such a solidity that could not be denied or doubted. I had not thought that that kind of peace was possible for me, never thought that that satiety and fullness was within my reach. But there it was. And I grabbed it with all eagerness, tying all the strands of my life to that pillar. It was so fresh and filling.

But the beast.

I came back from lecture one afternoon to see a note for me on my door. It was from the Hall Warden, and it indicated that I was to see him immediately. I did not even enter my room.

He confronted me with the accusation of illegally accommodating two squatters in my room. I denied this, explaining that it was only the previous year that I had squatters. He looked at me for some time before dismissing me. I was about to open the door to go when he called me back.

"You would like to complete your studies in this school, I guess?" he said.

"Certainly, sir."

"I speak to you in confidence because something in your face reminds me of a lost vision. You'll need to be careful over your activities in the Reformers' Academy. Some people are not happy with you."

"The Academy does not exist anymore, sir," I explained. "It died with the events and crisis of last session."

"Be careful anyhow. The Academy may be dead physically, but its ripples are not over with some persons in positions of authority. You will need to be careful over all that you do. Life had appeared so straightforward, but age and experience have taught me that it is not so. If you have to survive in our kind of society, dilute your vision with some sweet sounding falsehood, and that is if you must live with any noble vision at all. Balance your vision with a sense of time and place. Otherwise you will get destroyed."

I thanked him for his advice and then left his office.

"Mix your wine with some poison," Julia mocked when I narrated everything to her. "This is the philosophy of the vanquished who cannot risk anything in defence of what they know to be true."

"I'm mainly surprised at his goodwill. I didn't think he was that kind of person."

"Countless are those who appreciate the good, the true and the beautiful, though they may not always speak out," she said.

"On the other side there are the many who are so irked by such selfless activities as the Academy's that they will use all they have to kill it. I wonder what is in their hearts."

"Do you forget that humanity usually chooses the robber to the redeemer, and that in spite of the good work, healing them and teaching and showing the true meaning of love, He still was nailed to the cross. Evil men stop at nothing. Always they fish out the hopes and lights of the world and attempt to drive them into the mouths of wolves and wild beasts of destruction. In spite of all, they could not stop His mission because nothing stops Him from His work. You, too, ought not let them frustrate such a noble vision."

"The Academy, you mean?" because I was sure of an under-current beyond the Warden's advice.

"Yes, the Academy," she replied. "You should not let it die like that. Why should you surrender to the wishes of the imprisoning forces? What more is there for you to do in this life? Join them and then bury yourself more in the depths of matter in the name of pleasure and enjoyment? You know there is no fulfilment in that."

"I know," I replied somewhat feebly. "But I still am confused about the matter. I didn't expect the whole thing to go that way. And then, the slaughter of Socrates."

"Socrates' task, at a level, was finished, and he had to move on – no matter the manner. Your love for him can best show in how far you keep this beautiful dream of his alive. So the problem is not in his murder, nor in the behaviour of your brothers in the movement. It all lies in you."

"In me?" I could not avoid asking.

"Yes, in you. Because your mind is still coloured by the thought of a heaven of idle bliss with music of the spheres wafting through the incense-filled air. Can't you recognize opportunity in every challenge? Do you not see that the way of the cross of struggle and suffering is the only way to bliss? You fall from the highest height, that fall swells your sack of wisdom. And then, when you act, look not for results in terms of what people say either way. Always stand in the strength of truth you recognize and don't listen to the noise around your action. Look within yourself and see if you can master that divide which still governs your perception and conduct."

"But can one fully master that divide?"

"Sure, but with the realisation that one can never completely go to sleep because we have mastered all and there is nothing else to strive towards. The struggle never ceases as we move from one mountaintop to another which is higher, although there is a point where it becomes effortless effort, and then all of life becomes a dance. Always there is a mountain to climb, with the force of gravity ever pulling us downward. But even that has its role within the cosmic dance."

"So I should resurrect the Academy?" I asked.

"You know what your heart tells you. There is much work to be done, and the Academy can help in giving vision and direction."

I knew, indeed, what my heart had been whispering to me, but I had thought it one of those outpourings from my unrelenting world of dreams. Now that another – more so Julia – had put a seal of assent on those stirring whispers, I knew there was more to the matter. So I went to work, and had nearly completely worked out plans on how to re-start the Academy when it happened.

I was in the library one afternoon when one of my lecturers walked in.

"Ah, Eno, so you are here reading while the whole school is burning," he said.

"What's the problem?"

"Your president has been stoned."

"The Students' Union President? Who stoned him?"

"No, I mean our own President, the Commander-in-Chief himself. He came to commission the school's water project. He was almost mobbed by angry students who were said to be protesting the bad state of things in the country. They threw all kinds of objects at him, and a dirty shoe is said to have hit him on the face."

"That's unfortunate," I said.

"It's not unfortunate. He got what he deserved, and now he can truly tell how popular he is."

"But violence won't solve anything. They should have used some more constructive way to protest."

"Nothing could have done it better. Let him have a bit of it too, after all he is lord and merchant of violence."

A week after this, I got a letter from the Students' Disciplinary Committee inviting me to come and explain my role in the attack on the President. As I read that letter, I realized that it was the last desperate attempt to see that I did not graduate. I was doing the final pages of my long essay, and we had about three weeks more to round off the programme. It seemed a perfect time for them to unleash the deadly blow.

But I was determined not to let them succeed. I was determined to fight till the very last drop of my blood was shed. Julia and I assessed the situation and concluded that it was almost impossible for the Committee not to find me guilty. Every available evidence to prove that I was not at the scene of the incident had to be used. My lecturer who met me at the library that day came to mind.

I went to him and, after explaining the situation, requested him to appear as a defence witness.

"I have a career to pursue in this school," was his frank reply.

"Yes sir, I know that," I replied, not entirely surprised. "Sir, you are about the only witness, and a credible one for that matter, that I have to prove that I was not there. I have to prove that to the Committee, otherwise I will lose everything in this school. Please sir, my future is somehow at stake."

"It's not something for you to beg me about. I will be committing myself, and invariably my career, if I appear as your witness. The university authorities will not forgive me for that, and you can be sure that I will pay dearly for such action."

"But, sir, you are only going to speak the truth—"

"Don't sound so naïve about things. You should know that things are not as easy as they may appear. In any case, whether

I appear or not will not change the judgement they have already passed. If you can, try and get a lawyer to institute a case for you in the court. This may be your only choice."

Again I returned to the Academy's lawyer, but he advised that I should exhaust the legal machinery in the school before proceeding to the court.

So I appeared before the committee, and it was still the same professors. The Chairman, still a professor of Law, told me that they had over two hundred memoranda from students suggesting that I was a major participant in the events of that day. Of course none of that memoranda was shown to me.

"It's possible that thousands more memoranda may suggest that I was not a participant," I fired back; for the war had begun.

And it hit them like a thunder bolt, totally unexpectedly. One looked at the other, open-mouthed in incredulity. It took some moments before the mouth could shut. The Chairman made to say something, but changed his mind. Embarrassment? Shock? Or whatever madness! But it held them in the grip of silence. The Chairman managed to break free.

"Give us an account of how you spent the day."

I told them everything I could remember about the day, from the time I woke up to when I went to bed, ensuring that I narrated in detail how I heard the news of the stoning of the President from my lecturer.

"So your claim is that you were never there," one of them asked.

"I was never there."

"And you were not remotely involved in any way?" another asked.

"I didn't even know that the President was coming."

"You expect us to believe that?" the chairman asked.

"Our earth is just one of the many bodies moving in the sea of space, as is our solar system. But always we are free to look the other way and claim that we are the only living beings in this sea of life."

It was a deliberate shot from me, and it hit them hard. Again in the grip of silence, teeth grinding. It was a good hit.

"You can go," the Chairman finally said.

"Is that all?" I could not help asking.

"Did you expect to go straight to jail from here?" the Chairman still. "You'll hear our verdict in two days."

I walked out of the room somehow relieved and at the same time with rising confusion. That certainly could not be all. They could not have believed me so easily. And no cross-examinations as such. The verdict must have been passed even before my appearance.

Aluta continua!

Outside the Senate Chambers Julia alone waited. No crowd of students waited at this most crucial time. Only Julia was there. And that was some inspiration. I narrated my experience, and we agreed that it could not be so simple and easy. The hearing, if one could call it that, was a sham.

We went to the lawyer who now wrote and dispatched a letter to the Committee. In it he thanked the Committee for its work and expressed the desire that justice was not only done but seen to be done in connection with me – his client.

On the day the Committee's verdict was to be announced, we waited and waited in vain; no word came from the committee or the University authorities. One day after, two, three, four, and still nothing was heard. The lawyer's letter seemed to be doing some work.

In the interval I completed work on my long essay and submitted it to the department. Julia completed and submitted hers too. Then we started our final examinations, and still there was no word. I wrote the examinations with fears of harassment, but there was none. Julia finished her papers on the same day as I did.

And that night we found ourselves again on the last floor of the Faculty building. The moon again was out and full, the sky softly illuminated by the glow of that moon, and gentle wind rocking trees back and forth. It was an evening and a world of soft sparkling light, and a lover's voice from one of the lower floors announced that heaven was near. I knew that was true.

We, Julia and I, we stood once more, hand in hand, eye to eye and spoke in measured whispers.

"But that every single moment of one's life were filled with such floods of fullness and satiety," I said, kissing her.

She took a little while to respond, a time during which much unspoken bliss passed between us. But did she, or rather did I really need to speak? Because her heart was in mine and mine in hers and each could tell what was in the other's heart. We could tell, so without words we spoke.

Without words.

Against what need will you measure and then appreciate that fullness? It has to remain so until we transcend our world of dualism.

You adorn my life with the radiant light of love.

Love is the main fabric of our world.

You picked the bits and pieces of a corpse and gave it a new life flaming with the fire divine.

But we receive that which we give much as a farmer receives his yield in the measure of the seed planted. That gift is to myself and my only glory.

And we stayed and stayed and stayed.

Soul-mate – she called within the one heart.

My own – because I could see the lighted substance of her wordless thoughts. So I answered.

Have you ever seen a bird of four wings soaring upward and upward into the bright blue sky?

Speak to me, my dear, light of truth new-born.

Or the hermaphrodite child of the sun completely bathed in the incredible brightness of the mother's rays?

Your light shines the truth of life I dream of. Speak on, my dear, lamp of the world.

My soul is enchanted by the splendour of that light

It is the splendour of the living truth of love. Speak on, oh radiant heart.

I am soaked in the satiety of light, that ultimate that all souls quest to behold.

The gift of light opens on to the world of love, dear child of light and love.

Sounds I hear are soft and mellow, and voices sing lullabies of tune celestial.

Breath of Truth, what can be greater than that harmony.

And we stayed and stayed and stayed, swift moments of inestimable pleasure and joy condensed into a moment in eternity. Because in that moment was an intensity of joy, that raging but serene joy that overflows the bounds of containment, that joy which, when you touch it, you will lose life itself in order to know once again. Because in that moment, in its joy was a flood of illumination of that hitherto translucent vision which had edged me on to various pursuits. Because in that moment, in its joy, was that light absorbed and known that I could now speak of the reality of heaven here on this most wretched earth. Wretched? Not with this joy, not in that light.

Soul-mate – still she called. Voicelessly. Wordlessly.

My own.

Though the sea be calm and the sky so bright, remember that time has claws and lion scatters the fold of gentle lambs.

This gift of life is ours to uplift or to besmear.

The wind is so gentle and the stars so friendly, but tomorrow has its unborn promises and plagues often blight the innocent.

This gift is ours, and whether for good or for ill, the choice always is ours.

The wind is so gentle, the season so mild, but even the wind can destroy, and harmattan a season.

The strands of light of which we are made are much stronger than any wild wind. What then is harmattan?

The wind is so gentle now and the stars so bright, but wild wind separates leaves from trees, and cloudy days spread darkness over bright stars.

Once harmony in the sphere of the soul is attained, sitting on red-hot coal isn't a feat.

But the sun comes and goes, and the moon is not always there.

The sun comes and goes, but everybody knows it will still rise.

And where will it all flow to?

To the deep source whence arise all.

What the path of approach, of ascent back?

To be deep down the deepest of pits and still struggle on after that vision, to stand before the lion and tame its anger and ride it home, to look upon the weak, the flat-fallen and give an uplifting hand, to stretch to the limits the length of one's chord of growth and then pour forth its waters of abundant life on all, that's all the worth of that gift. That's its meaning, that the Word.

Our testament!

Our testament!

So be it to the end

So be it to the end.

We left there late, our mouths wordless but hearts overflowing. I returned to my hall after seeing her to hers. But then she was with me all night as we floated through the universe as a blazing ball of intense light, singing and rhyming. And then she was floating above my bed, smiling and unceasingly waving goodbye, until I was woken up in the morning and told that she, my Julia, had been attacked and murdered in her room.

And that same day too, the Students' Disciplinary Committee announced my expulsion from school.

THE FIRE FESTIVAL

CHAPTER 17:

ASHES

A t the premises of Redemption Centre I found my gallon. It was dented at different points. I picked it up and continued my journey, caring not whether the gallon could still hold water. Utterly exhausted now, I continued my journey, my search for water, determined more than ever before to pursue my quest even into a scorpion's hole. For thinking of the life of the citizens of Ganchi, my narrow escape from death, I was now filled with a burning zest for life. My room now stretched out a warm open hand towards me, and I knew I could not disappoint by returning without water. Thinking of the cell, my room now had a magic attraction.

I sauntered on, making my way through a beehive of forlorn humanity, faces tight and hard with desperation. I sauntered on through that world and yet withdrawn from it, into my own.

How we live our lives knocked here and there by suffering and death and all that seeks to destroy. How from the very claws of death and the grip of non-being we snatch that survival. And an inward turning to comprehend the bases of being, to have a glimpse of the roots of the bewildering tree of dualism – that inward turning itself is the planting of the grain of anguish.

This is my tragedy. Are you cursed so to seek as I am?

Maybe better to flow in the river of innocent abandon and not-knowing than seek and thereby hang from that bewildering tree. Because there is much that brooks no understanding. The heart of life is as deep as the ocean, and yet I find no space, my own space, in it. The crops grow and die in their own season, and the sky now and then weeps upon a scotched world. Many seem full and even throw away – though I know not if they know the meaning of joy – but more are starved and pained and sad. The endless ocean of life, however, continues to flow.

But without space for me in her heart.

She continues to flow. But to what goal – do you dare ask? With all this suffering and deprivation and slow death, to what end? Do you stir that fire in you?

I sauntered on, making my way through that beehive, faces tight and hard with desperation. And the desperation in me was now inciting a mutiny in my stomach, as if the soldiers in that stomach were on rampage. And then almost suddenly I became aware of pains all over my body, pains seemingly increasing almost with each beat of the heart. As my freedom from that infamous Republic of Ganchi filled me with a certain measure of appreciation of life, it also intensified my desire to live that life as I wanted it, as I always saw it in the glittering world of my dreams. So my fate was now pegged. As always.

Either I find water today or I perish in the effort. For my cross I've found, and I will bend or break with it. Because so is the path of ascent. So it was in the beginning when the Word broke through the void of primordial chaos. So it is now for those who can take that kingdom by violence. And so shall it be world without end without end without end. Today, I seek water, I seek the cleansing water of life, and other things may be added thereafter. But think of the travail of that Great One as humanity rejected His light and chose the darkness of evil. Think of His agony.

Oh wonder that is humanity!

And so we choose, in daily life, the robber instead of our redeemer. More the reason why the beast won't let me be. And more why my life is a festering feast of flies. What more is there?

Bisimilahimohammadinjesusnameamen!

A child beggar, perhaps about six years old, was sitting in the middle of the road with vehicles passing her on both sides. In the mad orchestra of that street life, she somehow stood out and her moan, perhaps practised, was above everyone else's. In front of her were different denominations of money thrown to her by passers-by. I had almost passed when I noticed her eyes, or sockets rather. For eyes she had not; it was like some wild bird had plucked them, and flies had found a home in those sockets. Some flush of pity forced itself down my spine and I unconsciously dipped my hand in my pocket. But, of course, there was nothing there.

Wretched as I was.

I sauntered on though, now taking a turn into Uka Street. A church signboard, with a large inscription of the words "Come unto me" welcomed me. And on the walls of the church were paintings depicting Jesus and the Apostles. Started His ministry at thirty. Could start mine too, though a little late. And I would stand at the pulpit every Sunday repeating in different ways: The measure you give is the measure you receive. Pay your tithe and give and give, and so shall it be given to you. Do not keep treasures for yourselves in your houses or in the banks where moth and rust and corrupt officials consume and thieves break into and steal, but give your treasures to the church your Father's house, for where you put your treasures, there will your heart be. And when you give, do not let your left hand know what your right hand is giving. You know, the Lord loves a cheerful giver. And so I will drain them stone-dry. And that is all that we have seen to pick of that teaching. After twenty centuries. And we turn it upside down for the sake of our own pockets.

Oh wonder that is humanity.

I sauntered on, gallon in hand, mind aflame.

And the church is the mill of the poor. There they pour their hearts and souls. And into it their little earnings. Of course in the hope of a means of escape, a superman to lift off their shoulders their load and then allow them escape into an eternal life of non-struggle and non-effort. That's better than to tell them that within them is the power they need to solve their problems; and that they, too, are gods. Tell them that, and your church will become empty. But tell them that Jesus will carry all their burdens away and bless them with eternal rest, and they will worship not even that Jesus but you. Because you hold their tickets to Jesus.

My people still are asses that are led to that stream of undiscerning devotion. And I am just a dreamer. Just a dreamer with no foot on earth nor in heaven, just a dreamer hanging in the waste void between heaven and earth. What a homeless wretch, you swine!

I sauntered on, gallon in hand, my whole being now highly heated up.

Because I'm that knowledge and that dam fit only for the waste basket and sewage of existence. Because I know or believe these things, yet my life is so so wretched that there is nothing of that knowledge in it. Tell me, which parched tongue has your wretched life bestowed the cooling drop on? Tell me, you wretched of all wretchedness, you feast of flies, foul stream of pus, abomination unheard of, on what parched tongue have you bestowed the cooling drop?

My demon it was, that demon that always wanted to sing me into raving madness. And now it was there with me in full glare in the street, to taunt and torment me to dagger-point. As if the extreme unction had not been administered. As if I did not know that my life was wretched. What is it I have not tried? How many times have I made such useless journeys as this search for water? Has all my life not been such a useless search for that cooling drop? And I keep moving down down the drain. For how long will I continue like this, tell me, how long?

You are the salt of the earth, you are.

Still I sauntered on, gallon in hand and the fires of anguish now burning away the bits and pieces of any will and hope left in me. But the whisper of that last statement tempered that heat, and I sauntered on. In spite of all. But now I made up my mind to shut that door into the refuse heap of my consciousness and inner life. I would feed my eyes and attention on that street, on external things. That way, the door would be shut against my demon.

A girl came out of a house just by, walked to the road and poured some dirty water into a pothole in the middle of the road. And as she poured, a car came out from a corner with some speed. The driver, seeing the girl, horned and applied the brake, and as the girl ran out of the road, the tyres screeched and one of them bumped into the pothole and splashed water on a passer-by dressed in white. And as the driver fired away, the victim could only employ what was available to him.

"Ogun will cut short your journey!" And then he spat out – perhaps a way of affirming that invocation of Ogun's wrath.

That statement was not meant for me, but I felt its violence. And I wondered what kind of fire there was in that heart which emitted such. Surely not the kind that was in harmony with life. Nor with himself. And so he walks about the street dragging his slime and looking for victims to empty it on.

But are you different? Are you?

I moved on though, trying to soak my consciousness in the life of that street. But always it came back to me as a circuitous stream flowing back to its source. Because I was still trying to think out a solution, an open sesame into the holy of holies of life.

Which has no space for me in her heart. And there used to be a borehole here. No, not here. Just ahead. O yes, there it is. Hm! Seems to have been made for rust and rust alone. Wonder if water ever came out of it. Maybe only on the day it was commissioned. And after that, Oya ceased to weep. And Isis too. So rust took over. Just the way the grains of my life rot away, never knowing that seminal joy of fulfilment. Remember –

"Good evening, Eno."

"Ah, Teacher, good evening," I returned, observing that he had some kind of quizzical look. The thick forest of his beard.

"What's happened to you? You look out of sorts, like you've been to hell itself."

It was good enough a joke to draw out some laughter from him. I joined him in that hollow laughter before replying:

"But is life in this land not worse than hell itself?"

"My brother, I agree with you. Look at this water of a thing. Where else in the world do you find people carrying on the way we do without water? It is only in such a useless land that such a basic necessity as water is not provided for, and nobody raises an eyebrow. Is this the way to live life?"

"All of life is a hell without water, all of life," I moaned.

"It's such a terrible situation because one needs water for a whole lot; cook, drink, wash and clean up generally. We can't do anything without it."

"Certainly not," I replied. What does he clean up? And still stinks like mad. As I do now. Clean up what? Armpits, the privates, the house or the rot within? Never cuts his beard. Oh, wisdom resides in the thick forest of a chin. Can't lose that for anything. Makes a sage. The Old Testament prophets. Wise men from the East. And the armpit too. All that sweat from there.

CHAPTER 17 | ASHES

Should serve quite some purpose if purified. Mop mop mop – What a mad world.

"It's a mad world we live in," I said.

"Indeed, it is a mad world," he eagerly followed up. "Can you imagine how everything is sliding from bad to worse? Imagine one of those little witches called students had the effrontery to say that the circle of sweat from my armpit was like a full-grown moon. Imagine! A pupil to a teacher. And only because I asked them to give me examples of simile. I wonder what this world is turning to."

"I really wonder too."

"Signs of the end, says my priest."

Always priests and priests and imams on our lips. Religion, so much in our mouths but not in our hearts and lives. Why won't they talk to you like that? Taking turns in your house. Bewitched by the lure of their unmined chambers, those little ones not so innocent anymore. Well, not much blame. Where one works is where one should eat from. Part of that natural order? The strong on the weak. And the cycle goes on and on but to what end? Say something. Say something.

"Not much of a sign of an end. Insolence is an all-time acknowledged fact of life."

"No no no, I don't agree at all," the teacher replied, pulling his beard. "I still remember our school days. Who was that student to talk to a teacher like that? It's completely different now, and these can only be indicators of the imminent end of the world."

Can't stand this lip-deep puritanism. Not now that this westering sun is eating up my little reserves of energy. Feeling faint. Hope you don't collapse in the street. They will say you're sick, not knowing its mere hunger. Don't fall. Shameful for –

But do you still have shame? Do you? Because –

"Nothing makes sense anymore. It must be the end of time spoken of in the scriptures", he affirmed.

Woe betide this nation for making the teaching profession the crumbs and fall-offs of the labour market. End of time? What will he teach his pupils? What's there to teach when we can't even form our own words and – inhale, inhale deeply. Bad if you collapse here. Inhale.

"Where do you hope to get water?" I asked as I breathed in deeply.

"Well, it's somewhere in Eku Street. A colleague told me that I could get clean bore-hole water from a house down the street, and it happens, if what I'm told is true, that I know the owner. So it seems there won't be much problem. But even if we don't succeed, there is another place still in that street."

"I'm glad I met you then. But who is this man of God so kind to make water available to us, the wretched of the earth?"

"He's a retired principal," he responded. "He was Chairman of the Local Government for a period of six months, that's before the military took over. And for that six months in office, he has three luxury cars and five houses to show for it. And ten chieftaincy titles too. He also increased his harem from two to five. I got to know this much through one of his daughters who is a student of mine."

I swallowed hard, the saliva slowly running down my parched throat. We walked on, the teacher now and then waving at people he knew. And the way he lifted his hand to wave; like a practiced Grammy Award winner or an Olympic gold medallist. But he still had more worries to pour out. Lend him your ears.

"Don't you think it's a shame that in a country like this, water is such a scarce commodity? What are we going to tell God? That inhabitants of an island should so suffer from lack of water. And the government dreams only of what new tax to impose on the people. What a country!"

Again I swallowed hard. Then I inhaled deeply. To speak now was becoming too much drain of energy.

"It's not surprising to me," I said, "I mean, considering the kind of people we have in power. But even then, it's still the natural order of things – the strong over the weak, the privileged over the unprivileged. So nothing is new."

"But that can't be true, it can't be true at all," he returned. "That a man who is supposed to protect children leads them into the very mouth of wolves. That is the story of our leaders, and we shouldn't be so quick in absolving them, shameless as they are."

I swallowed hard again in an attempt to push down the welling disgust. You can deliver that sermon to some little children. Or to your students – but not to the not-so-innocent ones. And say it with your heart stifled. Why not tell him off? Easy with him, easy.

"Who is free anyway?" I asked.

And the teacher shrank, visibly. We walked in silence a while, and I had that much needed space to inhale more deeply. Because the foul stream from his mouth now ceased to flow. That I was no lamb descended from Heaven to wash away the sins of the world was clearly known to me. But to know this and still speak so caustically of other people. What sacrilege!

"Free from what?" he could not help asking.

"Free from life's blows and slaps and stains of shit. Free from life's powerful pull of gravity which sees us drinking of and swimming and finally drowning in the sea of mud life. This is so easily our life that more often than not, we don't even realize that there's something wrong with it."

That does it. I may not be interrupted for sometime. Goodness! See his expression. So changed and hostile. The world would be a better place if each individual took just a dose of truth each day. And heaven here on earth it finally would be. Reflect on it, brother. It is good for your growth. Bitter chloroquine for your malarial conscience. Swallow it. Only its bitterness shall deliver you. Just same for many Christians and Muslims who say so much about Jesus and the Holy Prophet. But only the truth presented by these holy Ones shall deliver. Not the exclusivist ticket of belief and self-serving morality. Only the liberating bitterness of truth. As I have been trying to swallow mine. Because life's –

"We shall soon get to Eku Street," he squeezed out.

"The street of hope," I replied.

Why we keep running away from what and who we are? Must be very ugly to ourselves that we can't stand looking into the mirror of conscience. Reminds me of that guy during our university days. Very wretched home he came from. First year told his room-mates that he had a glorious time in secondary school; chauffeur-driven and with all the money in the world to spend. He had just started experiencing difficult times there at the university. Second year, with a new set of room-mates, the story became that he had a glorious first year. Hard times had just started for him that year. And so the story continued until everybody knew how wretched he was. How can we change if we don't accept what and who we are? The spirit of –

"Did you see today's newspapers?" he asked.

"I don't bother these days. There is little or nothing to learn from them."

"There are reports that the Muslims beheaded somebody in the street for blasphemy."

"They must be executing the law."

"But how can you kill in the name of God? That's satanic. I wish it was when my pen used to flow. I would have done some verses in protest."

"But that too will be satanic. You know the decree on satanic verses. They are executing God's decree."

"Why can't they leave God to execute His decrees Himself?"

"Respect the words of holy books, that thy days may be long. I suggest you don't write those verses. But if you think you must, then don't rush the –"

"But we can't continue to swallow everything just like that. The other day it was a church burnt to ashes. Only two weeks ago it was a woman burnt to death for suspected adultery. Who knows who will be next? If the government refuses to curb these excesses, somebody should at least speak out. We can't continue like this."

"Until philosophers are kings, only then will this our country have a possibility of life and then behold the light of day."

The commonwealth, maybe in the world of forms. His best of all possible worlds. Thy kingdom come here on earth. Where there will be no more sorrow. And injustice and filth and mud water. Just the sparkling water of abundant life. Touch me, touch me now.

"That day may never be. No sane philosopher can play our kind of politics," he said.

"Then let him play his kind."

"But it won't work here."

"Has it worked anywhere yet? No one is free."

Oh, I've shot a fiery one again. And he burns in rage. Why does he take it so personal? Or is it like a prostitute called a prostitute? Why they even choose that sort of living. Victims of society or violators of the air of decency? Money? Any joy in it? Accommodates all. Stenches of all kind. And diseases too. Must completely kill one's sense of discrimination. All weather. Lots of contraceptives too. Certainly. Babies spoil business. And – ooh! Heavy boobs this one's got. Good material for the profession too. But only for the high-paying. In a practiced seductive voice. Just a car, a boutique and a bank account to maintain all. Hot straight legs she's got. Mini to show it off. No, she's only advertising her goods and their potentials. Getting to a time when they will start booking for ad spaces on TV. Come and climb the blissful mountain of my hips. Season the smoothness and warmth of my straight legs. Modernity, or is it civilization they call it, can you explain its obsession with sex? Why are we so base?

"This is the beginning of Eku Street," the teacher announced. "The house is not far from here."

"That's good to hear. I hope we succeed."

"I can't see why we shouldn't. I think the man knows me. And even if he can't remember me, the children are my students."

"It looks like you have some chance then," I said.

"I don't see why we shouldn't succeed."

Could Ruth have walked this distance? Or even half of what I've gone through today – but that's connected with my lot, my evil life. Still she can't fight hard enough, that's when she fights at all. Surrenders everything to Jesus in prayer. Can't fight hard. What's the difference anyway? Those of us who believe we fight. All roads leading to the same slime. Dike and so much noise about power and courage. The dream world of imagination of Hilary. All leading to this hole. All with this same disease of a gaping heart. And this festering dustbin life of ours with this narrow path passing through the refuse. My life is all a refuse heap of dreams, my life is.

"You must be familiar with this path," the teacher.

"I can't quite say. Does it lead to any prospect of water?"

"No, nothing of that sort. It's a short cut to your area, and it passes through the Anglican cemetery. I thought you might know of it."

"Well, yes I do, but the thought of passing through the cemetery makes the hairs on my body stand. So I've used it only once."

"It makes a statement that its entrance is a refuse dump and then it goes through a cemetery," he said.

My life is a cemetery of dreams.

"Sure that picture is apt enough, and in it we may locate all of our life."

Again, he appeared to be touched by my statement. But he quickly shook it off and said:

"I'm getting sick of this teaching profession. It's so unremunerative these days, more so in this useless and hopeless country of ours. In other countries teachers have comfortable homes and even own cars. Here we can't even feed well with what we are paid. And all because of a stupid set of idiots called leaders who don't know the importance of education."

"The teacher's reward, they say, is in heaven," I responded.

"Not with me. At all at all! I can't wait to roast to death in this godless land. I have never liked the idea of running away from my home and becoming an exile. But I see I don't have a choice anymore. I'll have to leave the country soon."

"But what difference does it make, I mean whether you continue here or elsewhere? Are we not always exiles even in our own country, I mean exiles of our dream-worlds?"

"Come on, Eno, what's come over you? Why this shouting tone of tragedy and despair in you? It's as if you can't find any positive and lasting value in anything at all."

What more could there be? The tragedy of this vast waste land. High above me that vision of the full-cream fullness of life. Between me and that vision the Atlantic Ocean. And I know not how to bring it down through that gulf to earth. And deep down the earth she lies. Decayed matter now. All that mattered. Just snatched her like that from me. Only God can tell what I'm still doing here. Only God can tell. Because – but there's no need for tears now, no need. It's no use at all. The heart itself is drained for this kind of violence. Just say something, say something. It should help.

"You know I always wonder if there truly is anything worth dying for in this land," I said, my despair easing somewhat.

"Why on earth would you want to die for anything in this useless land?"

"Maybe that's putting it in a harsh manner. Is there really much beauty you perceive in this world that could make you sacrifice all in order to have? I mean, is there anything, an idea, a principle or vision for which you could lay down your life if that's the only option?"

He dipped his hand into his breast pocket and took out a stick of cigarette and a box of matches. Lighting the cigarette, he inhaled and closed his eyes in relish before puffing out. I looked up at the setting sun but could still not stand its mellowing fire. Again he inhaled and closed his eyes. It took a while before he returned to our common and ordinary world to say:

"I don't think I want to follow that line of argument," as he continued smoking.

"So you plan to escape from the country?" I asked.

"Sure. I would have left a long time ago, but I stupidly kept thinking that we could salvage it."

"So isn't there anything here anymore to salvage? Are we now beyond redemption?"

"Who cares anymore about salvaging or not salvaging this god-forsaken land? What matters now is that there are greener pastures out there, and I want to take my place there."

"Who made or created those greener pastures, and why —"

"Enough of your "who' and 'why', for here is the house of promise," he interrupted.

"You mean the Chairman's house, the house with the bore-hole?"

"Yes, this is the Chairman's house."

Not that I could see much of a house; for the fence was almost as high as the house itself such that one could hardly see the roof from outside. And the gigantic iron gate did not alleviate the impression of a maximum-security prison.

"Do you think we stand any chance here?" I could not help asking. "Will they allow me too to fetch?"

"But they know me. And since we are together, they can't turn you back."

"Well, it's just that I have this funny feeling that the gate is not inviting at all."

"Scatter your funny impressions to the wind and prepare to fetch clean water."

Then he pressed the bell near the pedestrian entrance. A voice rang out through a speaker-like gadget on the wall:

"Who are you looking for?"

"I'll like to see the Chairman," replied the teacher.

"You'll like to see the Chairman?" the voiced repeated.

"Yes, the Chairman."

"Which Chairman?"

"Your boss, I mean the man whom you work for," the teacher said. "Or is there any other Chairman around here?"

"What is the name of the person you are looking for?" the voice insisted.

"His name, his name –" and the teacher turned to me.

"Do you remember his name?"

"I know nothing about him," I replied. "But I thought you said his children were your students?"

"Yes," the teacher replied, still struggling with himself.

"I'm still trying to remember the girl's surname."

"What about her first name?" I asked.

"Even that has slipped from my memory. But I'll get it, it's hanging somehow. It's there, just like a sit – yes, Sylvia is her name, Sylvia."

"What about the surname?"

"I still can't get that. But the daughter's name should serve."

"Well, I hope it does," I replied.

The teacher pressed the bell again, and the gadget grunted.

"I remember the daughter's name," urgency now in his voice. "Her name is Sylvia and she is my student."

"What is the name of the person you are looking for?" the gadget insisted.

"Please help me, please help," the teacher now descended.

"By the way, did he give you any appointment?"

"No, but I'm sure he –"

"He sees nobody without appointment."

"Please help me," the teacher continued.

Just then a tiny portion of the gate opened from inside and a pair of eyes peered through the hole.

"Who are you?" the eyes asked.

"I'm a teacher at the Secondary School."

"He teaches the Chairman's children." I added.

"Which Chairman?" the eyes still.

"The   former Chairman of the local government," the teacher now." I'm sure he won't mind seeing me. Or is this not his house?"

"What's the purpose of your visit?"

"Well, I thought he could be of some assistance?"

"Assistance? In what way?"

"I understand there is borehole water here. I came to see if I could get one or two buckets."

"You came to see if you could get one or two buckets?" the eyes repeated.

"Well, something like that?" the teacher's balloon of egotism was fast losing air. The fire of my desperation was rising and rising.

"Are you sure you are not making a mistake?"

"Mistake? You mean there is no water here?" I could not hold myself.

'I haven't said anything either way, coconut head," the eyes attacked me. "Did anybody tell you that the Water Corporation was located here?"

"I'm told there's bore-hole here, and I'm sure the Chairman won't mind my fetching," the teacher came in.

"Which Chairman, anyway? And what's his name?"

"But I've told you that –" the teacher tried to say.

"Get the hell out of here before I release the dog," the eyes finally ordered and then retreated.

The lot of a stunted sinful soul.

In my mind I nodded my head repeatedly as the episode once again stirred remembrances of things past and of everything good that would not come.

That extreme unction. That extreme unction.

But the Teacher could not be quiet as he paced up and down moaning:

"You see what man can do to his fellow man. Can you see? This goat of a guard! What does it cost him if he allows us to fetch water? And he will do anything so that the Chairman will not know that I'm here. Can you see man's inhumanity to man? That's how we block other people's progress, the more to the destruction of this damned and god-forsaken land! We are a wicked people. We are wicked, and I hate this land. I truly hate this land with all my heart. Just because of water! Ordinary water. Making this illiterate guard behave to me this way."

"You need not worry about him," I said. "What's important now is how we can get water before it becomes dark. You did speak of a second place in this street."

But there is so much baggage of self-image we will hardly drop except by force. He clung to his:

"I'll have to find a way to let the Chairman know I'm here. That's all we need. As soon as he knows it's me, he will attend to us."

"But are you sure this is the right place, I mean, are you sure this is the Chairman's house?" I asked.

"It's supposed to be. It should be anyway, which other building around here looks like a house where the Chairman would live?"

"I wish you were sure."

"I am. This is the place. Don't let that illiterate guard deceive us. This is the place. Only if the Chairman can get to know that I'm here, that will be the end of our problem. And I'm sure he'll even give us go-ahead to come anytime we need water. I wish the Chairman would come out. I pray he comes out."

But the mystery of the heavens. That mystery behind the clouds. Because just as the teacher said that, the gate opened, and the eyes which had spoken to us – a pot-bellied and piggy forty-something-years-old-looking man – he stood at attention by the gate.

"That's the Chairman, that's the Chairman coming," the teacher announced excitedly. "It's the Chairman, thank God. Our problem is solved. You'll see."

And then the car, a metallic grey Mercedes Benz with tinted glasses, emerged somehow in a stately manner. The car had not even reached the gate when the teacher started shouting.

"Good evening sir, good evening sir."

When, finally, the car got to the gate, the guard saluted in military fashion, and the teacher shouted more 'good evening sir'. But the car rolled out of the gate, gathered pace and drove off. As it passed us, I peered into it but could only faintly see through the tinted glasses a surplus of white *agbada* covering almost the whole of the back seat.

The ways of men. If men were God.

"Maybe he is not the one," I consoled the teacher whose mouth remained open from incredulity. Or perhaps that pinprick deflation of his balloon. The fire was raging in him.

"What do we do? Night is almost upon us now." Because as that glass-cup of hope was so hopelessly dashed, darkness was now increasingly descending on me.

Still the teacher had no words.

"You spoke of a second place. Is it far from here?"   I asked, confused about how next to move but concerned about helping the teacher, one way or another, out of the mire of that embarrassment.

Still he had no words for me. And I could not even be sure that he was still conscious of my presence. His mouth still remained open, and I saw through his eyes that he could still see the Chairman driving off without even a wave at him, and I saw how he saw himself crash, in that moment, from the mountain-top of esteem to the bottom-level emptiness of the most wretched. So he saw himself. And I watched him re-live that moment a thousand times, I watched and watched until I, too, almost became drunk with that embarrassment.

I knew his pain as he knew it. Do you understand?

"Father, let this cup pass from us, let it pass," I murmured.

Perhaps that cup did pass, but not as I expected. For the teacher suddenly turned and started moving away fast and determinedly.

"What about the second place?" I was confused. I tried to follow him. This was pointless because I had no such strength. I was now struggling to take some deep breathes.

He broke into a run.

And I watched, his figure receding and receding while the eddying darkness of which he was the centre closed in on and swallowed me. That darkness intoned:

The sacrilege of
The sinful one
The evil one
Whose stain of life
Splashed on

The white-cloth of existence.
Oh sacrilege! What sacrilege!

CHAPTER 17 | ASHES

THE FIRE FESTIVAL

CHAPTER 18:

THE INITIATORY FIRE

t was I who was at the centre of that whirlpool of darkness. I was now practically a dead dry leaf in the hands of the winds of that nightfall, and it swept me hither and thither the fringes of consciousness, through that dark street and the short-cut that began at the refuse dump and passed through the cemetery, on and on and on as I struggled to hang on to some level of awareness.

Ceaselessly it sang:

You are evil

You are evil evil

You are evil evil evil

You are evil evil evil evil evil evil evil.

On and on and on it swept me, and still I managed to hold on, somehow, till I reached the place I recognized as my place of residence. Somehow, the darkness lifted a little, and I heard a familiar female voice moan:

Had I wings like the dove
Had I wings like the dove
I would use it to fly to God
I would tell Him that this world is too harsh
This world! This world!
It's too harsh.

"You have the wings," it declared as I entered my room.

"I have the wings," I said listlessly. Then I staggered to the bed and stretched out my bones. Rather like a corpse.

Again the darkness lifted a little, and I saw that I could see much better than ever before, that I now knew that I knew.

"Life is a series of unrelieved gut-rot," it announced.

I smiled a smile of gull.

And shreds of broken dreams and shattered glass-cups of hope. More the reason why many a hermit did retreat in search of that word-key, that open sesame. Yes, only that word. And stillness, the stillness of fullness and identification.

"Calm in the midst of storm, calm," the voice whispered.

Alas, beyond that calm and seemingly unaffected repose of the hermit lies a tumultuous world of conflicts. Alas the search for the tree of life is laden with vile fruits. Why bother? Why stir? Why jostle?

"You have the wings. That which must be done must be done. Because you have the power." Again it declared.

What have I not tried? Where have I not searched? What else am I supposed to do? Where is all that glitter and gleam of abundant life? Where are you? Surely not in the bare wretchedness of this life here on earth. Nor is that fantastic promise of heavenly bliss, a heavenly nothing, so inviting anymore; for why must we go through this muck of earth life before we savour the other worldly gain of heaven? What use in coming here if we cannot transform that muck to mirth? What use the bewildering fruitfulness and riches of this earth if the juice of joy and life is stowed away in some other-worldly vault? What purpose?

"You vilest of vile dreamers! What if you had died in that police cell?"

Indeed, what if I had died. Oh, settle it with God who sees the strong triumph over the weak and remains quiet. Settle it with Him who watches the innocent perish at the hands of the wicked. He who watches from His almighty, from His infinite bliss, as we struggle and fail and struggle and fail. Our Almighty Father, ever merciful, omniscient and omnipotent. And He watches and remains silent over the destruction of His creature. And He watches and allows sinners – who is free indeed – to suffer eternally without any hope of redemption.

"And He watches and remains silent. What if Presido had slashed your throat?"

What if he had! Entry into what gain? Just death, senseless death. And that's all. And that's how it was in the beginning, is now and ever shall remain. Death, the way of all dreamers. Take an inventory of them all. Osiris, Tantalus, Socrates, Jesus, Gandhi, Luther King Jnr, and many more. How did they all end? This life!

"She has no space for you in her heart."

No she does not, and most faithfully. Nothing of her juice. And think of the Sets and Pilates everywhere to be seen. Are they not the ones who quaff the joy of the juice of the world? Who is it that downs that full cup of the juices of the vine, this vine of life that is only hell for me? She has no space for me in her heart at all.

"But the sounds soft and mellow, the voices singing lullabies of tune celestial."

Damn those sounds and voices. What raging hunger of the stomach has ever been quenched by sounds and voices? The ant labours very hard to make itself a hole, but it must step out to find its meal. And once it does that, it becomes a meal for the fowl. The fowl takes lots of care to find a suitable place for its eggs. But it is not enough that man has other things to eat; both fowl and eggs are delicacies. And the strong man destroys the weak and appropriates his possession. And the heavens do not even stir. Thunder does not roar.

"Oh no, they stir by pouring rain and sunshine on all alike. Thus do they stir."

And that is the deepest of all mysteries, the mystery of the cosmic heart as it tends to all, both good and evil.

The Chairman stole the people's money to enrich himself and increase his harem. You know how many chieftaincy titles and accolades that followed? You think anybody will consider you a possible candidate for even the most worthless honour?

"Your sound will be hollow and noise to the soul."

Yes I know. The sheer lifelessness of that debased materialism, the bare barrenness of the soul, its total lack of that raging joy, that just juice of a just life. The Chairman is rich and respected. I'm poor to the bones and worthless and non-existent in the roll-call of the life of our land. Which is better? Which to choose?

But I saw that land from afar and – Damn it, for I see and see and see so much life, but all that I know is death. Snatched her from me just like that. Deep down she lies. All that mattered, all that could have given you the strength and confidence to face all. Deep down she lies. And you are here burning in the heat for an abiding place. More to your sorrow and ruin.

Your plague is that of dreaming.

I agree. Remember the saying about all one's eggs in one basket. So you have channelled all your life's energies into the phantom of a dream. Can't you learn from people around you? When they want to look, they rather peep, hoping to see what's unwholesome. But you'll rather thrust all your head out in the belief that you'll see the best. And when they want to enter, they enter with only one leg, leaving the other behind. But you don't only enter with your two legs; you just jump in, and when it is a pit, headlong. Can you see what piece of rubbish your life is? Can you see?

Yes yes I can. But what can this be? Where is that giant pillar of life? Where is it all now, the splendour of that glory? Where is it now, the vision and all its glitters?

Messed up your life thinking of what you could put into the soil, dreaming about the glory of actualizing that dream. Fuck you man! People think in terms of what they can take and benefit for themselves, not in terms of what they can give. Everyone would rather receive than give, and everything thrives on deceit and oppression. Hahaha! What a piece of rubbish your life is! Doomed and damned. He doesn't show any support for all that futile and feverish dream. Doomed and damned, you shit! You piece of rubbish! You waste of all wastes! Most wretched of all wretchedness! You deep of darkness! Befouler of all that is holy! You abomination unheard-of! Damn and fuck you!

Yes yes yes. Now I know that I did not know. Now I know. That the blazing furnace of a dream is just the way of loss. That all is a harvest of darkness. Hahaha! I had not thought that death had undone so many. Now I know. Now I know. But it's been because of you, light of the world; because of you, image of truth newborn. Yet between me and the image of your face is that magnet, that primal gulf, the way of loss, which is the way of my life. O God! How long must I shout for help before it comes? How long? Isn't there some saving hand to lift me from this wreck? Tell me, God! Mortal man, shall we receive good at the hand of God and shall we not receive evil? Nothing to be done. I want a hero, an uncommon one, especially in a land where every bit of sanity is snatched from one like some birds snatch away joy from the bosom of a mother. Therefore all hope abandon all ye who enter here because nature presents to me nothing which is not a matter of doubt. And they snatched her from me, all that I had and could hope to have. Not yet I loved, and loved to love, I sought what I should love, loving to love. But nothing to be done now. Once the veil of maya falls, everything becomes one. Enough! They all are goat-herd who submit or abandon their will to another. I came and announced the death of God. I came and destroyed the false foundation on which they built. Thus speak I, and I speak in grief, not exultation, because I pity no more. Today I am a god in my own kingdom. I shall obey, my Lord. Alas, what are the roots that clutch, what branches grow out of this stony rubbish, out of this heart of darkness, this wasted generation? Things rank and gross in nature possess it mainly, and the ceremony of innocence is drowned. It is too much Lord, the pillar of fire I can't find.

"Not if you still try."

"Who still wants to try?" I retorted. "And to what end anyway?"

"That interminable ocean of longing could not have dried up entirely."

"I don't know and care not anymore," I put up. "And, please, don't trouble my life."

"But you can –"

"I cannot anything anymore, and please get the hell out of my sight."

And I stared, stared hard indeed. Even rubbing my eyes did not change anything. He was sitting right there on the chair in my room. I mumbled a few inaudible and incoherent things before I found my voice.

"Who the blasted hell are you?"

"Why worry? A little assistance in your present situation won't be out of place," he said with perfect composure.

That worsened it for me, and I flung all care to the wind and made straight for his throat. But I found myself struggling with the chair.

"All that won't help," he said. He was standing near the chair. "Why don't you return to the bed?"

And I returned, my lips shaking from a wild onslaught of shame.

"It's like the story of a farmer luxuriating in the verdant dream of abundance only to wake up to the stone-reality of a harvest of drought. Or like the story of a group basking in glimpses of the end of a ritual just begun but never to arrive. But in spite of all that, the courageous, instead of wearing themselves away in sorrow, still find a way out."

"What else is there?" I queried.

"What else is not there?" he fired back. "That you sit here heaping huge layers of garbage on God or on yourself."

"What else is there?" Still I queried.

"What else is not there? That in spite of so much that is possible, your best is just a groping and floating on the gulf of inertia; that in spite of the fire and the fever, you can't even raise your head to say 'yes, I am,' that in spite of – "

"Enough!" I cried, for just then the *suya* knife of his words sliced through my chest, and the weight of the years came crumbling and dropped heavily on my heart. My shoulders sagged.

"How uncharitable of you!" Again I cried. But the charitable tears did not fail to flow, because of;

The sacrilege of
The sinful one
The evil one
Whose stain of life
Splashed on
The white-cloth of existence.

The dustbin of the years was overturned before me, and it reeled out every bit of its muck and grime. And the tears poured and poured like Noah's flood.

"Enough of that! Enough of that weakling stuff. That's all what your life has been, always moaning and frittering away that fire that could have been more profitably used."

And I, the only adult in the house taking the last words of a dying parent, turned still, all attention.

"Acceptance is not in the dictionary of anybody worthy of the name human," he continued. "Life is lived at the cost of great sacrifice and ruthless struggle against the forces of denial; a man suffers famine simply because he has buried his last tubers of yam in the hope of a better yield. This is the secret of translation, and it underlies the success of all geniuses. But above all, nature is the prime initiator of this spirit of sacrifice in order to translate to that which is higher; for the first bed of the baby in the world is a pool of blood – the maternal blood of creative sacrifice."

"But in many ways that blood has remained still ever since the downing of hemlock," I put in. "And even when he had almost exhausted existence by logic, he was still confronted by that gulf."

"And he accepted?" he asked excitedly.

"He made his illogical jump, of course."

"That's the spirit!" he shouted.

"What spirit"

"The spirit to leap where movement seems impossible; the spirit to leap, when everything is said and done, into Hamlet's undiscovered country; the spirit to do that which must be done when nothing else is there. It is man's most courageous assertion of his freedom of choice and his rebellion against the absurdity of existence. It is a great triumph of life over the tragedy and death of inauthentic living. It is the final act of sacrifice for freedom. One wrung breaks, you step on another. The choice is yours."

The years, that dustbin that was my life, it poured through my consciousness in torrents of vision. Its slaps and stains, that putrefaction called my life, that pit-latrine stench, its sack burst open and poured and poured on me.

She never had a space for me in her heart. So faithful an unlover. Ever closing and narrowing me in, into it, stench, away from its juice. Oh, the futile fever of my struggle, that lusting after the indefinable. The burning hollowness of my sound, its noise.

She has no space for me in her heart.

Only my Julia did. Only. And I will be your companion forever and ever and ever. Which pact we sealed in the oneness of our heart. And I have remained here all along groping, groping. You befouler of holy atmosphere, breaker of sacred pacts, Judas the betrayer! Show me your thirty pieces of silver. Show me.

Of this, too, I had no evidence, nothing to show for it.

Okay now. At least opportunity beckons. For a definite act of rebellion and rejection. For a final redemptive act. No more to circle after the blablabla of this debased existence, never again to wobble after that unreachable fountain. I will be your companion. In the light of new possibilities of a final redemptive act. I will be, I swear.

I got up from the bed, walked to my camping gas cooker and turned open the knob. What more is there in sight, what more? Dragging a curse along the whole length of my life. Now release is in sight. All my life I have been a fugitive and wanderer. All my life. Come over now, and I will show you your bride, the wife of the Lamb. Nothing more. Because I have picked every aspect of it and turned each up and down. What more is there? Shards and shadows of broken dreams in the huge heap of the garbage of life.

What more?

Even then, I was desperate for something, just anything that could make me nod my head in the affirmative. I was desperate for a share of life, my most faithful unlover. I was, even at that last minute. That hunger raged within; but death beckoned with a soothing smile.

"Lead me, Oh Lord, from darkness to light," I said. Because I was tired and lost and confused of everything. Of death. Of life. Of everything and anything I could think of.

The room was now covered with tinder clouds of gas – I could perceive (and even see) it - and the box of matches I could always reach even with my eyes closed.

And that which must be done must be done. For this denial. Of the full-cream full-cup of life frothing at the brim. Because if life had loved me even a little, if life had just a little space for me in her heart, it would have blessed me with its succulent juice of joy. But in the vast riches of this wide world, I knew no saving harmony. And the fire of its despair raged on infernally.

"Lead me, oh Lord, from the unreal to the real," I intoned.

Because I was not sure of anything. So I took out a stick of matches, ready to strike. Because we all are flies in the festering feast of existence. Because the boiling pot of life only dries up that soothing juice of joy and fulfilment; all that truly matters. Because the harmony of music is not of this world. And I must seek it wherever it can be found. Because this soul-stirring melody of the flute as I hear it now cannot of this world be; this world of pain and sorrow and suffering and discord. Because there is naught else. Naught else but the arrows of denial and despair. What more! Farewell then, my beloved, most callous most faithful unlover.

"Lead me, oh Lord, from death to immortality," I said as I lifted the matches to strike. Because I was utterly lost.

And then I felt the need to say the last word, one last important word. It came, somewhat unbidden:
Lead me, oh Lord,
From darkness to light,
From the unreal to the real,
From death to immortality.

But it was a circle of light, soft but bright, at the centre of my room that attracted me. Or was there truly no light?

Slowly I moved towards it. Slowly, too, it moved towards and settled on my window.

Was it not beckoning at me?

Slowly I moved towards it, reaching that window just as the light passed through it.

Was it beckoning?

Gently, very gently, I opened my window. And slowly, almost imperceptibly, the sound of the music of that flute wafted in with the cool breeze of the night, encircling me, seeping through me and spreading its fire throughout the dead universe of my being.

There still was fire.

To which I revolted and quickly would have struck the matches. But the voice of a stray chick wailing inconsolably resounded in my heart. I tried very much to muster energy to stifle the roots of this reverberation in my heart. This was to no avail. That woeful wail held me hostage.

Because there still was fire.

The chick emerged from wherever and came directly under the security light near my window. And – do chicks actually shed tears? – I could feel those tears flowing profusely. In truth, I tried very much to hold myself, but my heart could not avoid shedding some tears.

Because of the one fire.

From a corner, too, a cock emerged and attacked the chick. It struck and struck, while the chick fell and wailed. And my heart jumped each time the cock struck the chick. My heart could not be steady. And it grieved me very much; that even up to this final point I could still grieve over another's grief.

All because of the fire of the heart.

"This is totally senseless and unholy", I found myself saying.

As my life is. And, indeed, all life.

From nowhere a black goat suddenly appeared, attacked the cock and drove it out of sight, the cock shouting as it ran for its life.

Is this absurd? Much less than life, much less.

The chick was still down struggling between life and death, and I simply watched, gripped by the puzzle and contradiction of the whole episode – as the episode of my life. The goat re-emerged, ran its nose up and down the chick and finally sneezed on it. And it was a burst of energy which blew the chick to its feet. It fluttered its wings and staggered away.

But it was not just the chick that that burst of energy touched. Was it that burst, the goat itself, or the whole episode? But in that instant, as I fixed my gaze on the goat, I saw through a veil, the veil of what had just happened.

And I became aware, once again, of that light. It encircled me. Immediately a flood of light came surging upon and through me, and I could see and see and see as my life, all existence became transparent, every episode of it. But then what can you say of the wordless? How much?

"Who are you?"

"A strand of light within the interminable ocean of light."

It was silence that reigned, that silence that speaks without words, a silence in which you know that you know. And there is no doubt.

"So why are you here?"

"To plumb the depths for experience and expression."

Again joy was the colour of that silence.

"What purpose?"

"The beautification of life through realisation of being."

"Why in the depths of sorrow and suffering?"

"Because sorrow is the fastest springboard for conquest. Because only in conquest do we come to our heritage. Because the beauty of music lies in harmony, and harmony is only when there is reconciliation of opposites."

I was joy-suffused, radiant in the certainty and surety of being. I was indescribably peaceful. And I knew that I was not and could never ever be alone. I knew it. And I knew many many other things. I knew without doubt that I knew them. And that knowledge filled up my cup, and I held on to that juice at the fire festival.

THE FIRE FESTIVAL

CHAPTER 18 | THE INITIATORY FIRE

THE FIRE FESTIVAL

CHAPTER 18 | THE INITIATORY FIRE

THE FIRE FESTIVAL

CHAPTER 18 | THE INITIATORY FIRE

www.ingramcontent.com/pod-product-compliance
Lightning Source LLC
Chambersburg PA
CBHW050659290626
47170CB00016B/2480